NO RIGHT WAY

NO RIGHT WAY

MICHAEL NIEMANN

W**O**RLDWIDE

TORONTO • NEW YORK • LONDON
AMSTERDAM • PARIS • SYDNEY • HAMBURG
STOCKHOLM • ATHENS • TOKYO • MILAN
MADRID • WARSAW • BUDAPEST • AUCKLAND

For
Joanna Wheeler-Niemann
The Love of My Life
October 15, 1940–September 11, 2018

W⦾RLDWIDE™

ISBN-13: 978-1-335-77266-4

No Right Way

First published in 2019 by Coffeetown Press, an imprint of Epicenter Press, Inc. This edition published in 2020.

Copyright © 2019 by Michael Niemann

This edition published by arrangement with Harlequin Books S.A.

For questions and comments about the quality of this book, please contact us at CustomerService@Harlequin.com.

Harlequin Enterprises ULC
22 Adelaide St. West, 40th Floor
Toronto, Ontario M5H 4E3, Canada
www.ReaderService.com

Printed in U.S.A.

ACKNOWLEDGMENTS

As always, my writing group Monday Mayhem helped me shepherd this story to its conclusion. Jenn Ashton, Carole Beers, Sharon Dean, Clive Rosengren and Tim Wohlforth kept my plot lines plausible and noted the typos and missing commas. Thanks also to Alison McMahan, who read a big chunk of the first draft and pushed me to spell out the visceral reactions of the characters. Fred Grewe patiently listened to me charting my progress and helped sort out questions. Of course, any remaining flaws are my own fault. I probably should have listened better.

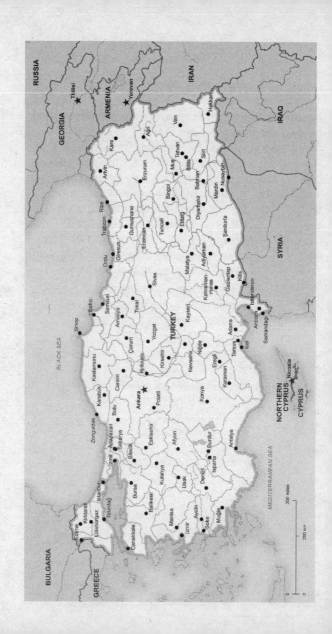

ONE

GETTING RID OF the woman's body turned out to be harder than Yesim Yaser had expected. It wasn't the size. She could have carried it on her own. It was a question of finding the right spot. She'd told her brother to drive to the edge of the vineyard, hoping they could dump it there between the grapevines. But, seeing how the road was closer than they remembered, she hesitated. Any car driving by the next morning would see the body. And the refugees picking grapes, they'd recognize her too.

Her brother, the driver, stopped the car. Its headlights illuminating the scene. Half a row of grapevines had been cleared away and the dirt was churned already. A couple of shovels still lay on the ground. She told the young guy, Korun, to do the digging. He was none too happy about it, mumbling something about always ending up with the shit jobs. She ignored him. She was in charge and her brother thought manual labor was beneath him. The young guy grabbed a shovel. It shouldn't take very long. The body was small and emaciated.

The first strike into the dirt ended with a premature thud. Not a rock. Something woody. Korun kicked away the dirt. A root. He moved a couple of feet and gave it another shot. Same result. After the third try he stopped. Whoever had removed the grapevines had just hacked the trunks off and left the roots in the dirt, figuring there was no reason to do all that hard work since they'd plant new seedlings and could let the old roots rot. That didn't help Korun. The roots formed a subterranean web. He needed an axe instead of a shovel.

Her brother said something about using the backhoe they'd seen parked on the other end of the vineyard. Typical. Anything with a motor and he was on it. Yaser told him to stay put. Driving the backhoe here and digging a hole would make a big racket and wake up the refugees in their tents. Korun leaned on the shovel and watched them argue.

The woman had struggled as he suffocated her, but it was nothing Korun couldn't handle. Even if she'd been at her prime, she wouldn't have stood a chance against the three of them. As it was, it only took Korun to finish the job. That's how weak she was, picking grapes every day and not getting a whole lot to eat. She must have been pretty once. Back when she lived in Aleppo and did whatever women like her did in Aleppo. But those days were long gone. She'd looked gaunt when they grabbed her at the store. Her eyes were dull with resignation and fear, like those of the other refugees.

Yaser made a decision. It didn't involve a backhoe or digging a hole, which improved Korun's mood. They got back in the car, her brother behind the steering wheel, his usual spot, Yaser in the passenger seat. The young guy sat in the back next to the dead woman. They drove toward the border. An easy drive, a little less than five miles. The distance wasn't the issue. It was the fighting on the Syrian side. Plenty of stray bullets landed in Turkey. Especially at night, when all kinds of patrols were afoot.

A mile before the border crossing, they turned east

onto a dirt road. Her brother switched off the headlights. Which meant he hit every pothole. Even in a Mercedes, the bumpy ride tossed the dead body against Korun. She turned around. In the light from the dashboard, she saw him making a face. Strange. He had no compunction killing her, but he couldn't stand sitting next to a corpse.

The car reached a narrow, tarred road and they turned south again. They were close to the border now. The shadows of olive trees looming to their left. The border lay just beyond them. They stopped. Yaser told Korun to carry the woman across the border and drop her. Another dead refugee. Not a Turkish concern. Korun wasn't so sure about that, saying that those stray bullets scared him. She told him not to get hit. He shrugged, pulled the dead woman from the car, took her by the wrists and dragged her past the olive trees.

He'd passed three rows when the tak-tak-tak of an AK-47 surprised them. She saw him dropping to the ground. She slid down on her seat. Her brother did the same. At least the Mercedes had enough steel in it to offer some protection. Korun disappeared from view. She was tempted to turn on the headlights to see where he was headed, but she didn't. It'd only make them a target. The hellish firefight that broke out in the distance confirmed her assessment.

Next thing she knew, Korun was back in the car. She asked him if he'd brought the body across to Syria. He said yes. She had her doubts. He came back too soon. But she wasn't going to check on it. Not with that fighting going on. With any luck, jackals would find the body and get rid of the evidence.

They drove back to Kilis. Yaser had a sense of accomplishment. The dead woman had been a threat.

They had eliminated the threat. The only worry was the car they encountered right when they turned back onto the highway. She didn't want any witnesses. But she couldn't do anything about it. The other car stopped and its driver motioned out of the window for them to stop. Yaser told her brother to step on it. As they sped away, Korun watched the car through the rear window. He said that it was doing a one-eighty. Her brother sped up more. The other car's lights faded away. Nothing to worry about.

THE OTHER CAR was driven by Valentin Vermeulen, investigator for the United Nations Office of Internal Oversight Services and at that moment thoroughly lost. He'd flown into Gaziantep's Oğuzeli International Airport in southern Turkey late that Wednesday afternoon, coming from Ankara for a meeting at the Gaziantep sub-office of the UN High Commissioner of Refugees. After landing, he received a text that the head of the office, Bilek Balbay, was out, inspecting the Kilis camp. Since Vermeulen was scheduled to visit the camp, he decided to accompany Balbay. Better to have someone with authority and knowledge along.

All of which meant that Vermeulen rented a car late that evening and drove the thirty-five miles south to Kilis. After taking the Kilis exit, he figured he was about to reach the city, but a road sign with words GÜMRÜK/DOUANE told him he was wrong. He was headed for the Syrian border. *Damn.* On top of that, the car didn't have a GPS, his phone was dead, and there were no street lights.

He saw a car turn onto the road and come toward him. It was the first vehicle he'd seen since exiting from the motorway. He stopped and cranked down his window. A wave of hot air slapped his face. He stuck his arm out and waved for the other car to stop. It looked like a large black Mercedes. And it didn't stop. It sped up instead. He turned around, intending to catch up to it. But by the time he'd finished the U-turn, the Mercedes' tail lights were a mere hint on the dark horizon. Vermeulen hit his steering wheel in anger.

He got out to stretch. Being lost in a country he'd never been to before was nothing unusual for Vermeulen. His job took him wherever the United Nations was active. Despite the briefings he received in New York, the old adage that no plan survives first contact with reality turned out to be true most of the time. The sound of automatic weapon fire sounded in the distance. He ducked behind the car without hesitation. He'd been to enough war zones to know how far bullets can travel.

Well, there was a bed waiting for him in Kilis. Since he was near the border, the city had to be in the opposite direction. He got into the car and raced back the way he'd come until he found the traffic circle where he'd taken the wrong exit from the D-850 motorway. This time he went straight ahead and reached Kilis.

After crossing what looked like a beltway, he drove into a dense network of narrow streets. Fifteen minutes of random turns later, he finally saw a man walking on the sidewalk. He stopped and asked for directions to his hotel. The man barely spoke English, but he understood the destination and mimed the necessary turns. Vermeulen found the hotel. There was a night porter who helped Vermeulen park his car and even lugged his suitcase up to the room. Although hungry, Vermeulen fell into his bed. Sleep was definitely the priority.

TWO

YESIM YASER WASN'T used to getting phone calls this early in the morning. She had crashed in her townhouse after the long night. Her mother accepted her living alone, even though she didn't like it. An unmarried woman should be living with her family until she moved in with her husband. Those were the traditions. Yaser wasn't having any of it.

Ever since her father had been killed in a mob shootout, she'd made it clear that she was going to live her own life. She was her father's daughter. She was meant to lead, not follow. Husbands or children weren't her ambition. Instead, she made it her mission to find the man who ordered the death of her father. What better way to do that than follow in his footsteps? Her uncle Ceylen was happy to let her join his organization. She was a hundred times better than her dishrag of a brother. Ceylen knew that and gave her opportunities to make her mark. She controlled a string of loan sharks, and ran a phone top-up card scam. All along, he took her to meetings where she had the chance to learn the names of the southern Turkish mob. One of those men was responsible. When the time came that person would pay.

Along the way, she'd used her position to learn as much about Ceylen's illegal operations as she could. The best thing was learning how to manage illegal cash. Her uncle's operation was an eye opener. Companies registered in multiple countries. Fake loans. Bent judges. Thinking of the millions involved almost made her head spin. A month ago, he made her vice president for those letterbox firms. He thought he was doing her a favor, help burnish her reputation without giving her real power. Just some paperwork filed at the relevant corporate registers. Except now she had access to the banking records of all those companies. Online banking was something her uncle's generation didn't do. They relied on their crooked accountants to manage their money. Online access told her when money was moved, when pay-offs occurred. Given time, she'd dig deep enough to find out who killed her father. For now, she played the eager apprentice. And that meant running his errands.

"Yes, Uncle. What can I do for you?"

"Did you deal with the matter?" Ceylen said.

"We did. It's a Syrian problem now."

"Nothing that will come back to bite you or me?"

"Nothing. As I said, we dealt with the matter."

"Why did you use my car?" Ceylen sounded a bit miffed.

"Because mine is too small. Besides I needed help." Did he really think she would put the dead woman in her BMW Z4?

"There are always rentals."

"Yes, but you taught me to be frugal. Why waste money and leave a paper trail?"

It seemed to mollify him. At least for a moment.

"Are you sure this was an isolated event?" he said.

How should I know? Who in their right mind would expect a pesky refugee to show up asking for a cash card well after the scam was over?

"I'm sure, Uncle. It was one of those random things. It won't happen again."

"A good leader expects random things. Make a plan so the next time something random happens you don't have to act hastily."

"I will. Good advice. Thanks, Uncle."

Right. If it were up to him, I'd be planning all the time and not doing a damn thing.

"WHERE IS ZADA?" Rima Ahmadi said to the three women who were picking grapes closest to her. She stood up and wiped the sweat from her forehead. Her clothes were damp, too. Across the rows of grapevines, some twenty others, more than half of them women, were doing the same thing. A gaggle of children, some as young as three, hung about. The older ones helped, the little ones sat in the shade. The pickers' arms moved rapidly, darting out to the fruit like snakes striking an unsuspecting rodent. Ahmadi was much slower. She'd only started at the vineyard three weeks earlier. Back at her home town south of Aleppo, she'd worked as an elementary school teacher after finishing university. Then the civil war arrived. Picking fruit for a living wasn't something she'd ever had to do.

"Yesterday, Zada said that she had learned something important," Ahmadi said. "But she never came back to the camp."

The camp being the jumble of tents where the refugees lived. To call it rudimentary would be an exaggeration. She'd come to Turkey late. Although the war started in 2011, it had skipped her town for four years. Until it didn't. When she made it across the border, the official refugee camp in Kilis was full. She would have liked to stay there. She'd heard people talking about the white containers repurposed for housing. They were tight, but bearable. There were places to wash clothes, shops to buy groceries, a little town just for Syrian refugees. Their camp by the vineyard only had a pump and a latrine.

"Zada was very bright and very brave," Ahmadi said. "I wonder what she learned. Did she tell you?"

One of the women, Rahel Besher, stopped picking and said, "No, she didn't tell anyone. You better pick grapes or the foreman will be angry again. We have to make our quota and when you don't do yours, it hurts all of us."

Ahmadi looked down. Rahel was right. She didn't pull her weight and the others suffered because of it. She concentrated on cutting the grape clusters with the dull knife and filling her basket. The others knew how to empty a grapevine with the least amount of wasted effort. She hadn't figured that out yet. She worked haphazardly, cutting here and there and then having to go back when she missed some. It was the worst job she'd ever had.

When she fled Syria, she'd brought her savings and stayed at a shabby hotel. She knocked on all doors she could find to ask for work. Anything, madam. I'm a good worker. But she was too late. Other refugees who'd come in the years before had taken the menial jobs in town that didn't require knowing Turkish. The local school had openings but not for an Arabic speaker. And, anyway, she couldn't have documented her qualifications. The certificates burned, just like most of her documents in the house after the missile hit.

The foreman came down the row to inspect the work

of the pickers. He was a stocky man with greasy hair, grubby clothes and a three day stubble. A cigarette dangled from his mouth. When he got to Ahmadi, he started yelling in Turkish. She didn't know what he was saying, so she kept her head down. He yelled even more and punched her in the back. She stumbled and her basket toppled to the ground, grapes scattering over the dirt. She looked up. He switched to Arabic and told her she was missing too many grapes. The anger in his face scared her almost as much as the shooting back in her hometown. She knelt, picking up the spilled grapes as fast as she could.

"You must pick all of them," Rahel said.

Ahmadi stayed on her knees, looked down and said *"Evet, efendim."* Being answered in Turkish with a polite "Yes, Sir" seemed to mollify him and he went on to the next person.

"Now you've made him angry," Rahel said. "Be careful. He's a mean man. Pull your scarf back over your hair. Don't give him any excuses. Or he will come after you."

Ahmadi had held back her tears until the foreman left. "How can you stand this?" she said, bursting out. "It would have been better to die at home than live like a dog in Turkey."

"Don't speak like that. Even a bad life is better than death. You are young. The war won't last forever. One day you'll go home, *insha'Allah*. Until then, stay away from that man."

Ahmadi hurried to catch up with the others. When her basket was full, she went to dump it in the bin at the end of the row. She noticed the foreman looking at her, she covered most of her face with her scarf.

By lunchtime, the temperature had risen well into the nineties. It was very hot for September. The workers sat in whatever shade the grapevines offered and drank water and ate the meagre rations they'd brought, a crust of bread, a few olives and raisins. The grapes they picked weren't for eating. They would be dried and processed into molasses.

Rahel said she was worried about her middle son. "He should be in school." They all knew what she meant. Most of them had families at the camp. Old parents who could no longer work, or children who were too young to be at the vineyard. But it was their teenage boys that worried them. They ignored their father's orders and hung out in Kilis instead of working. School was out of the question.

"I'm worried about Zada," Ahmadi said. "It's not like her not to come to work. Did any of you see her at the camp?"

"I saw her yesterday afternoon," a man said. "She was headed to town."

"By herself?" Ahmadi said. Kilis was an hour's walk from the camp. Not a safe thing to do for a woman alone.

"Yes, by herself."

THREE

Vermeulen met Bilek Balbay, the local UNHCR official, the next morning at breakfast. Both had stayed at the same hotel and Vermeulen recognized the man from a picture in the briefing materials. Balbay was barely thirty, if that, with a dark suit, a fashionable two day stubble and neatly trimmed hair and mustache. Vermeulen introduced himself.

"Oh, Mr. Vermeulen. What are you doing here? I didn't expect you until Monday."

"How odd. The people in Ankara told me that everything had been arranged. I arrived in Gaziantep yesterday, only to find that you'd left for Kilis."

"I'm sorry, but we're really busy. There's a war going on just across the border."

"I'm aware of that," Vermeulen said.

"It'd be better if you go back to Gaziantep and wait there for me. I have a lot on my schedule for the next two days."

"I understand, but checking up on the Kilis camp is part of my assignment. If I could just tag along, I promise to stay out of your way."

"Hmm." Balbay's face radiated his displeasure.

"Well, I'll let you get on with your breakfast."

Vermeulen went back to his table to finish his coffee. The icy reception was no surprise. Dealing with bureaucrats had been a constant annoyance of his professional life. First as prosecutor in Antwerp, Belgium, where he specialized in financial crimes after law school. Then, after his marriage fell apart, as investigator for the United Nations. Bureaucrats never liked anyone looking over their shoulders. Especially not someone like Vermeulen who wouldn't leave well enough alone and dug deeper. Balbay was simple another specimen of the sort. It would take a good amount of patience on Vermeulen's part to get along with him. He saw Balbay take a phone from his pocket, get up and walk out of the dining room. The man was probably already warning his staff that a UN investigator had arrived.

When Balbay came back into the room, Vermeulen approached him again. "Let's just get this out of the way. I'm here to do my job. I understand that it is inconvenient for you, but that's what it's going to be. With a little cooperation, everything will go smoother and I'll be out of your hair. So, if I could join you for the tour of the Kilis camp, it would make my job much easier."

"I understand that you have a job to do," Balbay said. "But it's not my job to make your job easier. I would appreciate it if the UN would send people whose mission it was to make my job easier."

Vermeulen rarely encountered such open hostility and on the occasions he did, it was usually a cover for something else going on that wasn't related to UN operations. He could pull rank and use his authority to put Balbay in his place, but he didn't want to go there, yet.

"I do understand that you are asked to achieve impossible goals without the necessary resources to do so. Believe me, if I had any influence, I'd use it to make your job easier. But my job is to make sure that the resources provided by the member states are put to proper use. I know, it sounds like the folks at UN headquarters don't trust you. They do. Still, we have to show that everything is on the up and up. The alternative is far worse. Member states will pull back, the funding dries up and you'll have even less to do your job. So let's just get this done."

Balbay hadn't expected this response. Vermeulen saw the lines on the man's face soften. Good. He needed as much cooperation as he could get.

"Okay," Balbay said. "I'm going to the camp in an hour. Meet me in front of the hotel."

Vermeulen used the opportunity to text his partner Tessa, that he'd arrived in one piece and that the job should take less than a week. With the seven hour time difference, it was too early to call. He first met Tessa, a Zambian freelancer for some of the top international news outlets, during an assignment in Darfur. Six months ago, they'd moved in together in New York City. Her globe-trotting days were over and she'd managed the release of a cache of secret documents she'd obtained helping Vermeulen unmask a nefarious land scheme. After that task, she and the two other journalists who managed the cache decided to put out a webzine in collaboration with a select group of writers around the world.

VERMEULEN STEPPED OUTSIDE the hotel an hour later. There was an odd mixture of old and new around him. Across the narrow street, a hole-in-the-wall shop sold bulk goods. A sign advertised bulgur. Several sacks filled with beans, lentils and grain leaned against the wall. An old man was busy scooping chick peas into a bag, weighing it, and, satisfied that it was the right amount, tying the bag and handing it to a woman. Next to it was an ATM and a bank. To the left of the hotel was an Internet cafe and to the right a fancy shoe store with flashy window displays. Before he could explore more, a white SUV pulled up to the hotel entrance. Balbay was at the wheel and motioned him to get into the car.

The drive out of town led through the same narrow streets where Vermeulen had gotten lost. In the daylight, he saw they were lined with trees that were surprisingly green given the temperature and time of year. He mentioned that to Balbay who told him that the rains wouldn't come again until October. When they reached the outskirts of Kilis, the buildings became more modern and the street widened to four lanes. Vermeulen recognized it from the night before. They passed the same traffic circle and headed toward the Syrian border.

Balbay started into a tour guide routine.

"The Turkish government has been very proactive. Within twenty-four hours after the first refugees came across the border, they put up the first tent camp. Now they operate twenty-two camps."

The traffic became sparser. Only those who had business there drove into the border region. It was too dangerous. The Kilis camp lay in a pocket of Turkish territory that jutted into Syria. Fighting could easily cross the border. Mortar rounds and rockets often did.

"That must have cost the government a lot of money," Vermeulen said.

Balbay nodded. "It took a while before the international community started to help out. Individual countries gave money to Turkey and soon after UNHCR started paying for the refugee allowances. But the cost of the camps was entirely paid for by the government."

They arrived at the entrance. It was different from any refugee camp Vermeulen had ever seen. Access was strictly controlled. Each car was stopped, pedestrians had to pass through a metal detector. A large group of people hung out by the entrance.

As they waited to be checked in, Balbay continued. "The Kilis camp was started in 2012. There are just over two thousand containers here. They are all the same, three rooms, electricity and water. They now house some sixteen thousand refugees. There are three supermarkets here, playgrounds for the children, schools, you name it."

He showed his ID to the guard at the camp entrance. Vermeulen showed his. They were waved through. The first thing that struck Vermeulen was how clean the camp was. There was no trash, anywhere. The last time he'd visited a refugee camp was in Darfur. The differences were startling.

The containers stood neatly aligned in long rows. Stone paths connected them to each other and the common areas. Each unit had an air conditioner and their inhabitants had tried to spruce up the stark lines with cloth awnings, chairs and other belongings they had rescued.

"Who runs the shops?" Vermeulen said.

"They are privately run. There are different owners so we have some competition. Since last year, with the help of UNHCR and the EU, we've been giving each family cash cards. They can use them to buy what they need in the shops. Much more efficient than vouchers or goods. They get to decide how to spend their allowance."

"How do you handle the distribution of the cards? Determine eligibility?"

"First, they have to register as a refugee. The humanitarian organizations collect the information about the recipients and vet them. Once that is all checked out, we distribute the funds to the organizations. They contract with a card issued and then distribute the cards to the recipients. The amount depends on how many family members they have. A financial contractor reloads the cards every month."

"That's a lot of money being distributed," Vermeulen said.

"That's true, but easier to manage than truckloads of food and other items. The shops take care of ordering the goods people want. We don't have to guess."

"What about the other refugees? The camps only house about ten percent of them, right?"

"Yes. They live in the community. As long as they are registered and we can keep track of them, they get cash cards, too."

Vermeulen knew that, of course, but he'd found that letting the people in charge explain their operation put them at ease with his presence. And that helped later on when the dicier issues came up. Such as how they kept track of all those cash cards floating around.

FOUR

AHMADI WAS READY to crawl into her tent and sleep forever. Her back ached from bending over all day. The grapes hung too low to cut them standing up and kneeling on the stony dirt was out of the question.

Zada still wasn't back from wherever she'd gone. The two women shared a tent. It had started as a cohabitation of convenience. Being a single woman in a refugee camp was difficult. The married women were suspicious and their husbands leered. In a matter of days, they became friends. Despite their age difference—Zada was forty, fifteen years older than Ahmadi—they found that their journey from middle class life to refugee was similar. Zada's husband died fighting with a rebel militia against the Assad regime. Shortly after burying him, her house was destroyed by a missile that killed her two children. Ahmadi hadn't lost a husband or children, but her parents' and siblings' fate had been the same. The didn't talk much about their loss. What was there to say? It was the trials of being a refugee that forged their bond. They had each other's backs through the daily misery of picking grapes.

Ahmadi needed to eat to keep up her strength. Resting first meant she'd miss the evening meal. Rahel had invited her after learning that Zada had disappeared. Which was kind, especially since Rahel's family was Christian and she was a Muslim. But Rahel understood

the precarious position of single women and the importance of protecting one's honor.

Back home, Ahmadi considered the idea of honor
old-fashioned. Being passed from your father to your
husband didn't appeal to her. She went to the university,
she could take care of herself. Or so she thought. In the
refugee camp that self-sufficiency had evaporated like
morning mist in the September sun. What little pay she
received for picking disappeared so fast. The agent who
got her the picking job got his cut, the tent rental took
another bite, leaving her with just enough for food. Zada
did the cooking. Another one of those things Ahmadi
wasn't good at. She'd never had to cook for herself.

She took two apples and went to Rahel's tent.

"Salam," she said when she entered. Rahel's husband sat in a rickety chair in one corner, her three children, including the teenage son, sat on the ground. They
were all bent over plastic bowls eating their supper.
The children returned the greeting. Rahel's husband
grunted something.

"I brought some apples," Ahmadi said.

Rahel took them and passed her a bowl of couscous
and thin stew.

"Shokran," Ahmadi said.

"Al'afw," Rahel said. "Sit. Enjoy the food."

Ahmadi squatted near the entrance and ate. The stew
was spicy, but all the peppers in the world couldn't make
up for the fact that it was mostly broth with some onions and bits of gristly mutton. Rahel cut the two apples Ahmadi brought into pieces, gave the biggest to
her husband, and the rest to the kids. She kept a couple
of pieces for Ahmadi and herself.

The tent flap opened and a woman looked inside and said that the police had found Zada.

"Where is she?" Ahmadi said, jumping up and almost spilling her food.

"She's dead," the woman said. "They found her body in an olive grove near the border."

Ahmadi fell to her knees, barely able to put the bowl down. She covered her face with her hands.

"Who found her?" Rahel said.

"Workers checking on the olive trees. They called the police."

"How'd she get there? How did she die?"

"I don't know. The men said they didn't see any injuries."

The flap closed again and the woman went to the next tent to break the news. Ahmadi stood, unable to move. Zada had been her guide in this crazy world. How could she go on now?

Rahel put her arm on Rima's shoulder. "Such sad news. You liked Zada very much."

Ahmadi held back her tears and sighed deeply. But she didn't break out in a wail. Zada's death was her private grief, nothing to be mourned in public.

"Stay here tonight," Rahel said. "It's not good to be alone when one is full of sorrow."

Ahmadi shook her head. No, she wasn't going to stay there. "Thank you for your offer, but I'll be okay. I'm going to find out what happened to Zada."

"What do you mean?"

"Yesterday, Zada told me she learned something important. Today she is dead. That can't be a coincidence. I need to find out what she learned."

"Oh Ahmadi, you are distraught. Stay here and calm yourself. This is for the police to sort out."

"The Turkish police? Haven't you seen how they disdain us? We are just Syrian refugees. One less to worry about."

"So you're going to investigate?" Rahel's husband said. "How far d'you think you'll get? You are right about the Turkish police, and they won't like it if you stick your nose into their business."

Ahmadi looked at him, frowning. Those were the most words she'd ever heard from that man.

"Thomen is right," Rahel said. "This is not a matter for a single woman."

"Listen, Zada knew that we weren't treated right. She wanted to make our lives better. Now she is dead. I'm going to find out what happened. Her death wasn't an accident."

"How do you know?" Rahel said. "Maybe she lost her spirit and her heart gave out. She was all alone in a foreign land. Without family. She had no one."

"She had me," Ahmadi said. "Thank you for the meal. You have been very kind."

She went back to her tent. Inside, she zipped the flap shut and began to search Zada's things. There was a suitcase and a large bag. She started with the suitcase. It was a wardrobe assembled not with logic but in panic. Several plain skirts, a dress wholly impractical for harvesting grapes, a few shirts, a silk blouse she'd never seen Zada wear. How do you pack when you have only a few moments and think you'll be back soon?

Ahmadi felt strange sorting through Zada's underwear and bras. Those were private things and she silently apologized to Zada for this violation. She found

two books, a Koran, several letters, an envelope with
pictures. Ahmadi took them out and spread them out on
the blanket. Pictures of a man and two children at different ages. Tears came to Rima's eyes again. So much
senseless suffering.

The ghastly image of her parents and siblings, all
dead in the apartment on the top floor, rushed back into
her mind. The only reason she was still alive was because she'd run an errand for her mother. *Quick, Rima,
there's a lull in the fighting. Get us some cooking oil. I
heard the shop got a delivery.* On the way to the shop,
she heard the screaming jet and the explosion. She didn't
give it another thought. There were attacks all the time.
She continued on and bought the bottle of oil. Only
when she returned did she realize that this time, the
missile had hit her house.

The street-side walls of their apartment had been
blown out. She saw the armoire in her parent's bedroom, the drawers askew, the bathtub teetering over the
edge of the bathroom floor. Her own room had taken
the brunt. The mattress hung over the edge, shredded,
and her clothes were spread out over the rubble above
and below, some hanging on bits of concrete and rebar.

She'd been lying on her bed when her mother had
asked her to get the oil. She would have been dead.
Dropping the bottle of oil, she raced up the stairs to the
fourth floor. Strangely, the stairway was untouched.
She reached the top. There were three apartments. Hers
was the only one occupied. The other two tenants had
left a year ago.

Rubble obstructed their door. She leaned against
it and managed to open a crack large enough to slip
through. The acrid smoke of the missile explosion lin-

gered in the hallway. All the pictures her mother had hung had fallen to the floor. She inched forward. The first body she saw was in the passage to the living room. It was her father lying on his face. Her mother's body was draped over the kitchen table, a piece of metal piercing her back. She couldn't find her brother and sister. The wall of their room had collapsed on top of them. Back in the kitchen, she checked her mother's pulse. There was none. When she turned over her father, she shrieked. Half his head was missing.

The rest of the afternoon, Ahmadi operated in a daze. She gathered the clothes that hadn't been scattered, her laptop, three of her favorite books, chargers for her phone and computer, and put it all in her suitcase she'd hauled up from the basement. The downstairs neighbors had stuck their head into the door, saw the carnage and alerted the White Helmets emergency response team. Men came into the apartment. They asked if she was okay. She nodded, unable to say anything. They brought body bags for the dead and removed the bodies of her mother and her father. Four of the men tackled the fallen down wall. She wasn't allowed to watch. But she knew when two more body bags were brought outside. The men left in a van and took the bodies to the hospital.

When she had packed her things, she went to the bank and took out all her money. Her parents had accounts there, too. Ahmadi didn't care. She went back to the apartment. The local militia commander was waiting for her.

"They are getting your family ready for burial. Please go to the morgue and help."

She nodded without understanding his words.

"Please," the man said. "Go and help wash your mother's and sister's bodies. The men will take care of your father and brother."

She nodded again, dragged her suitcase by the handle and walked toward the town center. The wheels bounced over the debris on the street. Someone would wash her family members, wrap them in a shroud and bury them. It would not be her. In town, she hired a driver to take her to the Turkish border.

Ahmadi rubbed her eyes. It had gotten dark in the tent. Zada's suitcase was empty. There was nothing that hinted as to what she might have found out. She rifled through the pile of things Zada hadn't put away yet. Nothing there either. Zada must have taken her phone with her, but just to make sure Ahmadi dialed her number. She was about to end the call when she heard a beep.

"Alo?" a male voice said.

Ahmadi sucked in her breath. She'd expected the phone to ring somewhere in the tent, not someone answering.

"Alo. Where is Zada?"

There was a hesitation on the other end. The man answered in Turkish, all she understood was that he was a policeman. She didn't say anything. Police was bad news.

"Who are you?" This time the man spoke rough Arabic.

"A friend."

"Your name?"

Ahmadi hesitated. Was she in trouble? She was registered as a refugee. But she needed to know about Zada, maybe get her phone.

"Rima Ahmadi."

"Where are you?"

"West of Kilis. At a vineyard."

"Come to police tomorrow for questions."

The call ended. Ahmadi stared at the phone. Should she go? The answer was obviously no. She couldn't miss work.

She had looked everywhere and found nothing that hinted at what Zada might have discovered. She put everything back in its place, zipped up the suitcase and put it in the corner. The last thing she did was put Zada's sleeping mat under hers. She stretched out. This was much better. Her eyes fell on something light where the mat had been. She grabbed the flashlight and found a scrap of paper. On it was a series of numbers, too long to be a Syrian phone number, but the right length for a Turkish one.

FIVE

TARIQ YAWNED AS he stepped into the workshop. The sun hadn't risen above the horizon yet. Inside, the fluorescent lights hanging from the ceiling created a flickering brightness that hurt his eyes. The room was a rectangular space without windows. There were fifteen tables with a sewing machine each, nine along the left wall and six more along the rear wall. The rest of the room held cutting tables holding bolts of fabric.

Five kids, two girls and three boys, stood around waiting. Tariq joined them. At eleven years, he wasn't the oldest or the youngest kid in the room. One of the girls was only nine. The oldest boy was thirteen. They sewed uniforms for *Daesh,* the killers who had occupied much of northern Syria. The foreman called them ISIS. The color of the fabric on the tables, green, told Tariq that today's order was for the frontline soldiers, the ones doing the actual fighting.

The day before, he'd worked until the sun set. When he was finally allowed to go, his stomach cramped with hunger. But when he got back home, he just wanted to go straight to bed because he was so tired. Home was a single room his mother rented for the four of them. His two sisters were too young to work and his mom had to take care of them. His father was dead.

The adults drifted into the room. Five men and ten women. The men were the cutters, rolling out the bolts of material, placing patterns on them and cutting with large scissors. Tariq figured that they had a system, because there was very little fabric left over.

The foreman came into the workshop. The waiting workers straightened. The orders for the day were just as Tariq had thought. Fighting uniforms for *Daesh*. Tariq and three boys climbed on the stools behind their sewing machines and started sewing the pieces together. Tariq only did the outside seams of the trousers, straight, but long. The other kids did similar seams. The women took the pieces and sewed the complex seams, attaching arms to tops, crotches, the zippers for the flies and the collars. Most of the *Daesh* uniforms consisted of tunics and trousers, but the battledress uniforms had buttoned fronts that also required the women's work. The girls mostly sewed on buttons or wrapped completed uniforms in plastic bags.

Tariq overlaid the two sides of the pants, slid them under the presser foot, held the fabric as straight as possible and lowered the presser foot. The first stitch of the day was always the scariest. The machine was not like the one he'd seen his grandmother use back home in Al Bab, where she'd turn the machine's pulley to get the stitching started and then step on the foot switch. The machines in the shop were designed to sew as fast as possible. The motor was always running and the moment Tariq released the clutch with his foot, the feed dog would yank the pieces under the needle and spit them out the other side. Even the slightest change while feeding the material, and the needle would race off the fabric or veer across the pants leg and mess everything up.

It had taken him two weeks to get the hang of it, the shop owner hitting him every time he messed up. The machine scared him. Releasing the clutch was like releasing a caged lion. He held his breath and stepped on the pedal. The motor engaged the needle and the feed dog. The pants leg shot toward him. He breathed out. It was a good seam.

He looked at the growing pile still waiting to be sewn and knew this day would be just as bad as yesterday.

KORUN TURNED OFF the road onto a dirt track. The van lumbered along, the springs and shocks strained past their normal use. He was carrying way more cargo than the van was meant to carry. It was still early, but the sun was up and he kept an eye out for the armored cars of the gendarmerie. They'd stepped up patrols after NATO complained about smuggling ISIS oil into Turkey. It wasn't a big problem. The increased patrols were mostly for show.

After three miles on the bumpy track, he reached what might have once been a barn. There were already three vans waiting. The drivers had lined up their jerry cans and waited for their turn. Korun parked the van and walked into the barn.

Inside, another man dressed in greasy overalls operated a primitive pump connected to a rubber hose that emerged from the dirt. The hose originated across the border in Syria.

"What's the price today?" Korun said.

"Five dollars a can," the pumper said. "Just got the text. Only diesel today. The infidels bombed a refinery yesterday."

Korun nodded. That'd be sixteen and a half lira per can, about four hundred for the entire load. It was a lot cheaper than diesel in Turkey. The boss would give him a bonus. He went back to his van and smoked a cigarette. After an hour, it was his turn. He filled twenty-four jerry cans, all his van could hold, and paid the pumper.

"Should I come back today?" Korun said.

"I don't know yet, text me."

Korun got into the van and drove back to the road. Thirteen hundred pounds of fuel taxed the van. It groaned with each pothole. He drove mostly in first gear. About a mile away from the tarred road, he spotted an armored car of the gendarmerie coming toward him.

"Damn," he muttered and slowed to a stop.

The cops stopped and pulled their vehicle across the track to block any possible escape. As if he was going anywhere with that overloaded van.

A sergeant climbed from the armored car and approached the van, his finger through the trigger guard of the submachine gun. Korun cranked down the window.

"Papers, please," the sergeant said.

Korun pulled out his license, rummaged in the glove compartment for the registration, and folded a fifty lira note inside. He handed the package to the cop. The sergeant unfolded the papers, took the money, and looked up at him.

"Where are you coming from?" he said.

Korun turned his head and pointed with his thumb behind him.

"Where are you going?"

"Kilis."

"What's in your van?"

Korun knew that the sergeant wasn't satisfied with the fifty lira. But he didn't want to give him more. Once you give in, it gets more expensive every time. It'd cut into his bonus.

"I think you should talk to your commander," Korun said. "I'm sure my boss has spoken with him."

The sergeant was not impressed. "What's in your van?"

What a stupid question. The stink of diesel was as thick as fog.

"Farm supplies," Korun said. He pulled out a twenty lira note from his pocket, took out his insurance letter from the glove compartment, wrapped it around the note and handed it to the cop. "Sorry, I forgot to give you my insurance."

The sergeant took the money, looked at the paper, and handed everything back to Korun. Then he turned and signaled the driver of the armored car to clear the track. He looked back at Korun and tipped his dark green beret with his right index finger.

Korun drove off, slowly, while texting the pumper at the barn that the gendarmerie was coming. Adding the bribe to what he'd paid for the diesel brought his cost to four hundred seventy lira, about a hundred and forty US dollars. At the going price, still a good deal.

VERMEULEN SAT IN the dining room of his hotel and finished his second cup of coffee. Fortunately, the hotel kitchen offered filtered coffee to accommodate tourists who didn't want to partake in the Turkish breakfast tradition of drinking tea for breakfast. The meal was ample, *simit*—which looked like a giant bagel—with butter and jam, two kinds of cheeses, tomatoes and olives. Vermeulen lingered. He liked breakfast and could never understand people who rush out of their houses gulping coffee from travel mugs.

He checked his phone and saw that Tessa had texted back, telling him that she missed him and to come home soon. He replied with a kiss emoji.

The tour of the Kilis camp the day before had been useful. It was the best run camp he'd ever seen. Everything worked, mostly because AFAD, the Turkish Disaster and Emergency Agency, ran the show. No infighting between various humanitarian organizations, which often duplicated some services while skipping others that were needed. The only role UNHCR played was funding the cash cards and helping staff the schools. There had been no reports of irregularities at the Kilis camp and his conversation with the camp authorities confirmed his sense that UNHCR's role there had not generated any complaints. This left him curious about the majority of refugees who didn't live in such well-managed camps. How did AFAD and UNHCR handle them?

That was a question Bilek Balbay would have to answer. Vermeulen had expected him at breakfast, but he didn't show.

After waiting a while, he inquired at the reception and found out that Balbay had left early that morning. Vermeulen pretended to be surprised and told the concierge that he was supposed to have a meeting with Balbay. Had he left a message? The concierge shook his head. Following a hunch, he asked if Balbay had left the hotel anytime during the last evening. The man behind the desk shrugged. He hadn't worked then. Vermeulen would have to ask the night porter.

Vermeulen stood at the counter, tapping his hand.

He'd experienced more than his fair share of rudeness, so Balbay's behavior was par for the course. Driving back to Gaziantep was the logical next step, but he didn't want to chase Balbay. Besides, he already had an appointment at his office for Monday morning. There was nothing to do until then. He turned back to the concierge and extended his booking for two more nights.

SIX

Vermeulen left the hotel and turned right toward Cumhuriyet Caddesi. It was the main street through the center of Kilis. He stopped at the ATM across the street, withdrew a thousand lira and continued on. There was a large square to his right. Something was either being erected or taken down. All he could see were piles of fabric. Adjacent to the square was a stately government building. A quick glance at the map app on his phone told him it was the governor's office and court house for the Kilis province. For a moment he considered the option of going inside and asking about refugees living in the community, but decided it was better not to show up unannounced.

The street was busy. Cars and trucks of all sizes jostled for space. Pedestrians crowded the sidewalks and darted into the streets, seemingly oblivious to the traffic. The ground level was all shops. The mixture of new and old he'd noticed the day before was apparent everywhere. Flashy storefronts with large glass windows, mannequins in modern clothing, and bold lettered adverts stood right next to a small pastry shop, a tiny watch repair place, and a cobbler, which by all appearances had been at their locations for decades. Vermeulen could tell the age of the buildings by the number of air conditioning condensers bolted to the walls above street level.

He reached a mosque. The name, Kara Kadi Cami, was affixed to the minaret. Its heavy wooden doors were closed. A little souvenir stand just outside sold postcards. He kept an eye out for hawkers, figuring that refugees subsisting outside of camps might fall between the cracks of the support system, or try to supplement their allowances through other means. The large influx had to have pushed up housing prices for everyone.

Sure enough, he saw an old man sitting in the shade of a tree by the iron fence surrounding the mosque. The piece of green cloth in front of him displayed pieces of jewelry. Next to him sat a boy maybe ten years old. As he came closer, Vermeulen saw three pairs of earrings, four necklaces and a dozen or so bangles, the latter made of silver, brass and copper. Vermeulen stopped, nodded a "Hello" and inspected the wares. It was clear that the man hadn't made these pieces. For one, his fingers were crooked with arthritis. And the metal was tarnished from long wear. He was selling his family's jewelry.

Vermeulen picked up a silver bangle. It was a slender oval with a round stone set on one side of its minor axis. The stone was as green as an emerald but opaque. A gorgeous gem. On each side of the stone was an intricate pattern that faded as the band narrowed at its major axis.

"How much," he said.

The old man looked at him without comprehension. The boy said something to the man. The man looked at the boy and replied. His voice was raspy. The boy turned toward Vermeulen and said, "Hundred lira."

A little over thirty bucks. A good deal for a special piece. He pulled out his wallet, took a hundred lira note from it and handed it to the old man. He accepted it and shook Vermeulen's hand with gratitude.

"Do you speak English?" Vermeulen said to the boy.

"A little."

"Are you from Kilis?"

"No, we come from Hamah."

"Is that in Syria?"

The boy nodded.

"Where do you live now? In Kilis?" Vermeulen said.

The boy shook his head. "No, tent."

"Where?"

The boy shrugged, then pointed down the street.

"Are there other refugees?" Vermeulen said.

"Yes."

"How many?"

The boy asked the old man something. The man looked at Vermeulen with suspicion in his eyes and replied. "My grandfather says, why you want to know," the boy said.

"I work for the United Nations." Vermeulen showed his ID.

The boy translated for the old man, whose face became animated. He spoke to the boy again, much faster.

"He says, you come and help us?"

Vermeulen hesitated. Strictly speaking, the answer was "No." His job was to make sure that money was spent properly and in accordance with the policies established. Better not to create expectations on which he couldn't deliver. On the other hand, this was his chance to see how people who didn't get into the camps fared.

"Maybe," he said to the boy. "But I want to see how you are living and if you are receiving the support you are entitled to. How far from here do you live?"

"We walk two hours and more," the boy said.

"I have a car. I can give you a ride back."

The boy translated for the man. The man shook his head and said something.

"He says, come back later. We must sell more."

"When?"

"Afternoon."

VERMEULEN HAD EXPECTED the old man and the boy to disappear. People in precarious situations usually tried to dodge authorities because they rarely improved their conditions and often made it worse. And the status of refugees in Turkey was precarious, the well-run camps not withstanding. The briefing documents Vermeulen received before he left New York made that clear. Although Turkey was a party to the Refugee Convention, the country had limited its applicability to refugees from Europe. Syrian refugees were officially "guests" of the government, and they were not allowed to work.

So, when he drove by the Kara Kadi mosque at four o'clock that afternoon, he was surprised to see the old man and the boy still on the sidewalk. They had moved the cloth with the jewelry to follow the shade cast by the tree. From what Vermeulen could tell, they hadn't sold much more.

He honked and rolled down the window. The boy recognized him and started rolling up the cloth. He was eager not to miss the ride. It'd beat walking back in the hot sun. The old man was slower, but followed suit.

"Can you tell me where to drive?" Vermeulen said to the boy.

"You go that way." The boy pointed out the rear window.

"I can't go that way. It's a one-way street."

The boy looked at him, forehead wrinkled.

"I can only drive this way," Vermeulen said, pointing to the front.

The boy nodded, but seemed puzzled.

Vermeulen merged into the thick traffic on Cumhurriyet Caddessi and looked for a place to turn. Without a map of Kilis, he could only hope that there was a parallel street that would let him drive in the opposite direction. He took a right turn and promptly found himself in a warren of narrow streets each of which was only a block long. He took a few more rights and got back to Cumhurriyet Caddessi. Following the street, he headed toward his hotel and tried a left turn by the large square that fronted the provincial court and government buildings.

"Is this the right way?" he said.

The boy shrugged. The old man said something to the boy. The boy responded, then said to Vermeulen, "Grandfather says, we go east."

Easier said than done. Somehow, he managed to get on a wider street that headed into the right direction. He followed it until the boy yelled, "Turn here."

Vermeulen slowed. "Which way?"

The boy pointed to the right. Vermeulen turned. They reached an intersection and the boy pointed forward. They crossed to Yavuz Sultan Selim Caddessi and the boy smiled. "Yes, we walk on this street."

There was a lot of construction on both sides of the road. Kilis was growing at a good clip. A barren stretch to their right had been turned into a parking lot for long semis. A bit farther was a stone crushing and sand operation.

It was a herd of goats, trotting very disciplined three abreast along the road, that told Vermeulen that they'd left the city for good. They crossed the highway on which Vermeulen had come from Gaziantep a couple of days ago and entered farm country. The road narrowed to a single lane. The land to the left was being tilled for new plantings. On the right, there were lush fields with vegetables and fruit trees. After a couple more miles, the boy said they were almost there.

Ahead he saw a vineyard that spread as far as he could see. There was a concrete block building by the road. It was two stories tall with a steel water tank on the flat roof. Next to the building was a large shed. In its shade stood at least ten large cases filled with grapes. A tractor with a front loader stacked the crates on top of each other.

"Drive more," the boy said.

Vermeulen passed the building and rows of grapevines. When they reached a break in the rows, the boy told him to stop. "We walk now."

Vermeulen could tell that the boy was relishing his role as guide as much as having gotten a ride rather than having to walk the seven miles from town. The boy led Vermeulen and his grandfather along a row of grapevines until they reached a clump of bushes. Beyond the bushes he saw an encampment. There were about a dozen tents more or less lined up on two sides of a central area. They varied in size from barely larger than a pup tent to ones accommodating an extended family. None of them were new. Some had cooking stoves outside. Off to the side stood two portable toilets. Closer to the grapevines were two spigots attached to wooden poles.

A handful of kids were playing in the central area, dust rising as they were trying to catch each other. Other children watched them, sitting nearer to the tents. Three older boys kicked a ball back and forth. A group of old men holding tiny cups sat in plastic chairs under a tree, staring at the newcomer.

The boy ran to a tent, hollering something. The tent flap opened and a woman smiled when she saw the boy. She came outside and scooped him up in a hug. The boy struggled against that much affection. The other boys around were watching. His grandfather caught up with them.

Vermeulen stood alone in the middle of the camp. It was a little after six in the afternoon. People looked at him, but nobody came closer. The old men under the tree had stopped talking but showed no intention of greeting him. It wasn't clear if there was someone in charge, some protocol, a person he should talk to first.

Football being a universal language, Vermeulen approached the older boys with the ball. He nodded to the one balancing the ball in the crook of his foot. The boy lobbed the ball up high and towards Vermeulen. It was meant to be a header, but Vermeulen wasn't about to head a ball he hadn't tested first. Instead, he raised his right leg, caught the ball gently with the arch of his foot, balanced it for a moment before passing it to another boy. The boys kicked the ball back and forth again. Vermeulen had become the fourth player. He'd passed at least one test.

The woman who had hugged the boy walked over to Vermeulen.

"Thank you for driving my son and my father," she

said in accented English. "It is a long way. They were happy you took them."

Vermeulen reached into his jacket pocket and pulled out the bangle.

"Is this yours?" he said.

The woman nodded.

"Here, take it back. It's too precious. I'm sure it holds memories."

The woman shook her head. "No, you bought it. We need the money more than we need the bracelet."

"You can keep the money."

"Did you buy it for someone?"

"Yes, my…" He hesitated. Lover seemed an inappropriate word. "…partner Tessa."

"Then I want you to have it."

Vermeulen wanted to protest but the noise of a car arriving got everyone's attention. It wasn't the car as such that made them stop, but its siren. A white and blue Fiat minivan slid to a stop near the first tent, *Polis* emblazoned on its side. The siren died with a whine but the lights kept flashing. Two cops jumped from the van and ran to the center of the camp. The little kids had already dashed into their tents. The boys playing soccer stopped and checked out the flashing lights. The old men sitting in the plastic chairs seemed not interested. Nothing they hadn't seen before.

The taller of the officers shouted something. Nobody answered. Nobody moved. He shouted again. The woman who'd been speaking to Vermeulen answered. The cop came up to her. It was then that he noticed Vermeulen. He said something to him. Vermeulen didn't understand and shrugged. The woman translated.

"He wants to know what you are doing here."

"I'm with the United Nations," he said and took out his ID. "I'm here to check up on the work of the refugee agency."

The woman translated haltingly, but the policeman stopped her. "You have authorization?" he said to Vermeulen in halting English.

Vermeulen nodded and showed him a letter from the Undersecretary-General of OIOS. It didn't really mean much, but the letterhead and the signature looked impressive.

"No, Turkish authorization."

"I don't need it. Check with your supervisor. I'm here on the authority of the Turkish government. I can call right now." Vermeulen pulled out his phone.

The cop had second thoughts. Having to deal with Ankara was above his pay grade. He turned back to the woman and said, "Where is Rima Ahmadi?"

SEVEN

THE QUESTION PRODUCED no reaction. People still outside their tents inched away and turned to leave. The second policeman, shorter and fatter, hollered something in Turkish. There was no answer. The first cop shouted again in English, "Where is Rima Ahmadi? We need to speak with her."

The space between the tents was empty now. Only Vermeulen and the old men under the tree remained seated. They looked at the two cops and seemed to enjoy the display of passive resistance. The second cop shouted again. Vermeulen could see the tent flaps move, dark eyes peering through the cracks, hoping the police would just leave.

"Why do you need to speak to this Ahmadi?" Vermeulen said.

"Police business. Not your concern," the tall cop said.

"Fair enough, but if you're looking for cooperation, you'd be better off explaining why you are here. I only just arrived and I can tell they're scared."

The fat cop said something in Turkish that sounded angry and the tall one replied. It sounded like he was trying to calm his colleague.

"What's Ahmadi done?" Vermeulen said. "Is she in trouble?"

"It's our case. Stay out of it," the tall cop said. Then

he turned around and shouted, "We will search every tent until we find Rima Ahmadi."

He followed with a statement in Turkish, presumably the same threat. Neither produced any results. The people remained in their tents.

Vermeulen thought he could hear the old men snickering behind him. That was a bad sign. He knew enough about people in positions of authority to understand that the laughter would only escalate the situation. Nothing irks police more than ridicule. Before he could do anything about it, a young woman appeared from one of the small tents.

She was of medium height, wore well-worn jeans and a cotton shirt. Unlike some of the women Vermeulen had seen in the camp, she didn't wear a hijab. Her hair was dark brown, fell down her shoulders and framed what Vermeulen immediately thought of as an interesting face. It wasn't pretty in the traditional sense. Her almond eyes were set rather far apart, making her nose look slightly off center above her thin lips.

"Are you Rima Ahmadi," the tall cop said.

"Yes," the woman said. She turned to Vermeulen. "Are you here because of Zada?"

Vermeulen hesitated. His role had just changed. He wasn't sure he liked that. But it was clear that his answer would determine what happened next. The logical response would be no. He didn't know who this Zada was. But he also sensed that Ahmadi had just put her trust in him. His presence was a check on the police. They wouldn't harass a UN official. Vermeulen had already pulled rank by threatening to call Ankara. It had worked.

If he said no, the cops would take that as a sign that

they could proceed with whatever they'd planned, which probably involved taking Ahmadi to the station. A yes, on the other hand would keep them at bay. He looked at Ahmadi. Her face was still like a plaster mask. But her eyes spoke to him with desperation. It wasn't really a question anymore.

"Yes," he said. "I'm here because of Zada."

Maybe Ahmadi knew he was faking it, maybe she was simply relieved that he'd come to her aid. She stepped toward him and told him in rapid-fire sentences that her friend Zada had disappeared the day before, that she hadn't come to their tent that night, that she'd tried calling Zada's phone and that the police had answered because Zada was dead. Her English was excellent. By the time the two policemen had processed Vermeulen's surprise answer, the balance had shifted towards Ahmadi and Vermeulen.

"Why do you want to speak with this woman?" Vermeulen said.

"It is not your concern," the tall cop said. "You are not her lawyer."

He got that right. Vermeulen was a lawyer. He'd studied law at Antwerp University, gotten licensed in Belgium before working at the Crown Prosecutor's office in Antwerp. He was well versed in criminal law. But he wasn't Ahmadi's lawyer, and he wasn't licensed to practice law in Turkey.

"I am a lawyer," he said and turned to Ahmadi. "Would you like me to be your lawyer?"

"Yes," she said with a smile that lit up her face.

"Now it is my concern," Vermeulen said to the policeman.

"You can't be her lawyer." The policeman was in-

credulous. He turned to his fat colleague and explained
what had just happened. Before they could point out the
obvious fact that he wasn't licensed to practice law in
Turkey, he played his trump.

"According to the European Convention on Human
Rights, she has a right to legal assistance of her own
choosing. She just chose me. The European Court of
Human Rights has asserted multiple times that this right
begins from the moment of first contact with the police."

It was the biggest bluff Vermeulen had ever pulled. It
was correct, but it didn't obviate the fact that he couldn't
practice in Turkey. For a moment he worried that he'd
overplayed his hand. Even a six-foot Belgian can't press
his luck this far.

The policemen looked at each other, then at Ahmadi
and finally at Vermeulen.

"We want to speak with her about her dead friend.
What she knows," the tall cop said. "When she saw her
last. Those things. We want her to come to the station
for the interview."

"Is that okay with you?" Vermeulen said to Ahmadi.

"Only if you come along."

"Of course." He turned to the cops. "She'll ride with
me. We'll follow you."

During the conversation, the rest of the refugees had
slowly come out of their tents. They watched the exchange and those who understood English and heard
snippets of the exchange came forward to talk to Ahmadi. A woman who seemed to know Ahmadi thanked
Vermeulen for his assistance.

"I'll bring Ms. Ahmadi back here when she's done
with the police."

ONCE THEY WERE on the road to Kilis, Ahmadi turned to him.

"Are you really a lawyer?"

"Yes. I am. Really."

"And did you come about Zada?"

"No, I didn't. But it looked like you could use some help there."

Ahmadi sighed. "Yes, that's true. Thank you very much."

"There is another problem," Vermeulen said. "I can't practice law in Turkey. It's only a question of time before the police get wise to that and then you're on your own. So, do you have anything to do with the death of Zada? If so, I advise you to get a proper lawyer right away."

"I know nothing about Zada's death. We shared a tent. She was a friend when I had no one. She told me she'd found out something that would make our lives better than picking grapes and being mistreated by the foreman. She never told me what it was and then she disappeared."

"Still, I doubt I'll make it through the evening without someone telling me to get lost. Tell them what they want to know, and I'll be quiet. Maybe we get you out of there without further problems."

"Why did you come to our camp?"

"I'm here to make sure that the UNHCR monies are spent properly and according to plan. I visited the Kilis camp and things there were fine. I had a weekend to spend and I wondered how refugees who didn't live in the official camps get along. I found the old man and the boy, who took me up on my offer to drive them to their temporary home."

"*Masha'Allah*, God has willed it," Ahmadi said and looked out of the window.

As they neared the ring road at the outskirts of Kilis, the preposterousness of his position sank in. He'd impersonated an accredited lawyer. For all he knew, he'd broken the law by doing that. He went over the exchange with the policeman in his mind. Everything he'd said was right. He'd only left out that he wasn't licensed.

"Zada never told you what she found out?" he said.

She shook her head.

"Did you look through her things after you knew she was dead?"

Ahmadi looked at her feet. After a moment she mumbled, "Yes."

"Did you find anything that would explain her disappearance?"

"Nothing. Just a phone number."

"Have you called it?"

She shook her head again.

"Well, let's get through this interview first."

They reached the ring road again and retraced the route Vermeulen had driven, but instead of driving to the city center, the police van in front of them turned right onto Inönü Bulvari. Half a block farther, they pulled into a driveway next to a tall building. The lot behind the building was filled with police cars.

EIGHT

THE FAT COP brought Vermeulen and Ahmadi to an interview room. He grunted something, then walked out. The tall one had disappeared the moment they came into the building.

The room was depressingly similar to all the interview rooms Vermeulen had had the displeasure of visiting. A Formica table, bolted to the floor, the veneer peeled off at one edge. Three steel chairs with loops to accommodate handcuffs. Vermeulen chose one of them, Ahmadi the other.

A crude image of a penis had been scratched into the table surface. Lots of affirmative graffiti surrounded it. There were plenty of words Vermeulen didn't understand except for the obligatory "fuck off," which was written with a marker that the janitor hadn't been able to clean up. Not for lack of trying. The surface of the table was pocked from the cleansers. They had taken off the surface layer, but the palimpsest of the words shone through.

"Can you think of anything Zada might have said that hinted at what she'd found out?" Vermeulen said.

Ahmadi rested her head in her left palm and closed her eyes. Vermeulen waited. Finally, she sat up again and shook her head.

"No. All she said was that it would make our lives easier."

"Okay. What do you think would make your life easier?"

Ahmadi looked at him with an expression that made him wince at how clueless his question must have sounded.

"What I meant was your life here," he said, adding in a gentler voice, "I know that ending the war and returning home would make your life easier. But I'm certain that's not what Zada had in mind."

Ahmadi sighed. "Where should I begin? Not having to learn Turkish, not being leered at by the foreman, having a decent washroom, not living in a tent, getting better pay, being able to teach again, even for free." Her voice drifted off.

Vermeulen held his tongue. He had to ask difficult questions, but he didn't want to upset Ahmadi. She was his only access point to the world of refugees who seemed to have fallen between the cracks of the humanitarian efforts.

"Did you register with the Turkish authorities?"

Ahmadi shook her head again. "We aren't allowed to work in Turkey. Which is fine for the refugees living in the official camps, but not for us. If we register then they know about us and find out that we are working illegally."

"Don't you think the police know this already? The two policemen who came today must have known that everybody in the tents worked at the vineyard. But they didn't do anything."

Ahmadi considered this for several seconds. "Maybe the police are paid, you know, *baksheesh*."

"That's a possibility. But if they are paid off, you don't have anything to worry about."

"What if AFAD finds out, they won't accept *baksheesh*. They send us back."

Vermeulen nodded. Just the kind of situation Joseph Heller had conjured up.

Before he could say anything the door opened and a short, stocky man with a shaved head the shape of an artillery shell, squinty eyes and an enormous mustache entered. His suit was of fine beige linen but looked like he'd lived in it for several days. The fat cop followed him through the door, but the man said something and the cop remained outside.

"What the fuck are you playing at, Vermeulen," the man said in loud English. "You may be a lawyer, but, as far as Turkish law is concerned, you could be the king of Siam. It'd make no damn difference. You got no standing and you know that."

Vermeulen waited. No need to upset an already irate man.

"Don't for a moment believe you fooled my colleagues. They let you tag along because, hey, why not grab two for the price of one. He wanted to lock you up. But I decided this is so fishy, it might be good."

"Your English is outstanding, Mr.…" Vermeulen said.

"I'm Inspector Demirel, and compliments won't get you anywhere. I studied at Boston University. So tell me what the hell is going on."

Vermeulen looked at Demirel and weighed his options. The man could be an ally or an enemy. The former would obviously be preferable, not only for the obvious reasons, but also because he was a man who did things his way. Something Vermeulen was all too familiar with.

"I'm here to check up on the refugee operations of the United Nations. Making sure all the money is spent as intended. You get the idea."

"So why aren't you doing that?" Demirel said.

"But I am. Part of that is, of course, checking with actual refugees to see what all that aid looks like once it's trickled down to those who are the supposed beneficiaries."

Demirel grunted something, looked at Ahmadi then at Vermeulen again.

"You're shitting me," he said. "No way you'd end up at some rundown tent camp doing UN work. Try again. What were you doing at the vineyard?"

"Exactly what I told you. Sometimes I have to be creative. If I only checked what the local UN bureaucrats showed me, I wouldn't do my job. I saw a couple of folks selling their family heirlooms in town. The rest was easy. What concerns me is why you want to speak with Ms. Ahmadi."

"None of your concern. Official police business."

"Well, she's asked me to help her. Why not let me sit in? I might not be licensed in Turkey, but what harm can I do?"

"Undermine Turkish sovereignty, create a fucking precedent, have my boss fire my ass, annoy the hell out of me. Need any more reasons?"

"Inspector, you and I know that nobody is going to fire you. You've already shown you are in charge here. And I promise, I won't annoy you. As to sovereignty and precedent, nobody needs to know."

A hint of a smile appeared on Demirel's lips as if his assessment of Vermeulen had turned out correct.

"Okay," he said. "But you keep your mouth shut. She answers my questions and that's that."

Vermeulen nodded.

Ahmadi had a bemused expression on her face. Having the two men in the room argue with each other kept the attention away from her. Now that Demirel looked at her again, her face turned expressionless.

"How do you know Zada Homsi?" Demirel said.

"We shared a tent at the vineyard. Yesterday she didn't come to work and last night she didn't come back to the tent. Then someone came and said she was dead."

"How long have you known her?"

"Not long, just a few weeks. Why?"

"Did she say where she was going?"

"No. She left in the morning without telling me anything."

"And when you found out she was dead, you called her phone?"

Ahmadi scratched her forehead.

"I know it sounds odd," she said. "I thought maybe there'd been a mistake. I couldn't believe she was dead."

"What do you know about her?"

"She came from Aleppo, lost her whole family after a missile struck their house. That's all."

"What did she do?"

"I don't know. She had two children."

"Did she say anything about going back to Syria?"

"No. Why would she? It wasn't safe in Aleppo. How did she die?"

"Any idea why she would go near the border?"

Ahmadi shook her head.

"Did she say anything at all that might help us figure out why she ended up there?"

Ahmadi hesitated. She looked at Vermeulen, who shrugged. The Inspector noticed it and pounded the table.

"What is going on here? What are you two hiding?"

Vermeulen sat up straighter. "Mr. Demirel. I've never laid eyes on Ms. Ahmadi before this afternoon. We had barely exchanged a few sentences before your colleagues showed up. So there's nothing going on. But it strikes me that Ms. Ahmadi might be a bit reluctant to deal with the police given her precarious status in Turkey."

"Cut the bull, Vermeulen. All Syrian refugees are honored guests of Turkey. But we do expect cooperation in return."

"That doesn't include a work permit, does it?"

"That's what she's worried about? Do you think I waste even one second of my time hunting down illegal workers? If I did, I'd be doing nothing else. So, out with it. What else do you know?"

Ahmadi squirmed a little, but answered, telling the Inspector that Zada had found out something that would make their lives easier.

"Did she say what specifically?" Demirel said.

Ahmadi shook her head again.

Demirel stroked his mustache. "There aren't that many things that would make a refugee's life easier. It all boils down to housing, food, or money."

He got up and adjusted his pants. "Well." He yawned. "Thanks for coming in. We have your numbers. The next time we ask you to come in, don't make us come out there. You are free to go."

Vermeulen and Ahmadi rose from their chairs, too. Demirel led them to the front door. As they left the building, Demirel handed him his card and said, "A word of advice, Mr. Vermeulen. Don't try to play the lawyer again. The next police officer you run into probably won't be as accommodating as I've been."

The two went to Vermeulen's car. Once inside, Vermeulen asked her why she hadn't mentioned the telephone number she'd found among Zada's things.

"I don't know," Ahmadi said. "I wanted to keep something private."

"Do you have it with you?"

"Yes."

"First, let's get away from here. Then we'll call it."

He drove a few blocks and pulled into a gas station.

"I'll call the number from my phone," he said. "No need to get you into trouble."

She handed him the piece of paper. He dialed the number and waited for the call to connect.

After three rings, a woman said, *"Alo?"*

"Hello. Valentin Vermeulen here. Who am I speaking with?" Vermeulen said.

There was a long pause at the other end.

"What do you want?" the woman finally said. Her English had a slight accent.

"Your name, please."

"My name is not important. What do you want?"

"I'm interested in the death of Zada Homsi."

There was another long pause. Finally the voice on the phone said, "I don't know Zada Homsi."

NINE

THE TALL COP waited in the entrance of a closed TekCell shop. He stayed in the shadows as much as possible because he was still wearing his uniform. The old man had impressed on him to never wear his uniform to a clandestine meeting.

This was different, though. Urgent. After the dead woman had been found in the olive grove, he'd told the old man that nothing would come of it. The old man hadn't said anything, had just nodded. As if that was a given.

And now it wasn't.

First someone calls the dead woman's phone that's sitting on his desk. The fat idiot answers. So now they have to go and bring the caller in. Then some United Nations lawyer just happens to be there when they go to pick her up. Not only that, he comes along and the Inspector lets him sit in on the meeting. How much bad shit could happen in one day? Not that it mattered. He couldn't care less about the dead woman, or her friend, or the UN guy. Nothing would come of it. He knew the Inspector. The man was just playing around, letting the UN guy think he was important.

Still, he had to tell the old man what had happened. He'd called the number they'd given him. He was told to wait in the shop entrance. It was hot there. The building still radiated the day's heat. He took off his blue beret and wiped his forehead. He felt the cool draft before his brain registered that the shop's door behind him had opened. A hand pulled him inside and the door closed again. The inside of the shop was dark, but the street lamps illuminated the display cases and a counter. The posters advertising the latest phones and plans looked like sepia photos in the yellow light.

He still hadn't seen whose strong hand held his arm and guided him past the counter through another door into a backroom. The door closed behind him. The old man was sitting in a chair. In the shadow of the rear corner stood someone else. The cop craned his neck to see who that was, but a gruff voice behind him said, "Eyes straight ahead."

The old man sat still and examined him. He looked no different from the other old men that sat in coffee-shops and read the newspaper. Short white hair, bushy eyebrows, leathery skin that had withstood the sun for decades, and a thin mouth that spoke of underlying cruelty. Despite trying, the cop hadn't gotten used to the man's x-ray stare yet. Those eyes were both ice and fire at the same time. He knew it sounded impossible but it was the only way he could describe it. The rest of the old man was unremarkable. A grey suit and a white shirt. Like any of the old men that sat at cafes, read the newspaper and looked at life passing them by. He could imagine him playing backgammon with others his age.

"What is so urgent that you have to come in uniform?" the old man said.

"The dead woman. Others are involved now. A man from the UN."

"Explain."

He told the man what had happened.

"What do you think the Inspector will do?" the old man said.

"I don't know. Maybe nothing. But he let the UN man sit in on the interview. That's not protocol."

"What do you know about the UN man?"

"Nothing. He pretended to be the girl's lawyer. The Inspector told him to stop that, but did nothing else."

"Did he say why he is here?"

"Something about refugees and United Nations. I don't know."

"You were right to contact us. We will remember your initiative. Now go. Make sure no one sees you."

The strong hand coaxed him into a one-eighty turn and back into the store. A phone rang. It must have belonged to the person in the shadow because everyone in the room looked in that direction. The man behind him stopped. The shadow moved into the light. It was a young woman. She was good looking, but he knew better than to stare at her.

She answered the call and said, *"Alo?"*

There was a pause. Then, switching to English, the she said, "What do you want?" Another pause. The woman said, "My name is not important. What do you want?" Another pause. The woman tapped something on her phone.

"Where did the UN man park?" the woman said to the cop.

"Behind the station," the cop said.

"Is he still there?"

The cop shrugged.

"What kind of car does he drive?" the woman said.

"A white sedan, Kia, I think."

"Plate number?"

"I don't know."

The woman looked at the old man and said, "I need a pickup and two men to go to the police station and follow the white Kia rental car until it is far enough away from the station. Then make it look like an accident."

While the old man dialed a number on his phone, the woman tapped her phone again and said, "I don't know Zada Homsi."

VERMEULEN LOOKED AT his phone after the abrupt end of the call. That was one of the strangest phone conversations he'd had in a while. It seemed as if the woman on the other end was merely stalling for time rather than answering any questions.

"She said that she doesn't know Zada."

Ahmadi shrugged. "Maybe the number had nothing to do with Zada. Maybe it was just some shop where Zada went to buy something."

Vermeulen considered this. His gut told him that the woman he'd talked to knew about Zada. He couldn't quite explain why. The pauses were telling. As if she was sorting things out, processing an unexpected call, maybe organizing something. Whatever that might be. He looked around but there was nothing out of the ordinary outside. Just a gas station—six pumps, a small shop, everything lit brightly.

"We better get you back to the vineyard," he said. Traffic was moderate. No rush hour, but still plenty of cars driving in both directions. He retraced his route back to the ring road, checking his mirrors occasionally. Nothing stood out.

"What's work like at the vineyard?" he said.

Ahmadi hesitated, looking out of the window.

"It's bad," she finally said. "The vineyard is bad. The foreman yells because I'm not fast enough. I've never done this work before. Then he leers at me, knowing I have no family to protect me. I live in a tent and wash in a bucket and I'm supposed to be grateful that I'm not being shot at or bombed in Syria. But I didn't choose this. I want my life back, and if I can't have that, I want to start a new life. Not be treated like dirt at that cursed vineyard."

Vermeulen knew better than to say anything. Being kept at arm's length, never wanted, often despised and treated accordingly, that was a given. He hadn't even thought about how heavy the expectation of gratitude had to weigh on refugees.

They reached the ring road and left the lights of the city behind. It was still hot and Vermeulen kept the windows up and the AC on. Since her outburst Ahmadi hadn't said anything. The silence in the car felt heavy. In the rearview mirror, he saw a set of headlights in the distance.

"I'm sorry," Ahmadi said. "I should have thought about my answer rather than blurting out how I felt. It's not that I'm not glad I'm here. There was no way I could have stayed in Syria. Coming here saved my life. But I had plans, I had hopes. Now I'm stuck in nowhere."

Vermeulen said nothing.

"You must think I'm a terrible person."

"No," he said, looking at her silhouette dimly lit by the instrument panel. "Not at all. I can imagine that everything that has happened to you has deeply upset your world. Everything is wrong-side up and all jumbled. You have every right to be angry."

As he focused on the road ahead, he saw that the

headlights behind him had come much closer. He steered towards the edge of the road to let the speeding car pass. Ahmadi noticed the maneuver and looked back.

"Oh my. That car is really going fast," she said.

The car's high beams were on, filling their Kia with bright light. Those high beams were also much higher off the ground. It had to be a truck. Vermeulen flipped the lever on the rearview mirror to cut the glare.

The vehicle came alongside their car. It was a pickup all right, high off the ground with oversized tires. Vermeulen slowed to let it pass. The pickup slowed too. It dawned on him that the truck was there for them. Adrenaline jacked up his pulse. He gripped the steering wheel harder. A moment later, the truck swerved into them. The sickening crunch made Ahmadi scream in horror. The driver's side windows shattered and hot air laced with burnt fuel filled the interior. Their car was being pushed off the road. His heart racing at a crazy beat, he tried steering against the truck. The little Kia stood no chance. He slammed on the brakes, hoping to lose the pickup. The tires squealed on the asphalt, but the Kia didn't slow down. Somehow, it had gotten hooked to the pickup. The passenger side tires were already off the road and the car shook as it bounced over the rough ground.

He stomped the accelerator to the floor. Whatever had attached them to the pickup came loose. The Kia shot forward. He steered it back onto the road. For a moment, Vermeulen thought he could outrun their pursuers. That moment lasted only two seconds. The pickup sped up again and slammed into their left rear. The Kia yawed like a rudderless plane. Vermeulen jerked the steering wheel to keep the car on the road. The pickup hit them again, forcing the Kia to the left. Vermeulen yanked the wheel to the right, desperate to straighten out the car. He'd turned too hard. The Kia shot off the road and bottomed out on a rut. The impact riveted the seat to his rear like a jackhammer. Ahmadi's screams had turned into whimpers. The car caromed across the field. The sight of a massive tree trunk in the headlights made Ahmadi scream again. Vermeulen twisted the wheel once more and slammed on the brakes. The Kia lurched to the right. The front wheels dug into a deep rut, bringing the car to an instant standstill. The airbag exploded into his face like a plank of oak.

VERMEULEN DIDN'T KNOW how long he'd been sitting in the car. The idling diesel engine of the pickup finally roused him from the trance he'd been in. It stood on the road, maybe twenty feet away. He couldn't tell how many were in the cab. He heard steps. Someone approached the Kia. Vermeulen's heart began racing again. He willed himself calm and slumped into his seat. Ahmadi wasn't moving either. Whoever was checking on them must have been satisfied because they went back to the pickup. The door slammed and the truck sped away. Next to him, Ahmadi gave a small moan. She sat slumped against her seatbelt, the deflated airbag covering her knees.

Vermeulen touched her shoulder. "Are you okay?" he said.

"Where am I?"

"We are stuck in a field. Are you okay, or do we need an ambulance?"

"I think I'm okay. My head hurts and my neck is sore, but I can move all my limbs."

Vermeulen unbuckled his belt and tried to open the door. It didn't budge. The pickup must have jammed it into the frame.

"Can you get out on your side? My door is stuck."

He heard the click as the steel tongue slid out of the buckle. The door opened. Ahmadi more crawled than climbed out the car. Once outside, she disappeared from view. He clambered over the center console and out of her door. He ended up on the ground, sitting next to her.

"What happened?" she said.

"We were run off the road by a pickup truck."

"An accident?"

"No. That wasn't an accident. That truck was aiming for us."

"What does that mean?"

"It means that my phone call to the number you found got someone's attention. That's why there were so many pauses. The woman I was talking to was arranging for us to be killed in an accident."

"How did they find us?"

"That's what I'm wondering," he said. "It must have been someone at the police. Maybe Demirel himself."

TEN

THE DEMAND FOR uniforms in Syria never ended. That's why there was no weekend off at the sweatshop. Tariq was there on Saturday like every other day of the week. He waited with the other kids for the foreman to come and tell them the day's quota. He'd had a cup of sweet tea and a slice of bread. It wasn't much, but kept his stomach calm.

When the foreman came, he brought with him other men and a van. The man unloaded four more sewing machines from the van and brought them into the factory. Everything else needed to be rearranged because the space was already tight. One of the machines was added to the row along the left wall, the others got squeezed in the rear after moving one of the cutting tables.

The diversion was a nice break, but Tariq remembered that he was paid by the seam. Fewer seams meant less money. He'd have to work longer. His heart sank again. One of the older boys poked him and pointed to an old man who was standing next to the van.

"That's the big boss," the boy said.

"Who is he?"

The boy shrugged. "I heard he's very rich."

"He doesn't look very rich."

"Not all rich people do."

Tariq was confused. "But why be rich and wear old clothes?"

"He puts his money into new sewing machines to make more money."

"So he can buy nice clothes then?"

"No, to buy more sewing machines to make more money."

Tariq shook his head. That made no sense at all. "Does he ever buy nice clothes or a car?"

The other boy shrugged again. "Maybe he doesn't care about nice clothes."

The old man saw the boys looking at him, came over to them and said something in Turkish.

Tariq didn't understand Turkish very well, but thought the man was asking what they were talking about. The other boy was more fluent and answered, *"Özel bir şey yok, efendi."* A smart answer, Tariq thought. If in doubt, just say, "Nothing much, sir."

The old man focused on Tariq.

"Türkçe konuşuyor musunuz?" he said.

Tariq said, *"Biraz, efendi."* Yes, he spoke a little Turkish. The old man said something about going with him. Tariq looked at the older boy, the unspoken question being, "What should I do?" The boy shrugged. Tariq could see the relief on his face that he'd been spared from whatever the old man was planning.

"Ta'ala ma'ee," the old man said, switching to Arabic, "Come with me."

They walked past the van onto the street and turned toward the city.

"Ma esmouk?" the old man said, again in Arabic. He must have decided it was easier to speak in Tariq's language. Tariq felt a little better and told the man his

name was Tariq. They stopped by a black Mercedes CLS 500. Tariq knew the model because it was the best car in the collection of car pictures on his bedroom wall. So the rich man did spend money on a nice car. A driver stepped out and opened the door for the old man. He gestured to Tariq to get into the car. Once both had settled in the plush rear seat, the man looked him up and down again.

"Tariq, I have a job for you."

"What kind of a job?"

"I want you to be my eyes and ears for a while. I will pay you well, better than at the factory."

"Okay."

"I will bring you to a hotel. There you will watch out for a man. Tell me where he goes. When he speaks to people, try to listen to what he says. When he talks on the phone, try to get close and listen, too."

The old man reached into a pocket, pulled out a mobile phone and gave it to Tariq. It wasn't like the fancy phones he'd seen in the windows of the mobile shops. But since Tariq didn't have a phone, it was the best phone ever.

"You know how to operate this?"

Tariq nodded. Of course.

"Good. There is only one number programmed. Call it whenever the man takes a car or a taxi. Try to get the plate number. Take a picture when the man talks with someone. And make sure he doesn't see you."

The old man said something to the driver, who handed an envelope across the seat. The man took it and pulled out a fifty lira bill. It was almost double the money Tariq made sewing uniforms for twelve hours.

"Here, your first pay."

The next thing he pulled from the envelope was a photograph.

"This is the man you must watch."

The picture showed a European man with rugged features and blond hair, with a strand hanging across his broad forehead. He sat in a room behind a table. He looked elsewhere, not aware that he was being photographed.

VERMEULEN OPTED FOR the big breakfast. *Menemen,* as the server explained, was a dish with tomatoes, peppers, onions, and eggs. He was glad he'd followed the man's advice. It arrived in a copper pan, piping hot and with an aroma that would have raised the dead. Slices of air-cured sausage and hot tea completed the meal. It went a long way toward restoring his bruised body.

By the time the rental car company sent someone to pick them up the night before, it was close to midnight. The driver examined the wreck, asked what happened and shook his head when Vermeulen told him that they'd been run off the road. Had they called the police? Vermeulen said they had, but that the police hadn't shown up yet. The driver shrugged and told them to get in. They could deal with the police later. Since Vermeulen had paid for comprehensive coverage— fortunately the UN wasn't pinching pennies there—the driver didn't seem to care that the car was smashed. A new car would be brought to the hotel in the morning. He drove them back to Kilis. Vermeulen insisted on paying for Ahmadi's room. She was too shaken to object.

Chewing on a slice of cured meat, he stared out the window at the roof top of the building across. A woman was hanging out the wash on a line that stretched from a chimney stack at one side to a pole fastened to the parapet on the other side. A scene from everyday life, of normalcy, repeated this very moment across the stretch of world illuminated by the sun.

The ordinariness of the woman's task didn't calm Vermeulen. He'd poked his nose into something and provoked an immediate reaction. The violence of the reaction was shocking. What kind of criminal would opt for the maximum response after a simple phone call? Obviously, the kind of criminal who had a lot at stake. Whatever Zada Homsi had gotten involved in was a high-stakes enterprise, one where murder wasn't the last but the first resort. And, as far as he could tell, it was none of his business.

He took Inspector Demirel's card from his billfold. It listed both his office and his mobile numbers. He'd have to talk to that man, even if he was the one who tipped off the driver of the pickup truck. The question was when. Now, before the police response to finding the wreck kicked in? Or later? He couldn't fathom any reason to postpone the call. Better to finish breakfast and get on with the job. He took a corner of bread and wiped the rest of the egg from the pan.

Demirel answered.

"Inspector, I have to ask you if you told anyone about our conversation yesterday."

"Sure, I filled in the cop who brought you in and filed a report. Why do you ask?"

"Someone tried to kill me and Ms. Ahmadi on our way back to the vineyard. A pickup ran us off the road. It was a miracle we got out unscathed."

"Ah, it was your car they found. A call came in but

when the patrol officers got there all they found was a smashed up rental car."

"Well, the rental company came faster than your colleagues."

"You didn't by chance initiate that crash, say by cutting someone off? The locals don't take kindly to inconsiderate drivers."

"Come on, Inspector. Once we passed the outskirts of town, the pickup sped up, came alongside and tried to push us off the road. I tried to get away, but it struck us again, that time succeeding in pushing us into the field. It was obvious he was aiming for us."

"If you're insinuating that I or someone at this post gave your information to some maniacal driver, I take exception. What a ludicrous idea. I didn't even know what car you drove."

Vermeulen considered that for a moment before continuing. "Here's what I know. I called a number Ms. Ahmadi had found. A woman answered. I asked about Zada Homsi. The woman said nothing and hung up. Next thing, someone tried to kill us."

"You had a phone number?" Vermeulen could hear Demirel's anger over the phone. "I asked both of you clearly if you had other information. You denied you had any. Now you tell me that you had a phone number. That's outrageous. You're impeding my investigation."

"I wasn't aware there was an investigation. All I knew was that your colleagues came to pick up Ms. Ahmadi because she called Zada Homsi's phone. What are you investigating?"

"You may think southern Turkey is the boondocks, but we treat the deaths we encounter with the attention they deserve. Why didn't you tell me about the number?"

"We didn't think it was relevant. But back to my initial question. Nobody knew we were at the police station. We called the number from a gas station nearby. How would the pickup truck driver have known where we were or what car we drove? Somebody at the station must have told someone."

"You're grasping at straws. The only explanation that makes any sense is that it was a case of road rage, which you must've caused by your driving. Either that, or you just lost control and smashed the car. Roads around here are narrow. Good day."

Vermeulen stared at the phone in his hand and had half a mind to redial the number and give Demirel some choice words. But Ahmadi came into the room. Her hair was still damp and she had a glow on her face.

"Come," he said. "Have some breakfast."

"Oh no. I couldn't. The room was already too much. But thank you. The best sleep I've had since I left home. And the shower. A dream come true."

She sat down.

"Nonsense. You've got to eat."

He called the waiter. Ahmadi ordered *Simit,* jam and tea.

"I just spoke with Demirel," Vermeulen said. "It wasn't a good conversation. He didn't believe that the hit-and-run was a deliberate attack. And he was adamant that no one from the police told the pickup driver."

"But it was an attack."

"I know. And it happened almost immediately after we made the call. That makes me think that the woman I spoke with on the phone already knew where we were. How else could she get someone to follow us so quickly?"

"Who is she? What does she want?"

"She'll let us know. I'm sure about that."

ELEVEN

TARIQ SETTLED IN front of a garage door. Time had scoured every fleck of paint from it. The bare wood looked as crotchety as an old man. He could see the entrance of the hotel where his target stayed. There was a tiny grocery store to his right. It had bulgur on sale, but the sign looked as if it had been there almost as long as the garage door. On the left was a store that looked empty. It was a good spot. Nobody would bother him sitting there.

He took out the phone that the big boss had given him. It looked brand new. He flipped it open. A rainbow colored logo exploded onto the screen. Once that disappeared, he saw the time and three icons. He tapped each. Nothing happened. Of course, it was an old model. He pushed the two buttons at the bottom of the screen and managed to access each app. One was for settings, one for texting, the last one for contacts. There was only one number in the contact list. No name, just a number. If his mother had a phone, he'd call her. She didn't. Which was just as well. The big boss wouldn't like him calling someone else. Better be safe. He put the phone back in his pocket and waited.

An hour later, he saw a car stop in front of the hotel entrance. The driver put on the emergency flashers and went into the hotel. Several minutes later, he came out again, followed by the man he was supposed to watch.

It wasn't difficult to spot him. He was tall and his face was just like the one in the picture. The man and the driver talked for a while. Then the driver put a piece of paper on the roof of the car and the man signed it. The driver handed him the keys and walked away.

The car was a white Kia. The plate read "27 UG 245," black on white. The man got into the car and drove off. Tariq got out the phone and called the number. The big boss answered almost immediately. Tariq told him what happened. The old man sounded satisfied.

"Good. Tell me the license plate again."

Tariq recited it.

"Next time, take a picture of the car. But be careful about it. Was there a woman with him?"

"No."

"Good. Keep an eye out. If he doesn't come back in ten minutes call me again."

Tariq didn't have a watch, so he checked the phone. Could he set an alarm? There had to be a way. He navigated to the settings app. The text was in Turkish, which didn't help. He looked for the option to switch the language to Arabic, or at least English. It had to be there somewhere. He clicked through the options, but nothing looked even vaguely familiar. He tried a few settings without results. One thing he did forget was checking the time. Or if the man had come back.

It was twenty minutes later when he realized that. *Oh no.* He'd blown it already. He swallowed to get rid of the lump in his throat. If he called now, the big boss would know he hadn't paid attention. Maybe the man had come back. Then it was okay that he hadn't called. But he wasn't sure. Tariq had to find out. He crossed the street and stopped at the entrance to the hotel. He couldn't go inside. They'd throw him out. He could see the reception are through the glass doors. There was a man behind the desk, wearing a funny uniform.

He had to find out, so he opened the door and walked inside. Mr. Uniform saw him and stopped what he was doing. He shouted something that Tariq didn't understand, but the intent was clear. *Get out.* He took a deep breath, unfolded the photo of the man he was supposed to follow and showed it to Mr. Uniform.

"He here?" Tariq said, using what little English he knew.

Mr. Uniform looked at the photo and said, "Go away."

Tariq could see recognition in Mr. Uniform's face but that didn't tell him if the man had come back.

"He here?" he said.

Mr. Uniform told him again to get out. He grabbed Tariq by the arm and began dragging him to the exit.

"What's going on?" a voice behind them said.

They both turned. It was the man from the photo. Tariq wanted to sink into the ground. He'd really lose his job now. The big boss would fire him. Mr. Uniform said that the boy was bothering the guests. A young woman was with the man. She had kind eyes. The man told Mr. Uniform to let go of the boy. Mr. Uniform snorted. He turned to Tariq, took the picture from his hand and showed it to the man. The man took the picture, looked at it, looked at Tariq, then back at the picture.

Tariq didn't know what to do next. He could try to run away, but Mr. Uniform still held him by his arm. Not that it mattered. The man he was supposed to watch now knew Tariq was following him. Big boss would be very angry.

"Ma esmouk?" the woman said to Tariq.

"Tariq," he said. He was surprised she spoke Arabic.

"Hal tatakallamu alloghah alenjleziah?"

"Yes, I speak a little English."

"Are you hungry? Do you want to eat?" the man said.

Tariq nodded. He was in a big mess, but the man sounded friendly, and he was hungry.

"It's okay," the man said to Mr. Uniform. "We'll take him to the *Kebab Döner* place around the corner."

Tariq thought of running away, but the calm voice of the man and the thought of a *Döner* trumped all hesitation. He hadn't eaten meat in a long time.

VERMEULEN WASN'T SURPRISED that someone was shadowing him. He'd almost expected as much after the attack the night before. Choosing a kid was a smart move. He wouldn't have noticed Tariq on the street. Neither did he recognize the photograph the kid had. No doubt, it had been taken at the police station. All interview rooms have a recording system. It wouldn't take much for anyone there to access it and get a screenshot. What surprised him was how fast everything had happened. Merely thirty minutes after he made the call, there'd been an attempt on his life. And eleven hours later, a kid had his photograph. It confirmed his assumption from the night before that those he'd disturbed with his call went for a maximum response. It also confirmed his suspicion that someone at the police had leaked his info.

There were three immediate suspects, the two cops who'd come to the vineyard and Inspector Demirel. Of course, any of them could have told others who were linked to the gangsters, but that seemed less likely. It was late when they came to the station. There weren't that many cops on duty. The tall cop, who'd disappeared the moment they got to the station would be the prime suspect.

They went to the restaurant around the corner from the hotel. It was a typical *Kebab* and *Döner* place. The *Döner,* a large conical slab of meat, was rotating in front of a red-hot upright heating element. In the tray below the meat lay a pile of red peppers and onions. The aroma of roasting meat filled the place.

"What do you want to eat?" Vermeulen said.

Tariq pointed to the *Döner.* Ahmadi ordered a *Tombik.* "Do you want one too?" she said to Vermeulen.

"Sure, it's almost lunch time. Let's eat. Who knows when we'll have another chance."

"Can I have Fanta?" Tariq said.

Vermeulen nodded and Ahmadi ordered the three lunches.

The chef—with the flair of someone who knows he's being watched—wielded a knife long enough to dismember large farm animals. In his other hand he held a tray. With each exaggerated motion of the knife, a paper-thin slice of meat fell and was caught expertly on the tray. He repeated the show for a while until the tray was laden with meat. He took three large pitas that had been toasting near the grill, sliced them open, filled them with portions of meat, peppers and onions, and topped it all off with slivered cabbage and a white sauce. He plated the sandwiches and brought the drinks.

The three settled at a table away from the window. Vermeulen didn't want to be observed and he figured that Tariq was glad nobody could see him eating with the man he was supposed to watch. Vermeulen let the boy eat first. Better to let him get comfortable before asking questions. The way Tariq attacked the sandwich, there wouldn't have been an opportunity for questions anyway. Ahmadi also ate her sandwich with gusto. Food security, one of the UNHCR buzzwords, was clearly not a given for refugees who didn't live in official camps. He ate his meal more slowly. It was very good, but it called for a beer instead of an over-sweetened soda.

Once the pace of the meal had slowed down, Vermeulen asked the first question. "Why were you watching me?"

Tariq swallowed a bite, took a sip of Fanta and looked at Ahmadi with a frown. She translated the question. Tariq nodded and paused. His face displayed the inner turmoil. He mumbled something to Ahmadi.

"He says he doesn't know. A big boss told him."

"You work for the big boss?"

Tariq nodded.

"You tell him where I go?"

He nodded again. He said something to Ahmadi.

"He says that he also told him the plate number of your car."

"What's his name?"

Tariq shrugged. "I no know?"

"Do you call him?" Vermeulen made the telephone gesture.

The boy pulled a flip phone from his pocket and showed it to them. When Vermeulen reached for it, he put it back in his pocket.

"The big boss pay you?"

"Yes. Good pay." He said more. Ahmadi translated. "He says that he usually works sewing uniforms, but he gets more for watching you." She shook her head. "He's so young. That's terrible."

She said something else. Tariq responded.

"I can't believe it." Ahmadi looked at Vermeulen. "He only gets thirty lira for ten hours. We make double that at the vineyard."

"I get fifty today," Tariq said.

Vermeulen did a quick conversion. That was about sixteen dollars. A plum job for the kid.

"Okay," he said. "I don't want to get you into trouble. So you keep telling the big boss what I do and where I go. But I want you to show me where you make the uniforms. I'll give you a hundred lira."

Ahmadi translated and Tariq considered this offer.

"Big boss no see me with you?" he said.

"No, we drive by the place and you can duck in my car. He won't see you."

Tariq thought more about it. Then he nodded. "Okay."

TWELVE

TARIQ'S DIRECTIONS TO the sweatshop were pretty much what Vermeulen expected from a boy who'd landed in a strange city. He alternated between being very sure about the right turn coming up and second guessing himself. With plenty stops and U-turns, they managed to reach the southern edge of Kilis, an area of light industrial buildings. When they passed a motorcycle dealership and a garage, Tariq said, "Stop." Vermeulen pulled over.

Tariq rattled out words until Ahmadi held up her hand.

"He says we're very close. He's scared to go further. The big boss has people who work for him. They will see him and tell the boss."

"What is the name of the shop we're looking for?" Vermeulen said.

Ahmadi asked Tariq who said, *"Selim Tekstil."*

"How far is it?"

"One right, one right," Tariq said.

"Okay. Duck down."

Tariq didn't need a translation. He scooted off the seat into the footwell and pressed against the door. Vermeulen turned right, followed the street and took the next right. A low building with a series of roll-up doors occupied about half of the block. Half-rotten signs advertised businesses housed behind the shuttered doors.

None of them looked as if they were thriving. Two were clearly abandoned. Near the far end he saw the sign *Selim Tekstil*. A phone number was listed below the company name.

The roll-up door was open and he saw boys and women behind sewing machines. Two cars were parked out front. A pickup truck and a tan sedan. The pickup could have been the one that tried to run them off the road the night before. It was the right height. Vermeulen couldn't see if the front was damaged.

Tariq said, "No stop, please."

"I won't," Vermeulen said. He turned left at the next intersection and found a parking spot next to a large dumpster. He checked the street sign of the cross street, Köker Caddesi, fished one of his business cards from his wallet and wrote the name and address of the shop on its back.

"Did you see the pickup?" he said to Ahmadi. "I need to know if it was the one that attacked us last night. Tariq can't check it, of course. I'd go, but a European walking here alone would be suspicious. Besides, they have my picture. Someone could recognize me. Would you go by and check?"

She looked at him, incredulous. "And a single woman wouldn't be suspicious? Did you see the men there? They'll be ogling me all the way to the next intersection. They'll remember me."

Vermeulen nodded and waited.

"I guess I could ask for work," Ahmadi said after a moment. "They'd wonder how I heard, but I'll just tell them I heard from a friend of a friend."

"Okay," Vermeulen said. "But don't go if you don't feel safe."

She opened the door of the car and said, "I haven't felt safe since I left home."

"I'll drive around the block and wait for you at the other end."

Ahmadi closed the door and walked back to the sweatshop. Vermeulen drove toward the next intersection. There was no left turn. He turned around, crossed Köker Caddesi and took the next possible right turn. The road didn't run parallel to Köker Caddesi. Instead, it veered away from it. He followed the street for a while, hoping for another cross street. There was none. He was headed for the city center. He stopped and entered the sweatshop's address into his phone's map app. Sure enough, the voice told him to turn around. He gave in and retraced his route back. He sped past the sweatshop, keeping his eyes straight ahead to avoid attracting attention. At the next intersection he pulled into the parking lot of the motorcycle dealership. There was no sign of Ahmadi.

Tariq had remained as small as he could make himself in the footwell of the rear seat.

"We go now?" he said.

"No, we wait for Rima."

"I afraid."

"I understand, but we can't leave her here."

After five minutes, Vermeulen started to worry. Asking for work had been her idea. It was a way to get close to the pickup but it also exposed her to questions. He didn't know how good she was at lying. He managed to wait another five minutes. Then he pulled out onto the street and drove toward the sweatshop. He slowed down as he approached and saw Ahmadi standing just inside the sweatshop and talking to two men. Their body language was worrisome. They had positioned themselves in a way that made it difficult for Ahmadi to get out of the shop. She was talking, her hands busy underscoring her point. Was she arguing? Scared? It was hard to tell.

He executed a tight U-turn, honked the horn and leaned over to open the door. The men turned to look at him. Ahmadi shook her head as if to say, "Go away." It was too late for that. One of the men approached the car. Vermeulen waved for Ahmadi to come. She shook her head. He waved again. She raised her hands. Vermeulen could almost hear her say, "What are you doing?" He nodded. At last, she hurried over. She passed the man and jumped into the car. Vermeulen burned some rubber as he peeled away, the acceleration slamming the door shut.

"THAT WAS THE stupidest thing you could have done," Ahmadi said, her eyes blazing with anger.

"I was worried."

"About what? That I couldn't take care of myself?"

"The two guys had you cornered."

"Yes, but they were giving me important information. Did you know they sew uniforms for *Daesh*?"

Vermeulen's face must have shown how bewildered he was, so she added, "You call them ISIS."

"I know who *Daesh* is," he said. "I didn't just come out from under a rock. You were in a dangerous situation and I saw that you needed help."

"If I needed help I would have called you."

"How? I was parked a block away."

"I would have managed. They were about to tell me

the name of their boss when you drove up and started honking."

"Did you see if the pickup truck was damaged?"

Ahmadi didn't answer. Vermeulen opened his mouth, but closed it again. That was the reason she'd gone there in the first place. Her anger puzzled him. After all, he got her out of what looked like a tight spot. Yes, a name would have been great. But her anger seemed over the top. Which reminded him that the attack the night before had overshadowed the fact that he had no business doing what he was doing. He'd let himself be sucked into something that had nothing to do with his assignment. It was time to extricate himself.

"You are right, I should have waited," he said. "My apologies. I think it's best I bring you back to the vineyard."

In the rearview mirror he saw Tariq's face, looking equally puzzled. He understood the angry tone of their exchange, but not much of what had been said.

"Would you tell him that I'm bringing you back and that I'll drop him by the hotel. There he can tell his boss that I never left."

Vermeulen put the car back in gear and drove back to the ring road. He followed it to the exit that led to the vineyard. The silence in the car was thick. It was interrupted by a phone ringing. Vermeulen reached for his phone when he realized it wasn't his ring. He looked to Ahmadi who shrugged. It wasn't hers either. Which left Tariq in the back seat. The boy stared at the phone in his hand as if it were a scorpion. One move and it would sting.

The ringing continued until Ahmadi said something to him. The boy flipped the phone open and said, *"Alo?"*

His voice almost croaked. He listened, then responded haltingly.

"I think it's the boss," Ahmadi said. "He's telling him that you haven't left the hotel, except to get a Döner next door."

Vermeulen wasn't paying attention to the road and hit a pothole. The noise was unmistakable.

Tariq listened, then talked again, more animated.

"He's telling him that there was a noisy car on the street. Maybe you better stop."

Vermeulen slowed down but didn't pull off the street. Stopping now would change the background noise.

The call lasted longer than Vermeulen thought it should have.

"What's going on?" he said to Ahmadi.

"Not sure. He is listening mostly."

Tariq finally flipped his phone shut. He looked crest-fallen.

Ahmadi spoke to him and he responded slowly.

"He's just gotten fired," Ahmadi translated. "Apparently the men at the sweatshop got your license plate and knew that you were at the shop and not in your hotel as Tariq had said."

She said more to the boy, who shook his head.

"He doesn't think the boss knows he's in the car with you. The boss just thinks Tariq wasn't paying attention." She paused, as if to think over the next sentence. Then she said, "Now we don't know the boss's name and Tariq lost his job."

Unlike Ahmadi, Vermeulen bit his tongue. There was nothing to be gained by continuing the fight. It wasn't his business in the first place. He had no authority and what he'd done already was enough to piss off his bosses.

"I already apologized," he said. "I will pay Tariq for his loss. I was scheduled to leave for Gaziantep tomorrow morning anyway, so he's lost only one day of work."

"You are leaving?" Ahmadi said.

"Yes, I do have a job. And that work will be done in Gaziantep."

"What about Zada?"

"You'll find out what happened. Inspector Demirel will tell you what he finds out, I'm sure. It's not like I was any help."

The last part was unnecessary, but he said it anyway. He'd gone out of his way to help her, had gotten run off the road for someone he didn't know at all. And all he got in return was grief.

"Are you pouting? How very adult," she said.

"Oh, give it a rest. I never even planned on being here this weekend. It's only because the UNHCR guy Balbay left town without talking to me that I ended up here. I have an appointment on Monday and that means I have to leave. And, no, I'm not pouting."

"But Gaziantep isn't so far. It's only forty minutes away."

"You seem to think I'm here on vacation with nothing to do. I have to check on how the UNHCR is spending its money here and that will take all my time."

"Can I have your number, please?"

"Why?"

Ahmadi hesitated, then said, "In case something new happens and I learn more about Zada."

"Sure." He recited it and Ahmadi punched it into her phone.

They reached the vineyard. Ahmadi clambered out of the car. She leaned back in and said, "I'm sorry. You've been very helpful. And thank you for the room. It was nice to sleep in a real bed and take a real shower. Good luck with your work. By the way, the pickup had quite a bit of damage on the front. It was the one that hit us last night."

She closed the door and walked past the grapevines to the camp.

Tariq looked after her, then at him. His expression said something akin to "What's wrong with you adults."

He was right.

Vermeulen drove back to his hotel and let Tariq out before driving into the hotel parking lot.

"You can call the boss and tell him I'm back."

VERMEULEN SPENT THE next hour wondering what to do with the information about the pickup. The logical thing would have been to call Demirel. But he couldn't be sure of Demirel's allegiances. Since he was leaving town anyway, he decided to let the thing be and do some touristy things, something he rarely had time to do on his assignment. The sights recommended by the concierge were interesting enough. A couple of mosques, an old bath house, long closed, and a Dervish Lodge. He whiled away over an hour at the lodge. It dated back to 1525, a few centuries after the life of the poet Rumi. The only structure left was the domed hall where the ritual whirling dances were performed. Twelve windows were evenly spaced around the dome above. Dust motes floated in the shafts of sunlight slicing through the space. He could almost see men wearing conical hats turning in their trance, their robes flaring with each rotation.

He stopped at a different *Döner* restaurant and had another pita filled with meat, peppers and yoghurt sauce. A stubby bottle of *Efes Pilsen* confirmed his suspicion that beer was a better accompaniment for the sandwich than Fanta.

Back at his hotel, he sat at the bar for a while, drank another beer and contemplated buying a pack of cigarettes. Even though he hadn't smoked for months now, he didn't think of himself as a non-smoker. When things turned sour, the desire for a cigarette came back. Each time, it seemed stronger. The two women in his life, his partner Tessa and his daughter Gaby, were adamant in their anti-smoking stance and he knew they were right.

He took out his phone and dialed his daughter's number. There was little chance she'd have time to talk to him on a Saturday night, but it was worth a try. She worked as the head of the Africa section for a large international logistics corporation headquartered in Antwerp, but her office was in Düsseldorf.

Their relationship was as good as a divorced parent could hope for. It hadn't always been that way. A decade and a half earlier, his life was consumed by his prosecutor job in Antwerp. Family became an afterthought. Eventually, Marieke—his ex—had had enough. She wanted out. The divorce was acrimonious. Gaby couldn't take it and ran away. Despite his good relations with the police, they were of little help. Just another runaway. He did everything in his power to find her. Eventually he found her, strung out on heroin, in a nasty squat. Rehab was hard. Gaby hated him. She got clear, but the estrangement lasted for a long time. It took almost a decade before they spoke again.

Her job gave her access to all kinds of information in the business world that would take the UN a long time to unearth. They hadn't talked in a week, so his decision to call her wasn't only to see if she could find the owner of *Selim Tekstil*.

She answered the phone rather quickly.

"Hi, Gaby, it's Dad. Just wanted to say 'Hi.'"

"Hey, Dad, where are you?" She sounded happy to hear his voice.

"Kilis, southern Turkey. Checking up on the UN High Commissioner on Refugees."

"Ah, I figured you weren't home."

"I've been known to stay up into the wee hours of the morning."

"I know," Gaby said. "But those days are long gone. More often than not, I wake you up when I call after work."

"You're confusing me with Tessa."

"Not at all. Anyway, what's going on with the UNHCR? Any particular issues?"

"Nah, just routine. The UN is spending a hell of a lot of money there. The powers that be just want to make sure everything is on the up and up."

"And is it?"

"Too early to say. I'll let you know if it changes. Could you find out who the owner of a company called *Selim Tekstil* is?"

"No problem, what's he done?"

"Again, not sure."

"How's Tessa?"

"We haven't talked since I left. She's busy, as always."

"Are you going to visit before you go back to the U.S.?" Gaby said.

"Sure. I should wrap this up quickly. I'll call once I know more."

THIRTEEN

THE VAN LUMBERED along the rutted track. Korun wrestled with the steering wheel, trying to avoid the worst potholes. He didn't have much success. The tires were trapped in the ruts like hamsters in a wheel, they could go around, but not sideways. The sun burnt hot even though it was only nine in the morning. The heat made the stink of fuel worse. The petrol and diesel had permeated the van completely. Even the metal of the body felt sticky with residue. He so wanted to smoke a cigarette, but he knew that cigarettes and gasoline weren't a good mix.

He carried a load of high-octane gasoline. The van groaned each time it bottomed out, which was pretty much on every pothole. He'd rigged a wooden shelf that let him stow ten more jerry cans. That was the absolute limit. The ten extra cans were off the books. A little down payment on his future. Maybe his own van. With a newer model, he could double the amount of fuel on each trip and make real money.

A car honked behind him. He jumped. The rear-view mirror was useless. The extra cans on the shelf blocked the view. The passenger side mirror had broken off. The one on the driver's side was cracked. He could make out a slice of what looked like a pickup. Maybe a military vehicle. There was no way to pull over, so he slowed down, waving his left arm out the window for the pickup to pass him. It managed to climb out of the ruts. It pulled next to him. It was a military vehicle all right, almost as ancient as his van. The tan metal of the body was rust-pocked. A bald man leaned out of the passenger side window and signaled for him to stop. He didn't wear a uniform.

Korun slowed to a halt. The pickup next to him followed suit. Three men jumped off, one stayed behind the wheel. They all carried guns. Korun resisted the temptation to get out. Better to conduct whatever conversation was coming from inside the van. He pushed down the door lock knob, but remembered that it didn't work.

"Get out of the van," the bald man said.

Korun shook his head. He took his pistol from the seat next to him.

"Get out. Now."

Korun cranked the window all the way down and rested the hand with the pistol on the frame. He made it look like a relaxed move. Just a gesture showing he was armed too. "No. What do you want?"

"We shoot you, if you don't get out."

"You won't do such a thing. This van is fully loaded with super. You fire at it, it'll blow all of us to hell. I got cans of gas right next to me. So, what do you want?"

"You are working for us now."

"Says who?"

"My boss."

"Who is your boss?"

The bald man was getting impatient.

"None of your business."

Korun smiled.

"You expect me to just turn over my cargo to you?

You must be dense. You can't shoot me, but I can shoot you." He stuck the pistol out the window and pulled the trigger. The bald man stumbled back against the pickup and stared at his chest, puzzled at the red blotch that was growing. Korun didn't wait for the bald man to get over his surprise. He fired twice more, hitting each of the men. Finally, he aimed for the front tire of the truck. It blew up with a loud bang. He put his van into gear and drove away. Other smugglers had spoken of a *Daesh* connected outfit trying to muscle into the petrol smuggling business on this side of the border. Well, he wasn't going to switch over to a bunch of fanatics stupid enough to believe that a bullet could ignite gasoline. The old man had treated him right. There was no reason to switch. Funny. As backward as *Daesh* was, they watched too many American movies. He drove as fast as he could to the Gaziantep-Kilis highway. No use getting caught by the police. He didn't have a permit for the pistol.

Once he reached the highway, he waited for a break in the traffic. The dirt track didn't just merge with the paved road. He had to drive up a steep berm which posed its own unique problem. To get up the incline he had to build up speed. But going too fast meant he could break an axle on his way up the berm, especially with the extra load. The crazy pattern of ruts told of many attempts to tackle this obstacle.

One pair of ruts seemed to offer the best route. They didn't go straight up, but took a less steep angled approach. The downside was that he couldn't see the road. That's why he was waiting for a break in the traffic.

The road was as clear as it was going to be. He gunned the engine. The van rumbled toward the incline, gaining speed. He jerked the wheel aiming for the right set of ruts. The tires found the right path. The van kept going faster. He smiled. He was going to make it. No problem. The asphalt of the highway appeared at the top of his windshield. The engine howled as it struggled to maintain speed. He pushed the pedal all the way down. The front wheels cleared the ruts and reached the solid dirt next to the asphalt. Just a little bit more. Finally, the rear wheels gripped the dirt. The van shot into the road. From the corner of his eyes, he glimpsed a white sedan. A horn honked. He yanked the steering wheel to the right. The abrupt change in direction was more than the tired shocks could handle. For a second or two the van teetered on its left side wheels. Then it toppled onto the tarmac. It slid for ten yards before grinding to a stop, the quiet glugs of gasoline pouring onto the road the only sound.

VERMEULEN HAD NOTICED the van, or rather the cloud of dust following it from the distance, but didn't pay further attention to it. He'd enjoyed another breakfast of *Menemen,* packed his things and gotten on the road to Gaziantep. He'd be there in time for lunch, find his hotel, see some of the sights and get ready for the Monday meeting with Bilek Balbay at the UNHCR sub-office.

The cruise control set to the speed limit of a hundred-ten kilometers per hour, he was fiddling with the music player on his phone. The van had gotten much closer to the highway, probably following a frontage road. He could see that it was an older model. He finally got the Bluetooth connection to work and The Clash started playing on the car speakers.

The Clash had been the soundtrack of his life ever since they burst onto the music scene in the late seventies. It was only in the past few years, that he'd moved on to other bands and genres. Today, though, he was definitely in the mood for The Clash. He tapped the icon of one of the early albums. *Police and Thieves* started and it sure sounded appropriate after dealing with the cops and the pickup trying to run him off the road.

He looked up and saw the van right ahead of him, lurching up the embankment and headed right for his lane. He leaned on his horn and slammed on the brake. The tires screamed on the road, the Kia fishtailed. The van lurched onto the road. Vermeulen steered to the left. The Kia's rear spun forward. He pulled the wheel to the right. The Kia stabilized, but the momentum carried it toward the van. The other driver must have seen him, but his reaction was exactly wrong. He turned too hard. The van hovered on two wheels before tipping over. Vermeulen yanked his wheel one more time. The Kia slid to a stop mere inches from the rear of the van.

The Clash sang that people should get out to avoid getting blown up. It was uncanny how, yet again, their lyrics offered right advice. The stink of gasoline was overpowering. Vermeulen got out of the car and walked towards the van. There was way more fuel on the road than could have been in the tank of the van. Through the open rear door, he saw a jumble of jerry cans, some busted open. He pulled out his phone and walked away a safe distance before calling the emergency number. After a moment of confusion, the person on the other end switched to English. He explained what had happened, that there had been a gasoline spill, that he was okay, but that he hadn't seen the other driver yet. Just then, he saw the passenger side door of the van, now on top, fly open. A man climbed out and ran across the highway, heading toward Kilis.

"WHY DO WE keep finding you in car wrecks?" Inspector Demirel said.

They were sitting in his office at the police station. Vermeulen was eager to get out of town. He'd had enough of Kilis.

"It's just as I told you, I was on my way to Gaziantep, the van suddenly came up the embankment, the driver lost control, the van tipped over, I barely was able to stop. The driver jumped out and ran away. That's all."

"Why didn't you stop sooner?"

"Because I had no idea that he was headed onto the highway. I thought he was driving on a frontage road."

"Had you ever seen the driver before?"

"I didn't see the driver's face, so I can't answer that question, but chances are very good that I've never seen him before."

"Your car was very close to the van, how come you didn't see his face?"

"Because I stepped away from the wreck to call the police. The air was full of gasoline fumes, it was hard to breathe. Why are you asking me all these questions?"

"That's routine when we have a major accident. We had to close the road and get the hazmat team in to contain the spill. Did you hear anything?"

"What, besides the van scraping across the asphalt?"

"I meant before the van hit the highway."

"No, I was listening to music. The Clash. They kinda drowned out other sounds."

"No way. You like The Clash?" Demirel was suddenly animated. "What were you listening to, 'Rock the Casbah?'"

"No, 'Police and Thieves.'"

"Ah. A classic. Listen, I don't want to keep you any longer. It's clear that you were just an innocent passerby."

"So what happened on the highway?" Vermeulen said.

"Sorry, you know I can't tell you. Ongoing investigation."

"The gasoline was smuggled, wasn't it? Legitimate transports would use a tanker truck, not jerry cans in a ramshackle van. The van came from the direction of the border, so I'm assuming that gasoline came from Syria. Which means someone in Turkey is buying fuel from ISIS. And if the van is anything to go by, the guy driving it wasn't the guy in charge. And you'd like to find out who that guy is. How am I doing so far?"

Demirel just shrugged. There was a hint of a smile on his face. Vermeulen couldn't quite sort out the smile. Did it mean Demirel was in on the smuggling, or did it mean that he had guessed right?

"Are you planning on coming back to Kilis?" Demirel said.

"Not if I can avoid it."

FOURTEEN

THE GRAPE HARVEST was almost over and the pickers got a half day off on Sunday afternoon. Ahmadi, like the other pickers, had mixed feelings about it. No work meant no pay. But the free time also gave Ahmadi a chance to dig deeper into Zada's death. She wanted to talk to those men at the sweatshop again. Find out who the boss was. Zada had become her obsession. Her death had been violent, even if the police didn't say as much. She knew that in her bones. It was the only thing she knew for sure. The rest of her life was unmoored. Since leaving Syria, she'd yearned for a guidepost. Something that helped her sort out what to do next. As sad as it sounded, Zada's death had become that post. She stuck her phone and her passport into her pocket and left the camp.

The sun was hot again and reflected off the asphalt of the one lane road. It'd be another hour before she reached Kilis and then whatever time it took to find the sweatshop again. She'd brought what little money she had to buy water and something to eat. She'd be all right.

Vermeulen sure didn't turn out the way she'd hoped. He'd been kind when the cops came to pick her up. He, too, knew that something wasn't right. Once things got dicey, though, he abandoned her. Just as well. He would have left eventually. Better now than later when it really mattered.

She heard a car behind her and stepped off the road and continued walking on the grassy strip between the road and a ditch. The car came closer and slowed. She rolled her eyes and kept her head forward. The car turned out to be a pickup truck. It slowed to her walking pace. She could hear the window being buzzed down.

"Hey, wanna ride?" the driver said. The accented Arabic didn't bother her. It was the familiar tone that set her on edge. Of all the drivers that could have passed her and offered her a ride this was the one she would've preferred to miss. It was the foreman from the vineyard. How come he never spoke Arabic at his job? She kept facing straight ahead and walked on.

"Hey! It's hot. I have air conditioning. I'll drive you to town."

She kept walking. The idea of getting a ride sounded appealing. She'd be in town so much faster. But that man was such a creep. *No. Be strong. Don't give him that satisfaction.*

"Come, don't be that way. I know I'm strict at work, but I have to be, for the boss."

"Nobody forces you to be mean," she said. "I don't see the boss standing next to you, telling you to treat us like dirt."

"You don't understand. If I don't keep the pressure on, we don't get the grapes in on time. Then I'm in trouble. Come, get in. I give you a ride."

"No thank you."

"Well, I'm just going to drive next to you until you change your mind."

She stopped and looked at the man. He must have

washed himself because his hair wasn't as greasy as usual and he'd shaved. Ready for an afternoon out on the town. She started walking again.

"Nice to have the afternoon off, no?" he said.

In Aleppo I had the whole weekend off, you idiot, she thought, but said, "Yes, it is."

"You have a husband? A boyfriend?"

"Yes," she said, appropriating Zada's story "I have a husband in Aleppo. He's fighting Assad and sent me to safety."

"He must not care much about you to make you live and work at the vineyard."

"That's none of your business."

"He's dead. Why else would you be here alone?"

"That's a terrible thing to say."

"There's no husband. Where are your kids? You are all alone."

The pickup inched closer to Ahmadi. She kept walking. The strip of grass next to the road got narrower, the ditch on her other side deeper. Finally, the foreman cut her off. He stopped the truck and got out.

"Don't be a bitch. Just come with me. You think you're something special? You're just another Syrian whore. Well, it's about time you acted like one. I'll show you what Turkish men can do."

He wiggled his tongue at her, which would have looked ridiculous if it hadn't been so revolting. But self-reflection wasn't on the man's mind. He stepped around the front of the pickup, starting to undo his belt. Her revulsion turned into anger. She had to get away from him. Ahmadi mirrored his movement by sidling around the rear. He reversed direction. She followed his example. They did this for a while, the foreman swearing at her. Eventually, he decided to just make a run for her. He was fast, but she was faster. He chased her around the truck a couple of times, then stopped.

"Come on, Rima," he said, breathing hard. "I know I've behaved badly. Let me make it up to you. I'll drive you to town and buy you a nice meal. I know some special restaurants in Kilis."

"I don't want to eat with you. I want you to leave me alone."

He rushed her again. She stumbled, but caught herself. They were both on the ditch side of the truck. He made a grab for her, missed and struggled for balance at the edge of the ditch. Ahmadi used the opening and raced around the truck. At the driver's side door, she grabbed the door handle, yanked the door open and jumped inside. She almost managed to slam it shut, but he'd caught up with her and tried to pull it open. She struggled to keep it shut. He was stronger and she couldn't hold it. So she let the door go. The foreman didn't expect that and flew back and onto his butt. She reached for the door again and slammed it shut.

A piercing scream followed. The foreman had gotten a hold of the door just as she slammed it shut and the tips of his fingers were caught between the door and the frame. He hollered and motioned for her to open the door. She did not. Instead, she put the car in gear and started driving forward. The foreman jogged alongside, his face contorted with pain. She sped up. When the man was running at a decent speed, she opened the door a crack and sped up some more. In the rearview mirror she saw the foreman shaking his fist at her while sucking on his smashed fingers. Now, that looked ridiculous. She smiled and drove straight to Kilis.

SHE LEFT THE pickup in the parking lot of a grocery store. Before she got out, she searched the glove compartment and found an envelope with money, a thousand lira. She took it, locked the truck and threw the keys into a dumpster. The store wasn't far from the sweatshop. If the men were there, she'd better have a sound strategy. There'd be no car to drive away with, should they decide to go after her. Her cover story of looking for a job wouldn't work anymore. They knew she'd driven away with Vermeulen. Or, maybe they didn't. All they knew was the license plate. Whoever they reported to had no reason to tell them who was driving the car. What if they didn't know the boss? That was only one possibility. There were too many.

The biggest question was what she would do with the information. Say she got the name. What then? Go to where the man lived? Then what? He'd call the police on her. They would be looking for her anyway because the foreman would have reported the stolen pickup. And that reminded her that she couldn't go back to the vineyard. The foreman'd be waiting for her.

She sat on a bench in front of a closed shop. What was she going to do? A young couple pushing a pram slowed down and looked at her with sympathy. The man took a five lira note from his pocket and gave it to her. Ahmadi was so surprised, all she could say was, "Thank you."

She remained on the bench for another half hour, earning a total of twenty lira, but also meeting undisguised hostility with the suggestion she should go back where she came from. The last passerby, an older woman spoke to her with such venom, she decided to move on.

Ahmadi reached the sweatshop at mid-afternoon. The roll-up door was open and the workers were busy sewing. She saw Tariq among them. At least he hadn't been fired yet. Only one of the men she'd spoken with on Friday was there. He recognized her and raised his eyebrows.

"I want to work," she said. Her Turkish probably sounded as bad as the foreman's Arabic. "I sew better than these kids."

It was a lie, but hopefully the man wouldn't find out.

He motioned with his head for her to go outside.

"What you want?" he said once they were away from the buzz of the machines.

"I want to work. I need a job."

"We don't need workers."

She pointed to the idle sewing machine. "I could work there."

The man shrugged.

"The boss says no more workers now."

Ahmadi cocked her head in what she hoped made her look cuter. "Come on, your boss won't mind once he sees how much more I produce."

"You want more money than the kids. The boss won't like it."

"Can I talk to your boss? What's his name anyway?"

The man looked around and back at Ahmadi.

"You can't talk to the boss. He's a busy man and got no time for refugees."

"Not even pretty refugees like me? Maybe I call him. What's his name."

"Oben Özbek and he don't take calls, not even from pretty refugees. Now beat it."

Ahmadi gave up. She had the name. That's what

she came for. She also had some money. If she found a cheap place to stay she could start looking for Oben Özbek the next day.

FIFTEEN

Since the airport lay south of Gaziantep, Vermeulen hadn't actually seen the city at all when he'd arrived on Wednesday evening. He'd gotten into the rental car and driven south to Kilis. Reaching the outskirts of the city now, he was surprised how much larger Gaziantep turned out to be. According to the map app on his phone, he was still a ways from his destination.

When he exited the Kilis highway, he found that he had to traverse much of the city to get to the district that housed the UNHCR sub-office. The Sani Konukoğlu Bulvari, a four-lane highway, sliced through the city north of the downtown area. It being Sunday, traffic wasn't bad and he was glad that he'd decided to come a day early. On Monday morning, the road would be clogged bumper to bumper. The northeastern section of Gaziantep looked like one of those new Chinese cities. Blocks after blocks of look-alike multi-story apartment buildings. Most of the streets were numbered rather than named. His hotel was just a mile away from the office.

On Monday morning, he decided to walk. He crossed the Duisburg Bulvari and wondered why a main street was named after a German industrial city. Maybe a lot of Gaziantep's men had worked there at one time.

Bilek Balbay greeted him at the door of the UNHCR offices. "Mr. Vermeulen, a hearty welcome to our humble offices. As you probably know, this location was only opened when it became clear that the offices in Ankara and Van were too far away to sustain our assistance program for Syrian refugees. We still have that just-moved-in look."

Vermeulen shook the man's hand and nodded. There were boxes overflowing with folders and papers along the hallway. The reception desk was squeezed next to the entrance. He could see three doors on either side of the hallway. A woman sat behind the desk, typing and staring at the screen.

"Thank you," Vermeulen said. "Glad I finally made it."

"First I need to apologize for my abrupt behavior in Kilis. I didn't expect you there and I had a full schedule. To top it off, I had a family emergency that caused me to leave early."

"Oh, I hope everything is well again."

"An aging parent," Balbay said and pressed his lips together. "It won't get better. Something we have to get used to."

Vermeulen nodded and made a sympathetic face. Balbay led him to the last of the doors on the right. The man's office was spartan, but so was everything else. The desk had seen better days. A laptop stood on it, screen folded up. There was no phone or fax machine. Maybe the UN had finally realized that installing such devices was a waste of money in the age of mobile communications. The rest of the desk was covered with paperwork. Balbay was definitely not a clean desk kind of guy. More banker's boxes full of papers were stacked against the walls, the lids barely fitting.

Balbay gestured to a chair in front of the desk and Vermeulen sat down.

"Well," Vermeulen said. "Let's get to it then. As you know, OIOS's job in Turkey is threefold—assess strategic planning and monitoring, your project management and adherence to the regulatory framework. Much of the work has already been done at the headquarters in Ankara. OIOS commends the local UNHCR representation for shifting its emphasis to the needs of Syrian refugees in urban areas. Since they constitute ninety percent of all Syrian refugees in Turkey it was the proper strategic decision."

Balbay nodded. "The basic needs are so large, it is difficult to focus on the more complex issues. But we're making progress."

"One of our recommendations is that better communication with your partner organizations that provide the necessary services would go a long way. But you'll get more detail on that in our final report. I'm only here to follow up on project management details."

Balbay's eyebrows arched. "What details? I've been meticulous in documenting everything."

"I'm sure you have. Some of this is routine. You know how occasionally details get lost when large numbers are summarized in a few categories. Specifically, I'd like to focus on two aspects, your contracts with partners who issue the cash cards to refugees and the procurement and warehousing of non-food-items."

Balbay shrugged, as if to say, "You're the boss." He led Vermeulen to an empty office.

"You can use this desk. I'll have the paperwork brought to you. How long do you think it will take?"

"That depends on the amount of contracts you have. Usually not more than a couple of days. As I said, the majority of the work has already been done. I'm just here to clear up the last open questions."

BY THREE THAT AFTERNOON, Vermeulen was deep into his work. The room had been used for storage and was only cleared to make space for him. Boxes stood piled against the wall. The desk wobbled. He tore a piece of cardboard from a box, folded it, and stuck it under one of the legs. One of the employees had brought him a cup of coffee, a kind gesture. The urge to smoke lurked just below his consciousness. He put another printout on the pile of completed documents. So far, so good. Balbay was running a clean operation, especially in light of the dramatic increase in demand for services over the last year.

When he got to the procurement of the cash cards, he noticed the first inconsistencies. One of the contractors had put out a request for proposals to which only one vendor had replied. He could see no evidence that the RFP had been properly advertised. He marked that for further scrutiny. Another partner, rather than advertising, had invited proposals from only three vendors. Another flag.

The non-food item procurement and warehousing turned out to be complicated. The office had acquired a lot more mini-fridges, hot plates and kitchen sets than were distributed. There was no indication if the remaining items were still in the warehouse. More flags.

His phone rang. It was Gaby.

"Hi, Dad, you have a moment?"

"Yes, go ahead."

"I looked into *Selim Tekstil*. It wasn't easy. The company doesn't appear in any of the business listings we have, it must be a small outfit. So I went to the website of the Turkish Ministry of Trade and there I did find a record. The company is owned by one Oben Özbek. There was only a PO Box address for him in Kilis."

"Great, thanks for checking it out."

"Why did you want to know?"

"Not sure it matters anymore. I'm in Gaziantep now, digging through piles of receipts and RFPs. I hope you didn't spend too much time on it."

"Nah. Don't worry. I did a search for the name and it turns out this Oben Özbek is a serial company founder. There must have been at least fifteen in the registry. I have no idea if they all still exist. You want his address?"

"Sure." He wrote down the box number on a slip of paper.

"In my world, anyone registering that many companies is usually acting as a front for others. So keep that in mind. Anyway, I'll let you get back to your work. Don't get a paper cut. Ciao."

Vermeulen leaned back in his chair and scratched his head. Acting as a front for others. Like letter box companies at some Caribbean tax haven. He thought of the web of companies involved in his last case. Transferring money until the origin was no longer traceable. How did a sweat shop fit into this? It hadn't looked like much. A bunch of sewing machines stuck into a large garage, sewing uniforms. But if it were a front for something else, something bigger, that would explain why Tariq got hired to watch him. But he was done with that. *No longer my concern.*

He took the papers related to the cash cards and looked up the partner organizations. Both were Turkish non-governmental organizations. Their English names were nondescript, Turkish Refugee Aid and TurkOasis. The correspondence, mostly printouts of email messages, used their acronyms TRA and TO. He'd have to visit them and quiz them on their odd procurement practices. He stretched his back and yawned. Something to do the next day.

The question of purchasing too many supplies was something Balbay could answer. He got up and went to the man's office. Balbay was on the phone, so Vermeulen signaled that they needed to talk and he went back to his office. All in all, he was surprised how few flags had popped up. The large increase in the flow of refugees to Turkey had caught all aid organizations by surprise. Everyone was scrambling to meet the demand. Those were exactly the circumstances when bookkeeping, proper records and followthrough were ignored.

Balbay stuck his head into the office. "You wanted to talk with me?"

"Yes, about all those mini-fridges and hot plates. It says here that you have over thirty-five thousand of each in storage. Why did you order so many more than you distributed?"

Balbay came inside and sat down on the spare chair.

"You can't imagine what it was like. Once we realized that the Turkish refugee camps weren't even making a dent in the influx, we had to act fast. Winter was coming, refugees were living in places that weren't meant for human habitation. We had to winterize and provide a minimum so people could at least cook and eat. You know they came across the border with nothing. We simply extrapolated from what we saw and ordered what seemed like a reasonable amount."

"Yes, I see," Vermeulen said. "And are you sure that the surplus is still in the warehouses?" As much as possible, Vermeulen followed the old lawyer rule to never ask questions to which he didn't know the answer. But occasionally, it was his job to be suspicious. Balbay's answer would say a lot.

"Of course, where else would it be? Their warehouses are secure. There are more fire extinguishers than are required by law, there are cameras, we've implemented an online inventory control system."

"You have? I'm looking at this office and I don't see the personnel level that can handle an inventory control system."

Balbay shook his head. "Of course not, we have contracted the warehousing and administration to an outside vendor."

"Was that a competitive bid?"

"No," Balbay said. "We were overwhelmed. People were streaming across the border, we ordered the non-food items and the winterization materials. Then the trucks started showing up and we needed to find space. A local trucking and logistics company stepped forward and offered to manage this aspect. We were grateful and accepted."

"Yes, but at a cost of over five million dollars. That was done without consulting the Procurement Service at headquarters. I can see why it was necessary a year ago. But have you since done a cost benefit analysis to see if the warehouse management would be better done in-house?"

Balbay looked out the window then back at Vermeulen. "No, we did not. It would involve hiring more people, getting more computers. We just don't have time for that. If anything, that should be handled in Ankara."

Balbay was right. It wasn't really his job. And he wasn't rattled. All good signs.

"Okay, I need some contact information on the warehouse company," Vermeulen said.

"Sure, the receptionist has all that information."

"Thanks for your cooperation. I'll have to do a few site visits tomorrow and then I can wrap this up."

Vermeulen called the two partner organizations to set up appointments for the next day. The first, Turkish Refugee Aid, was happy to have him come at nine in the morning. TurkOasis' phone kept ringing until the call cut off. There was no answering machine.

SIXTEEN

AHMADI SPENT THE night in a filthy hotel. It wasn't the kind that rents rooms by the hour, but it might as well have been. She didn't even get undressed before going to bed. A world apart from Vermeulen's hotel only three nights before. On Monday morning, she found a discount store, bought some fresh underwear and a cheap top, and went back to her room. At least the shower worked.

After the shower, she went to a grocery store, bought a roll and two oranges, and found a bench in a small park off Cumhuriyet Cadessi. It was time to take stock. She couldn't go back to the vineyard. The foreman would kill her. On the other hand, the grape harvest was almost over and the agent would move them to a new place. Probably apricots or oranges. If she could hide from the foreman for a couple of days, she might be okay.

No. That part of my journey is over.

She thought of the suitcase and her clothes. They were lousy reasons to go back to that wretched existence. They were from a different life, a life she wouldn't be returning to anytime soon. Letting them go wasn't hard. What her new life would be, she didn't know, but she was certain that her skirts and blouses would be unsuitable outfits.

There was one picture of her family in the suitcase,

taken just a few weeks after the protests against the Assad regime had started. Back then, they'd all thought it'd be over soon, like in Tunisia and Egypt. They'd never imagined it would turn into a civil war. Her parents were smiling, her little brother squinting in the sun light. It was her sister's face that struck her. It was radiant. The kind of radiance that came from believing that the future was going to be glorious.

Tears flowed down her cheeks. The picture was her most precious possession. *Take a taxi and get it.* She couldn't get up. The weight of reality pressed her to the bench without mercy. *Let it go.* She wiped her face. Her family would live in her memories. A taxi would be too expensive and she had to be frugal. There was no foreseeable income in her future.

She ate the last bits of roll and orange and got up. That's as far as she got. As determined as she was to start over again, she had no idea what to do next. Zada had always known that. She never stood still. Find out what happened to Zada. *Yes, but how?*

A woman walking by stopped and looked at Ahmadi standing as if rooted to that spot.

"Sen iyi misin?" the woman said.

Ahmadi was so caught up in her thoughts, it took her a moment to sort that the woman had asked her if she was okay. The woman was in her mid-fifties, dressed in a dark gray pant suit, white blouse and heels. She gave Ahmadi an encouraging smile. Her face was round and soft. She had short gray hair and wore wire-rim glasses.

"Iyiyim, teşekkür ederim!" Ahmadi said, even though she wasn't fine at all.

Her accent must have given her away, because the

woman switched from Turkish to English, "Do you need help?"

Of course I need help. But one doesn't start one's new life by asking strangers for help. Zada hadn't. But she wasn't Zada. Tears welled up again. She shook her head.

The woman wasn't persuaded. "Have you heard of the Women's Center? They can help, and if not, they know who can."

"Is it in Kilis?"

"They work in Kilis, but their closest office is in Gaziantep. Let me call and see if someone's here in town at the moment."

The woman took out her phone, dialed a number and spoke to someone in Turkish. After some back and forth she asked Ahmadi, "Do you have a way to go to Gaziantep?"

Ahmadi shook her head. The woman continued her conversation on the phone. When she ended the call, she looked pensive for a moment, but must have arrived at a conclusion because she said, "Come with me." She took Ahmadi by her arm and coaxed her out of the park and along the street.

"I can drive you to the Center in Gaziantep, but I can't do it right away. I'll bring you to a café where you can wait for me."

"You are very kind. But it's not necessary. I can find my way to Gaziantep. There must be a bus."

"The bus only goes twice a day. I have a meeting with a client. That should last an hour. Then I'll drive you."

They reached what looked like an expensive restaurant. The woman led Ahmadi into the air-conditioned interior. A waiter approached. The woman said something to him and gave him a twenty lira note.

"Wait here," she said. "My name's Deniz Nazarayan, by the way. I'll be back in an hour."

"I'm Rima Ahmadi. Thank you."

The waiter brought her a cup of coffee and a sandwich.

DURING THE TWO HOURS it took for Nazarayan to return, Ahmadi considered what had happened that morning. In her experience, well-dressed women didn't stop and talk to refugees. If anything they picked up their pace to hurry past them. Nazarayan hadn't. Not only that, she'd offered to help. *Why?*

She'd heard stories from some Syrians who'd been here for a couple of years and who spoke of the friendliness with which many Turks had greeted them back then. They also warned her that the mood had changed. "Be careful," they'd said. "The Turks are hostile now. Try not to stand out. Keep out of their way, especially the men."

Who was this woman? Before she could answer that question, Nazarayan strode into the cafe.

"Sorry, that took much longer than I expected. A difficult client. Men…," she winked, "…they make even the simplest things complicated."

She plopped into the chair next to Ahmadi and called for the waiter. The man came immediately.

"A coffee." The waiter took the order in English without any reaction. She looked at Ahmadi. "Would you like another one?"

Ahmadi shook her head.

"Just one coffee then, Kadri."

"Yes, Madam Nazaryan."

"He knows you?" Ahmadi said.

"He sure does, I'm a regular here. Kadri is my favorite waiter. Did he take good care of you?"

"Yes, he did." Ahmadi hesitated a moment. "Why are you so nice to me?"

"Maybe because I'm a nice person. Maybe because I'd rather not meet you under far less pleasant circumstances. Probably both. I'm a lawyer. Two thirds of my business, the part that pays my bills, is real estate. But I'm also a lawyer on call for the Women's Center. I see what happens to vulnerable women in this country. You've never heard of the Center?"

"Uh, no."

"It started out working against honor killings, but it now focuses on preventing any kind of violence against women. Female Syrian refugees have become our fastest growing group of clients these days. Are you ready to go?"

Ahmadi nodded.

"Are there any things you need to get. A suitcase, maybe?"

"No, that's all lost."

"Poor child. Sounds like you've had a hell of a time. Have you registered with the authorities?"

"No, I haven't. Since I was working illegally, I thought it better not to."

"You must register. You get free healthcare and a little cash. The healthcare alone is worth it. The authorities usually look the other way when it comes to working without a permit. Not because they care about the refugees, but because those who employ them are glad for the cheap labor. Where did you work?"

"At a vineyard south of the town."

"Bad work?"

"The worst."

"Doesn't surprise me. My countrymen, the emphasis being on men, can be terribly ruthless when it comes to exploiting those who have lost all. You're single, right? You have any trouble with men?"

"Mostly just nasty looks, but yesterday the foreman tried to corner me."

"What'd you do?"

"I smashed his fingers in the door of his pickup before driving it to Kilis."

"Ah. That's why you can't go back. Good for you. What did you do with the truck?"

"I parked it at a store and left it there."

"Good." She finished her coffee. "Let's go. I don't want to get back too late. It's my turn to cook."

During the drive to Gaziantep, Ahmadi told Nazaryan a little about her background as a teacher in Aleppo. Nazaryan told her about her family and her work.

"My parents were progressive Armenians. I was the firstborn and instead of trying for a boy, they decided there was no reason that I couldn't fulfill all the hopes parents have for their firstborn. So I got to go to school and university. But I'm Armenian and so I'm suspect in Turkey. How about you? Do you have any siblings?"

Ahmadi was awed by what this woman had achieved. Compared to her, she felt inadequate. She told her about her family, growing up and going to teachers college. "But they are all dead now." Nazaryan didn't say anything. Ahmadi was glad she didn't. What was there to say?

Being frozen on that spot in the park, not knowing what to do next had turned out to be the best thing that could have happened to her. Ahmadi wasn't a very religious person, but it seemed to her that Allah must have had a hand in what had happened that afternoon.

They reached the outskirts of Gaziantep and the traffic slowed considerably. Nazaryan had made a couple of calls to alert the staff of the Women's Center that she'd be arriving. After a half hour of slow traffic, they exited at Atatürk Bulvari. Four blocks later Nazaryan stopped in front of the Center.

The hand-off was pretty quick as Nazaryan had to make her way back to Kilis. She gave Ahmadi her card. "What's your phone number," she said. Ahmadi recited it as Nazaryan punched it into her phone. When Ahmadi's phone rang, Nazaryan smiled. "We'll talk soon."

The head of the Center, Ayla Erkin, took Ahmadi inside. The center was tiny, consisting of three rooms—a reception area, Erkin's office and a meeting room. The furnishings were sparse and second hand. Erkin took Ahmadi into her office and began the intake process. Her manners were business like. In response to Ahmadi's raised eyebrows, she explained that they had to keep track of all people served. The funders required that. Once name, home address and passport number were entered into the computer, Erkin turned to Ahmadi.

"I'm sorry, this might be difficult, but I have to ask. Have you been assaulted in any form, sexually or otherwise?"

Ahmadi recounted the episode with the foreman. At the conclusion a hint of a smile appeared on Erkin's face. "That must have been a scary experience, but you stood up for yourself."

She typed a few more things, then scooted her chair over to face Ahmadi. "Tomorrow, you must go and register. It's really important. You can go to a doctor, you'll get a small stipend. You are a teacher. There may be a chance to work in a school for Syrian kids. We'll see. Do you have any money?"

Ahmadi nodded. She hadn't told anyone about the thousand lira she'd taken from the pickup truck. Better to keep that episode to herself.

"Enough for a room?"

"I don't know, I have a thousand lira."

"Hmm. That'll do for tonight, but it won't last very long. Let me make a few calls."

Erkin dialed a number on her phone, waited for the call to connect. Apparently there was no answer because she left a message. She called another number. The same result. The third call connected with a real person. Erkin said something about needing a bed. The conversation lasted a few minutes. Finally, Erkin ended the call.

"I found a place for you to stay tonight." She wrote an address on a chit of paper. "Come back tomorrow morning. Someone will be here at nine. We'll tell you where to get registered. Do you have anything besides what you are wearing?"

"No. I couldn't go back to the vineyard where my suitcase is."

She pulled open a drawer and pulled out a plastic bag. "Here are some basic toiletries for tonight. Your hostess will have a towel. You need tampons or pads?"

Ahmadi shook her head.

"The house is close by. Just go left from here. You'll cross a big boulevard at the end of the block. After the intersection the street name changes to Ordu Cadessi. Follow the street for two more blocks until you reach Mehmet Tolaman Sokak. That's the street on the paper here. See you in the morning."

SEVENTEEN

AHMADI CAME BACK to the Women's Center the next morning. She was an hour early. Her hostess had been very nice and the bed comfortable, but she didn't want to impose more than necessary. She did linger in the shower, though. It boosted her energy. She stopped at a kiosk and bought a cup of tea and an egg sandwich. So far, her new life had been promising.

Ayla Erkin showed up right on time and opened the office. "Have you been waiting long?"

"No. Just got here myself."

"Have a seat. I have to get everything going here."

Ahmadi watched as Erkin started up her computer, checked the telephone for messages, and started an electric kettle. Her moves were unhurried, a routine she'd performed many times before. It calmed Ahmadi's nervous energy. There'd be enough time to get things done. Her new life didn't have to start all at once.

Erkin's mobile dinged. She checked and frowned. Turning to Ahmadi, she said, "Slight change of plans. My assistant just texted me that she's sick. I had planned for her to take you to get registered. I can't do that because I have appointments. Do you think you could do it on your own?"

Ahmadi shrugged.

"It's not difficult. You have your passport, right?"

"Yes."

"Do you have any other ID?"

"A driver's license."

"Good. Hide your passport well. Make sure nobody steals it. Without it you'll have a lot of trouble. Anyway, you need to go to the Directorate of Migration Management office to register. I'll write down the address for you."

"Is it far?" Ahmadi said.

"Yes. I wrote down the instructions. You walk several blocks then take the tram. Then walk some more."

"Does the registration cost anything?"

"No, but the tram does, and you'll want to eat something later. If the registration is completed today, you can also get a cash card. You can use it at any ATM. It's not much, but it helps. Can you do that?"

"I think so."

"Good. Come back here when you are done. We need to sort out how you can get some income. We're open 'til 5:30 this afternoon. If it takes longer, call me. I'll make sure you have a place to sleep."

VERMEULEN'S VISIT TO Turkish Refugee Aid was short and the office manager answered all questions to his satisfaction. TRA had invited the three proposals directly because they had worked with each vendor before and knew them to be reliable partners. They went with the lowest bid, which was below the prices previously paid. He saw no cause for concern.

The visit to TurkOasis turned out to be rather different. The building was at the given address, but the office where the organization was supposed to be was empty. There was a sign on the door with a phone number. Vermeulen dialed the number. A woman answered.

He identified himself. The woman switched to English. He asked about the office. The woman said it was for rent. What about the previous tenants, TurkOasis? The woman hesitated a moment before saying that she had no idea what he was talking about.

"How long has the office been vacant?" he said.

"Perhaps, uh, eight months or so. It is not…how do you say…a good location. But the owner will not rent for cheaper."

"So this NGO has never been here?"

"Uh, no. The last occupant was an accountant and he retired. That is what I remember."

"Have you ever heard of TurkOasis?"

"Uh, no. What is it?"

"It doesn't matter, thank you very much for your help. Good day."

Vermeulen went back to his car and sat, the window open, hoping for a breeze. It could just be an honest mistake, maybe the numbers had transposed, maybe it was a "Boulevard" instead of a "Street," or something like that. His gut told him the opposite. Things just felt off. There was no reference to a different address in the paperwork he'd seen. No indication of an impending move. No past addresses.

Part of him just wanted to be done with the job, visit with his daughter and then go home to Tessa. He could do that. Sign off on the paper work, submit his report to New York and then fly to Düsseldorf.

But there was this other part, the one lodged in his reptilian brain, that smelled blood. Someone was scamming the UN, stealing from destitute people, people who'd lost everything. What sick mind would even contemplate that? All the weird stuff that had happened this last week, disjointed and vague, bubbled up. There were no obvious logical connection, but the synapses deep inside his brain were already linking them. This wasn't going to be a quick report.

He started the car and drove back to the office. Balbay was the first thread. He'd pull on it and see what else came unraveled.

BALBAY SEEMED GENUINELY taken aback. His face looked drawn and his fashionable two-day stubble more like a bad shave.

"I don't know," he said. He'd been saying that ever since Vermeulen got back to the office.

"Didn't you visit their location?"

"No. There was no need. Our communication was via the phone or email. She came here for the final signature."

"Who came?"

"The vice-president, a Ms. Yaser. Everything was fine. We were glad to be working with the organization. The record of their past work spoke volumes. They had a lot of experience."

"Had you worked with them before?"

"Mr. Vermeulen, I started this job last year. I hadn't worked in the aid field before. My background is in shipping and distribution. UNHCR hired me because of that, not because of my experience in non-profits."

"So Ms. Yaser could have completely made up her identity, come to this office and you wouldn't have been any wiser?"

"No." Balbay wiped his forehead and rubbed his hand on his pants. "They were registered with the authorities. It wasn't a made-up organization."

"They contacted you first?" Vermeulen said.

"Yes, we published the request for proposals in the usual outlets. You have to remember there was terrible pressure to get things moving. We needed to get cash into the hands of the refugees, otherwise it would have been a humanitarian crisis. Can you imagine what would have happened if people had died in the streets?"

"So TurkOasis replies to the RFP. How? Did they ask questions? Want clarification?"

"No, they sent in a complete proposal, filled out correctly. It was a surprise, really, because many NGOs don't do that. They forget things, or they don't have the right accounts, what have you. Usually, there's a back and forth until they get it right. But TO got it right the first time. I thought it was a sign of their professionalism."

"And the proposal was to buy and distribute cash cards to qualifying refugees."

"Yes, about $2.5 million worth. They also requested funds for renting cars. They needed to get around to verify eligibility."

"How much?"

"About $100,000. But they ended up spending more than double that. They requested a contract waiver after the fact. We saw no reason to deny that. Southern Turkey is large and houses the most refugees."

Vermeulen shook his head. "How did you find out about their past work?"

"They submitted past project proposals and their final reports."

"And you didn't follow up and check if these were real projects?"

Balbay squirmed in his chair. "You don't understand.

It was more like a panic. Things needed to get done. Everything they did was professional. I had no reason to doubt their credentials."

Vermeulen paged through the paperwork in front of him. It struck him that, as Balbay had said, only the name of the vice-president showed up.

"Who's the president of the organization?"

Balbay's eyebrows arched. "Hmm. Good question. I don't know."

"Can you look it up in whatever register these out-fits are listed?"

"Sure."

Balbay began typing on his laptop. He frowned, and typed some more. When he turned to Vermeulen, his faces had the pained expression of someone who's just seen his career swirling around the drain.

"It appears that the listing is no longer active."

"They went out of business?"

"Yes."

"And you didn't know this until now?"

Balbay shook his head.

"You had no inkling that the NGO was about to close?"

More head shaking.

"Can you at least find out who the president was?"

A few keystrokes later, Balbay said, "No. Once a list-ing is inactive, such details are no longer accessible."

"Do you even know if any money was ever put on the cards and distributed to refugees?"

"I'm sure it was. That was their contract."

Vermeulen took a deep breath to calm himself.

"Mister Balbay, unless you are playing dumb, it must have dawned on you by now that TurkOasis was a sham operation. So, it stands to reason that none of the funds you allocated were spent as intended."

Balbay slumped in his chair. "No. That can't be. We did our due diligence. The organization was real. That woman sat here in my office. You have no evidence to make such accusations."

Vermeulen could see that the man was being gripped by panic. That wouldn't help.

"Okay," he said. "Let's not jump to conclusions. First, we need to find out if the cash cards were ever ordered and if any money was put on them. Get me the contact information of the vendor. That should be in the papers you have."

EIGHTEEN

YASER AND HER uncle sat in the back room of the Tek-Cell shop in Kilis. Out front, there was moderate customer traffic. She could hear the buzzer of the front door every time it opened. The murmur of voices bled through the door when the sales guy came to the display with the cheaper phones near the back of the store. Sure, the iPhones and Samsungs drew in the buyers, but once they heard the price, most opted for some Chinese model. It didn't matter. Sales at the store were an afterthought.

"Have you wrapped up the operation?" Ceylen said.

Her uncle's bushy eyebrows moved as if they were caterpillars. She'd never get used to them. She wanted to laugh, but the thought also creeped her out.

"Yes, uncle. I put it to bed. I made a hair above two million in cash. The refugee agency was so desperate, it was almost too easy."

"Everything is buried deep enough so it can't point back at you, or me?"

"Yup. Our digital presence is erased, there's no trace left of TurkOasis."

"What about the registry?"

"It'll just be another record among millions. The only concrete thing there is the address and that's fake. Your contact at the registry still has to remove my name. That's all."

"Any loose ends you can think of?" he said.

"Well, the van crashing on the Gaziantep road. I'd call that a loose end, but that wasn't my responsibility. Honestly, I didn't think it was wise to use the vans we rented with the refugee money for oil smuggling. That wreck is not easy to explain away."

She watched him, saw his face harden. *Good. Challenge him. Turn attention to his mistakes.*

Ceylen's face softened into a smile. "The student teaching the teacher." He nodded as if lost in thought. "The times are changing, indeed." The smile disappeared in a flash. "But you should first learn to walk before you run, before you criticize someone who's already finished the race. Nobody will connect the crashed van with your operation."

"Unless they check the rental contract."

"The office manager knows better than letting someone see that. I ask again. Any loose ends on your side."

She had her thumb already between index and middle finger, ready to signal him to fuck off. The nerve of lecturing her after he'd made such a blunder. But she took a deep breath and kept her hands under control.

"None that I can think of," she said. "What's happening with that United Nations man? You were going to deal with him. That kid find out anything?"

"No. I should have known better. Never pay your employees before they do their work. For all I know, the boy had spent the day at some *Döner* shop, blowing his money on food instead of watching that man. I had to put the fear of Allah into him. The good news is that the investigator has left town. The boy overheard him talking with the concierge."

Another blunder. The old man is losing it. Her phone rang.

"Alo?" she said.

It was the woman from the property management company in Gaziantep she kept on a small retainer. "A man called about the empty office."

"Who was he?"

"I didn't understand his name, but he said he was with the United Nations."

Yaser's mood soured instantly. "What did he want?"

"He asked about TurkOasis."

She got up and walked away from her uncle's desk. Talk about loose ends. Vermeulen knew that the address for TurkOasis was fake.

"Did you tell him that they never rented that office?"

The woman answered in the affirmative. Good. The address was a dead end, just as she'd planned.

"What happened?" Ceylen said. "You look worried."

"The UN man checked on our fake office."

"In Gaziantep?"

"Yes."

The old man shook his head. "Are you sure all your tracks are hidden? I cannot afford any international attention right now, especially not for a measly two million dollars."

Yaser wanted to roll her eyes, but knew better. "Yes, uncle. He won't get any farther. The rental agent knows nothing. It's another dead end like all the others. He's a bureaucrat. He'll give up and go home. He's got no reason to dig deeper."

Ceylen wasn't satisfied. "Remember the proverb, 'Be thy enemy an ant, see in him an elephant.'"

Now Yaser really did roll her eyes. "Uncle, enough with the ancient sayings. He's going home."

Ceylen shook his head. "The ant would go home, the elephant would root deeper. I'll go to Gaziantep tomorrow and see if we're dealing with one or the other."

She got up, barely able to contain her anger. Now he was muscling in on her job. She managed to squeeze a "Thank you" between her thin lips and left. Outside, she wanted to shatter the window. Instead, she kicked a rotten apple that had fallen from the fruit stand a couple of shops down. It soiled her shoe.

She got in her BMW and drove to her condo. She couldn't stand playing the apprentice much longer.

At home, she fired up her laptop and started scouring the transaction history of one of the bank accounts. Whenever her uncle annoyed her, searching for her father's killer calmed her down. She picked a different account and plugged in the date range during which her father had been shot. This account showed few transactions and all those were for amounts too high to be a payoff for a hit. She logged out and connected to the next account. This showed mostly wire transfers to accounts in other countries. Another dead end. Mob hits weren't done by foreigners. She was about to log out and check the next account when it occurred to her that just because money was transferred abroad didn't mean the killer wasn't Turkish. Her uncle's network had links all over the place, especially in Germany. What better way to hide the killing than to hire a Turk there, have him do the hit and go back?

The usual procedure was to pay half in advance and

the remainder after completion. She knew how much it cost to have someone killed. Add to that the extra cost for a high value target and foreign travel and she had a pretty clear range of what to look for.

When she saw the first transaction, a fist clamped around her heart. The amount was almost exactly half of what she had estimated. It had been transferred three weeks before her father was killed. The numbers on the screen blurred. She gripped the edge of her desk so hard, it hurt her fingers. If she could have ripped the wood apart, she would have. The tears were pure anger. They burned her cheeks as if they were acid. She took a deep breath and continued scrolling for later transactions. An identical amount transferred the day after her father was buried. She might as well have found the actual gun that killed her father.

She got up, breathing fast now. Part of her couldn't believe it. Family trumped everything. Family doesn't kill family. That's what she knew. But there was another voice, the one that told her that blood mattered more than relations. Her father had been killed by her mother's brother. Others would think it bad, but not as bad as killing one's own blood kin. She disagreed. She would kill her own blood.

NINETEEN

EARLY ON WEDNESDAY, Vermeulen was back at the UNHCR office. Balbay was already there. His desk looked like a recycling dump.

"I've pulled all the paperwork for the vendor used by the TurkOasis. I wanted to make sure you have all the information necessary. TO received a bid only from CrescentCard."

Vermeulen nodded and took the documents Balbay handed him. The bid by CrescentCard had proposed to issue around twenty-five thousand cards.

"Who vetted the recipients?" Vermeulen said.

"We gave TurkOasis a list. They contacted each household, had them fill out a questionnaire regarding cash resources and other assets. They did spot checks to make sure the information was correct. Finally, they determined the maximum amount depending on family size. Once that was done, the registered head of household would get a text message telling them where to pick up the card."

"So the amounts distributed varied?"

"Yes, because of family size. As I said before, most arrive here with nothing more than the clothes on their back. We have determined a standard amount per person. You multiply that by the number of family members and you have your monthly allowance."

"How much is on the cards when they are distributed?"

"A month's worth. After that the contracted bank reloads them every month."

Vermeulen brushed a lock of hair from his forehead. "So there are at least three parties involved. TurkOasis, the card vendor CrescentCard, and the bank."

"That's correct."

"I have to talk to all three."

Again, Balbay's answers were to the point and didn't seem nervous or evasive. If anything, he seemed solicitous and eager to help Vermeulen.

"Do we have the list of recipients?" Vermeulen said.

"Yes, it should be here. Let me look."

Moments later, he returned with a fat stack of papers. Printed on both sides of each sheet were lists of names and phone numbers. Many, but not all, also listed addresses.

"These are the recipients," Balbay said.

"Do you know if they all got cards?"

Balbay shook his head. "You know we don't have the personnel to check on each refugee. That's why we hire contractors. However, the card numbers are printed in the last column. So they must have gotten their cards."

Vermeulen paged through the stack of papers. The list of names went on and on. Each represented a life disrupted, thrown out of its trajectory into a tailspin. These were the innocent victims of machinations orchestrated far above their station, the trampled grass left behind by fighting elephants. The thought that someone was scamming them out of the few dollars that would ease their suffering a little made him furious. Unmasking such scammers was the reason he did this job.

He turned a few more pages. More names. More lives. His eyes had already reached the bottom of the sheet when his brain signaled a familiar name. He did a reverse scan back to the top of the page. Yes, there it was.

Zada Homsi, no address, but a phone number he recognized.

"I know this woman," Vermeulen said. "And I know for sure that she didn't have a cash card."

"She must have. There's a card number listed behind her name."

Vermeulen dialed the number of Inspector Demirel. The call rolled over to voicemail. He left a message asking the inspector to check Homsi's phone and see if it had received a text message from either CrescentCard or TurkOasis.

He was pretty sure there wouldn't be one. What had Ahmadi told him about Homsi? That she'd found out something that would make their lives easier. Was it the cash card? Or, rather, that they should have gotten one, but didn't? On his phone's calculator, he added the card numbers except for the rightmost one, multiplied the sum by nine and divided that by ten. The result made him shake his head.

"This is a fake number. It's not a credit or debit card number. The last digit doesn't match."

Balbay stared at him.

"It's a simple calculation based on the Luhn algorithm," Vermeulen said. "The rightmost digit on any bank card is a check digit, used to verify the other numbers. Banks use this algorithm to create card numbers. Accordingly, the last digit should be a zero, but it is a three. So this is a fake number."

Vermeulen worked the algorithm for five more cards. Four of them were also fake, but one was not. He scratched his chin.

"It looks like some of the cards are real. I don't know what's going on. Let's call CrescentCard. We need to know for sure," Vermeulen said.

The call confirmed Vermeulen's fears. Although the company had indeed been retained by TurkOasis to produce and preload cash cards for refugees, the order contained far fewer cards than listed in the contract with UNHCR. Instead of twenty-five thousand, they ordered only five thousand. CrescentCard's management even debated if they should take the job because it seemed too small. In the end, they figured that it was a pilot project and doing it well could lead to more in the future.

Once the cards had been produced and loaded, they'd been distributed at various locations around Kilis using text messages to inform the recipients where they could pick up their cards. Yes, they had worked with Turk-Oasis, specifically with a Ms. Yaser. Their communication had been via email and phone calls. There had been one Skype call. Why all these questions? Was everything in order? Vermeulen assured the man it was and ended the call.

"What do we do now?" Balbay said.

"We find out who's behind TurkOasis. Contact the person you dealt with, this Yaser. I'll figure out how to find the person in charge."

BACK IN THE temporary office, Vermeulen fired up his laptop. There were a number of ways to finding who was behind the TurkOasis. Locating its online footprint was the first step. Enlisting Gaby's skills would be the second, although she might not be able to help. Her databases focused on businesses, not non-profits.

Although he had no reason to suspect that Balbay or anyone in his office had a part in the fraud, they shouldn't be excluded. Better to keep them in the dark about his efforts to locate the mastermind behind this swindle. He switched the browser to private mode.

The initial searches didn't yield anything. The few links highlighted by the search engine led to web pages that mentioned TurkOasis. Most of those were mere mentions from the UNHCR website. None of them had links to the organization. He tried narrowing the search to Turkish websites only and several variations of the search terms. The result was a long list of links in Turkish he could not understand. Using the translate function brought some sense to the list, but no new information on TurkOasis.

An hour of combining various search options later, he came across a website that had a link to TurkOasis. That wasn't unique. He'd seen several before, but none of them linked to their website, just to other organizations which mentioned them. He clicked the link expecting more of the same. This one was different. A domain name clearly referring to TurkOasis popped into the address bar of the browser. The little circle spun around and around. This was it. He'd found the digital trace. After what seemed a long time, the spinning circle stopped. An error page appeared informing him that the server could not be found and asking if he could possibly have misspelled the URL. Since he'd followed a link, he knew he hadn't. That left two scenarios. Either the address was no longer active, or the originating website had misspelled the URL. Since TurkOasis had erased so much of its existence in a relatively short time, the first scenario was more likely.

It was time to use a trick he'd learned from Tessa, the WayBack Machine, a service that had been archiving websites since 1996. He directed the browser to its address and typed in the non-functioning URL for TurkOasis. The little wheel spun again, but this time results appeared on the screen. According to the Way-Back Machine, TurkOasis' website had been up for nine months. It had captured six versions of the website during that time. The last archive was saved two months ago. Vermeulen chose the latest version.

There was nothing remarkable about the website. Nothing splashy. A rather rudimentary design, which made sense for a sham operation. A generic banner picture showing a city scape. Some introductory paragraphs he couldn't read. There was no option to display the site in English as he'd seen on other websites he'd visited. He tried the menu options one at a time and arrived at what appeared to be an "About Us" page. There were photographs of a middle aged man and a young woman. The man's photo looked like a stock photo. No actual man would look this airbrushed. The woman's photo had to be real, assuming that Balbay had actually checked the website, he would have noticed that the woman who came to his office was not the one in the photo. The names under the photos were Özbek and Yaser.

He sucked in his breath.

Özbek.

There was that name again. The same as the owner of the sweatshop. He didn't know if Özbek was a common name or not, but it would have been one hell of a coincidence to have two different people with the same name pop up in the same investigation. Running the page through the translation service simply showed that the two were president and vice president of TurkOasis. There was no further information about them. He sent the two photos to the office printer for his own benefit.

Before giving in to disappointment, he checked the remaining five versions of the website. On the third version, an email address appeared under the woman's photograph. He copied it into his notebook. The rest of the information remained the same. The street address on the contact page was of the vacant office he'd visited earlier. It also remained unchanged until he came to the first version. That address was different.

Balbay came into the office, sporting a hangdog expression. "The email address I've used to communicate with them doesn't work anymore. My message came back as undeliverable."

"Was it this one?" Vermeulen pointed to his notebook. Balbay nodded.

"That was to be expected. They have erased their online presence quite thoroughly. But they forgot that digital information never disappears completely. I've located a different street address from the one you had." He pointed to the screen. "Any idea where that might be?"

Balbay looked at it and shook his head.

"Well. I'm going to find out. In the meantime check on the car rental company they used for the vehicles. That's the only other lead we have."

TWENTY

THE ADDRESS VERMEULEN had found on the WayBack Machine belonged to a five-story building on one of the numbered streets in the southeast of Gaziantep, near the university. The structure seemed newer, painted the same creme color over stucco he'd seen all over the city. There was a grocery shop and a café at street level. The grocery store featured vegetables still in wooden boxes. The cafe was not very busy. Three tables stood outside in the shade of the second floor balcony. Only one table was occupied by a couple of old men, drinking coffee and reading newspapers. The other floors looked very much like apartments. Each corner unit had a balcony that protruded beyond the footprint of the building. He could see outdoor furniture and a few plants on the lower ones. A man was leaning against the railing on the fourth floor, smoking a cigarette. He looked at Vermeulen with idle curiosity.

Vermeulen circled the building to locate the entrance, only to find that it was between the grocery store and the cafe, partially obscured by the boxes of vegetables. The glass door was locked. Next to it was a communications panel with twenty buttons, each labeled with a name under a plexiglass cover. He was glad that the founder of modern Turkey, Kemal Atatürk, had switched from the Ottoman to the Latin alphabet. At least he could read the names. Not that it made any difference. There wasn't a business address and none of the names looked anything like Oben Özbek.

Yet another dead end. The UNHCR lack of due diligence was quite startling. Entering into a multi-million dollar contract with an organization that didn't have a real office seemed inconceivable. Still, he had to cut Balbay some slack. As long as the people seemed on the up and up, and the paperwork checked out, there was really no need to visit the organization's office. If anything, site visits should have focused on the refugees who were supposed to get the cards.

He took a seat at one of the empty café tables. A waiter appeared and he ordered a coffee. As far as he could tell, this fake NGO had stolen two million dollars, more if the car rentals were added. There was no trace of the principals. He had the names of the president and the vice-president, but they were probably fake, too. Someone had set up a perfect scam.

The coffee came and Vermeulen yet again had to suppress the urge to buy cigarettes. It didn't help that the old men at the next table were smoking. Instead, he took out his notebook and pen. His usual approach to baffling situations was to draw diagrams of what he knew, what he suspected and look for possible connections.

A large black Mercedes pulled to the curb just a few feet away. It was one of the more luxurious models. The driver stepped out of the vehicle and opened the passenger side rear door. An old man stepped out. His clothes—plain and a bit worn—stood in sharp contrast to the car. He had short white hair, busy eyebrows and a thin mouth. He could have fit in with the other old men reading their papers. He looked around. His eyes came to rest on Vermeulen, lingered for more than just a moment, then moved on to scan the rest of the surroundings. There was something professional about the gaze, like a threat assessment by someone used to dealing with danger. And something more sinister. The thin mouth hinted at something dark. The appraisal must have been satisfactory because the driver closed the door and accompanied the man to the entrance. He had his key ready and opened the door for the old man. They entered and disappeared from view.

Vermeulen had felt the piercing intensity of the old man's gaze. It had created a feeling of familiarity in Vermeulen. Hadn't he seen that face before? His first thought was Özbek, the president of TurkOasis, but the picture on the website showed a man at least twenty years younger. The driver appeared again and drove away. It did seem odd that someone with a driver and a fancy Mercedes should live in an apartment building when a mansion would be more fitting. Maybe the old man's mistress lived here.

He went back to his diagram. There wasn't much on the page. A box labeled TurkOasis, one for the UNHCR, a third one for CrescentCard plus two arrows connecting them. Money flowed from UNHCR to TurkOasis, a fraction of that continued on to CrescentCard. That was precious little. Of course, lots had happened. There was the dead woman Homsi, her friend Ahmadi, and the attack with the pickup. He couldn't conceive of any way they could be related to the cash card scam. Next came Tariq and the sweatshop. Again, something weird was going on, but it wasn't the case he was investigating. The overturned van with the gasoline had to be a random accident. If he'd left Kilis ten minutes earlier, he wouldn't even have been involved.

He motioned the waiter and ordered another coffee and a baklava. The waiter said something that Vermeulen didn't understand. The man held up his hands as if to say, "Wait, wait." He came back with a plate of something that didn't quite look like baklava.

"Güllaç," the waiter said. He looked at Vermeulen with an expectant expression. Vermeulen nodded. The man disappeared and brought another coffee. The pastry was still flaky, even though it was drenched in milk. There were walnuts and pomegranate seeds between the layers. It wasn't as sweet as baklava. Vermeulen enjoyed it very much.

He was on his last bite when the black Mercedes rolled up again. The driver stepped out, walked to the entrance. A few moments later, he reappeared with the old man. Vermeulen got a better look at him. He had bushy gray eyebrows over deep set eyes, a nose that must have gotten broken at one point in his life. He could have been one of the pensioners who were sitting at the other table if it hadn't been for the thin-lipped mouth that hinted at a ruthless streak. His tan skin was creased from decades of exposure to the sun. His clothes, linen shirt and pants, were spot on for the climate, as were his leather sandals. He was definitely too old to be Özbek from the website. But then that picture could have been a stock photo. The driver opened the door, the old man got into the car, the driver got in the front and drove away. Vermeulen checked his watch. He'd been inside for fifteen minutes, rather short for a visit with a mistress.

Just to make sure, he got up and walked to the entrance of the apartment building and checked the names again. Still no Özbek listed. He went back to his table and motioned the waiter for his bill.

THE DRIVER CHECKED on his uncle through his rearview mirror. He hadn't expected to pick him up again so soon. Ceylen looked as pale as if he'd seen a ghost. He'd gotten out his phone to make a call. The driver looked ahead again. After work traffic was beginning to spill onto the street.

Behind him the old man was talking on the phone. "He's found the address," he said.

The driver heard the voice of the other party. It was his sister, and it sounded like she was in trouble. He smiled. Serves her right.

"The UN man, who else?" Ceylen was saying. "He was sitting right outside, drinking coffee as if he were waiting for me."

So that's why he called me back so soon.

"How is that even possible? I thought all that information had been deleted."

A pause.

"Are you sure? How did he find the apartment? Didn't you always use the fake address?"

More squawking from the phone.

"No, I don't think he recognized me. How could he? We've never met. But he's seen my car."

That's something to worry about. A flashy Mercedes attracts attention. It better not mean they'd be changing cars. The driver liked driving the CLS 500 far better than the old Toyota.

"I don't think we can afford to ignore him," Ceylen said.

The driver wondered what was going on. Usually his uncle gave orders when he was on the phone. This conversation sounded different. His sister had weaseled herself into the old man's graces. It was the only reason he was talking this way. If it had been anyone else, heads would be rolling.

"No, I don't agree," Ceylen said. "We have to stop him before he becomes dangerous. The thing in Kilis wasn't even part of his job, but he stepped in and helped that woman anyway. This here concerns his job. He isn't going to let it go."

The driver thought about that. They were probably talking about the man drinking coffee outside the apartment building. He'd noticed how his uncle had stiffened when he first saw him sitting there. And his uncle wasn't easily startled. The coffee drinker hadn't looked dangerous. He wouldn't be afraid of him in a dark alley. Why was the old man so worried?

"No. This is the worst possible time for someone to sniff around my operations. I cannot afford that kind of scrutiny. Not now. What?" Ceylen paused. "You don't understand. If he knows about the cash card scam, there's nothing to stop him from checking the warehouse. Your operation may be over, mine aren't. I will take care of it. It's gone far enough," Ceylen said and ended the call.

About time she got put in her place.

AHMADI SETTLED INTO her room at the hostel. It was simple—a bed, a chest of drawers, a small table and a chair—but clean. The last couple of days had been unbelievable. First, she had registered as a refugee. The process took time, but it wasn't like she had any place to be. The woman doing the processing wasn't terribly friendly, but she did what was necessary and Ahmadi walked out of the office after four hours with a card that said she was a registered guest of the Turkish government.

After a quick lunch, she stopped at the office of Refugee Aid and, with a whole lot less bureaucratic hassle, got a cash card with some money on it. It wasn't much, but in combination with the money she had taken from the foreman, it should be enough at least for a while. Afterwards, she stopped at a couple of shops and bought new clothes. They weren't good quality, but they were all she could afford and the clothes she was wearing were past their use-by-date.

Back at the Women's Center, Ayla directed her to the hostel, where a room had just freed up. This was nice because she didn't want to impose any longer on the woman who had given her a bed two nights in a row.

The best news of all was the possibility of a job. She'd hoped to be teaching at a Syrian school in Gaziantep or Kilis, but there were no openings. More than enough teachers had fled the country before her and had taken those jobs as they became available. Instead, Ayla asked if she wanted to work on a survey of women refugees in Kilis. The Women's Center had received a grant from the European Union to survey refugee women in five cities including Kilis. Her status as a refugee and her being Syrian were an asset. It would make it easier to approach the women.

The questions ranged from the basics, such as original residence, time in Turkey, education and profession, to more difficult topics like reproductive health, their experiences in Turkey, their desire to return to their homes and other future plans.

"The pay won't be great," Erkin said. "But it'll be much better than living on your cash allowance alone."

It wasn't a difficult decision. She'd make it back to Kilis and find out what happened to Zada.

TWENTY-ONE

VERMEULEN STOOD UNDER the shower and let the water massage his shoulders. It didn't quite manage to rinse away his miserable day. The sun had beaten down without mercy. The investigation had screeched to a halt. He had no clues and no clear idea what to do next. Balbay had gotten in touch with the agency where the no-longer-existing TurkOasis had rented vehicles. They had rented cargo vans rather than cars, which explained the higher cost and the request for more money. It didn't explain why they had rented vans in the first place. One of the vans still hadn't been returned. Vermeulen would check up on that the next morning. He didn't hold out much hope. Whoever they were, the swindlers had covered their tracks very well. He got dressed and decided to go out to eat. He needed a beer and food. There was a restaurant in the hotel, but he wanted a walk, and with the sun setting, the temperature might be more temperate.

A breeze made the evening stroll pleasant enough. His hotel faced an intersection of four-lane streets and the prime spots on the corners had been claimed by the detritus of globalization—Burger King, Pizza Hut and a Turkish attempt at an American burger joint, named Big Yellow Taxi. He walked north on the street that led to the UNHCR office. There were a few grocery stores and a café. They wouldn't do. He had set his mind on a real restaurant with a menu and a waiter. He passed the mosque he'd admired earlier that morning. The setting sun bathed its metal dome in a golden hue. Cars were parked next to it, probably for evening prayers. He lingered for a moment and took a deep breath.

Admitting defeat wasn't easy. Even worse, the crooks were gone. No one at UNHCR could really be faulted. Sure, they should've checked more carefully, but the conditions were too dire to mess around with deep background checks. So, chalk one up for lessons learned, or rather, to be learned for the next time. *Right, when pigs fly.*

He continued to the next intersection. There was a bakery that was about to close, no restaurant. Maybe the side streets had what he was looking for. He took a right, hoping that the street layout was sufficiently linear that he would find his way back to his hotel. More apartment blocks lined the street with an occasional grocery store at ground level. He even passed a large public pool. What he didn't find was a restaurant. The Yellow Taxi joint would have to do. He strolled south again at the next intersection. His stomach had already made peace with the idea of a burger and urged him forward.

The sun sank below the mountains in the west and the street turned dark. Street lights were beginning to flicker on. There was little traffic here, even though he could hear the cars on the four-lane road a block away. He didn't see pedestrians either. Definitely evening prayers. He reached another intersection and looked left and right. There were no telltale neon signs. Just street lights and more apartment buildings. He kept going south in the direction of his hotel.

The sky had turned night blue. He usually liked these evening moments, these in-between times. But today it reminded him too much of the state of his investigation to be enjoyable. One last attempt tomorrow, then off to Düsseldorf. It wasn't the first time one of his cases appeared intractable. If anything, that was the norm. But he didn't remember a case with such a dearth of clues.

The next block contained a small park, its trees black shapes against the dark sky. A man came toward him wearing a light shirt and pants. Vermeulen felt an odd connection with the lone walker. Two men alone on a dark street. Was he hungry too? Maybe he knew of a restaurant. Before he could make up his mind whether to ask him for directions to an eatery, the man stepped towards Vermeulen and, pointing to a cigarette, said, "You have a light?"

By habit Vermeulen reached into his pocket. Then he remembered that he'd stopped smoking and wasn't carrying his lighter anymore. He looked up, trying to remember the Turkish word for "sorry," when a car pulled to the curb next to him. He hadn't heard the engine until that moment. He glanced at it. It was black. The way its motor purred, it had to be expensive. He turned back to the lone walker and, realizing that the man had spoken English, said, "Sorry, I don't smoke anymore."

That startled him *How did he know that I don't speak Turkish?* He wasn't dressed like a typical tourist. The car's door opened and the dome light came on inside. He looked at the man getting out of the driver's seat. A flash of recognition. It was the old man from the apartment building. *What's he doing here?*

Before he could process the signals coming from his synapses now firing at high speed, something very hard hit the base of his head. His brain shut down before the pain could register.

THE PAIN DID REGISTER, however, when Vermeulen woke up. In fact, the booming of a bass drum right inside his head was the first thing he noticed. Each beat triggered a wave of pain that gnawed its way to his extremities. He wanted to touch the spot where it originated, somewhere near the base of his skull. He couldn't. His hands were tied behind him to the chair he sat on.

Opening his eyes had no noticeable effect. He was in a dark room. Not even the sliver of light that usually sneaks under the bottom of a door. The air was hot, reminding him that his throat was parched. The sweat blooming on his forehead condensed into drops that ran down his nose and made spots on his pants. He moved his head gingerly. There was a background hum that reminded him of the sound of air conditioning in office buildings. But given the heat in the room, that couldn't be it. He strained to hear anything else, but the pounding inside his head blotted out whatever there might have been.

The *how* of what'd happened wasn't difficult. He'd gone out for dinner. He'd been knocked unconscious and brought to this place. He wasn't at all sure about the *why*. Except for the real estate agent, he hadn't spoken to anyone outside the UNHCR office. The rest of the research he'd done online. As far as the people behind the fraud were concerned, they didn't even know that their scheme had been discovered. Which left his brief entanglement with Rima Ahmadi. And that just didn't make sense. He'd dropped that and gone on to another city.

The beat in his head was unrelenting. He tried to move his head back, thinking that sitting slumped forward must have put a kink in his neck. The zinger that shot from his neck to his scalp proved him right. He kept moving his head back, a fraction of an inch at a time, remaining just this side of the pain barrier. It took a while, but, finally, he sat upright. He turned his head to the right in minute steps, then repeated the same process on the left side. The next step was raising his chin. That didn't go too well. The pain at the back of his head flared like a struck match.

The cautious stretches had lessened the pain a bit. He listened again for any sound that stood out from the hum. Nothing. His fingers did a little exploring. His hands were zip-tied to a folding chair, one to each side. It could have been worse. He stood up. The chair—a rather flimsy thing—hung from his wrists. More an annoyance than an obstacle. His pants felt light on his hips. They must have emptied his pockets.

He turned around. The darkness was no longer uniform. A sliver of gray interrupted it. He inched closer, afraid of stumbling over furniture. The gray came from behind a curtain that covered a glass door. He looked behind the curtain and saw a balcony and beyond it the lighted windows of other buildings and street lights below. It looked like he was being held on the third floor.

His back toward the curtain, he pulled it back and examined the room in the dim light that came in. Other than the chair he was dragging around there was no other furniture. There was another door on the opposite wall. That was it. He checked the balcony door. It had a door handle. He pushed it down. Nothing happened. Pulling it didn't change that. He felt along the hinge side of the door and found a lever. About to try it, he heard a door slam. A slit of light appeared under the door.

Decision time. Sit back down, or take the chair and attack whoever comes in. The pissed-off part of him wanted to smack the chair against the head of whoever entered. Give them some of their own medicine. But he decided to sit back down. With his wrists tied behind him to the chair, he could swing it using his body rotation and do some damage, but he'd never get his arms up high enough to hit someone's head. It wouldn't be enough for a knockout. And there were bound to be more than one. Whoever came in second would get to him for sure.

He closed the curtain again, hurried to where he'd sat before, coaxed the seat down, and plopped onto the chair. He didn't want the light to blind him once the door opened, so he slumped into the chair and closed his eyes.

Let them think I'm still out cold.

The door opened. Vermeulen peered through his eyelashes. A dark figure stood there, outlined by the bright light in the corridor. A man. That's all he could see. There was something in his hand. It glinted in the light. The figure stepped forward. Vermeulen couldn't make out what the glinting thing was. The answer wasn't long in coming. The hand holding it thrust forward towards Vermeulen's head.

TWENTY-TWO

A JET OF cold water hit Vermeulen's face. He snorted and shook himself, a reaction he regretted instantly when a new wave of pain flooded his head. He opened his eyes fully. The man's face was still obscured by the glare of the light flowing through the open door. He was tall and bulky, and held an empty glass pitcher in his hand. Not the kind of guy you'd want to take on. The man turned and switched on the light. Before he left the room, he turned once more and Vermeulen recognized the driver of the black Mercedes.

He looked around. A ductless air conditioner was mounted high on the wall. It was obviously not running. His wet hair kept dripping on his pants. He wanted to wipe his face. No chance of that happening unless he found a way to untie himself. The chair was flimsy enough, but it would take an effort to break it and make a lot of noise.

An old man came into the room. It was the same man Vermeulen had seen earlier at the apartment building. The driver was right behind him, carrying a chair. The driver put down the chair and the old man sat and clasped his skeletal fingers. The water drying on Vermeulen's face made his skin itch.

"What do you want from me?" he said in heavily accented English.

Vermeulen looked at the man and said, "Since I don't

know you, nothing, except being untied from this chair. After that you can explain to me who you are and I might be able to answer your question."

The man examined Vermeulen's face. His dark eyes radiated disbelief.

"You come to my address, yet you say you don't know me. This is hard to believe."

That was a clue. But not a very useful one. "I came to an apartment block. That's not the same thing."

"What was the address you were looking for?"

"I don't remember off hand. It's in my phone. Untie me and I'll tell you."

The old man raised his hand. The driver had already taken Vermeulen's phone. He took it from his jacket and pushed the home button. "It's locked," he said.

"Tell him your code."

Vermeulen hesitated. It didn't really matter. If he ever got his phone back, he'd change the code. He told the man.

"Where is it?" The driver said.

"Check the Note app. It should be the first note."

The driver did so and showed the screen to his boss. The old man's jaw muscles tightened. Which told Vermeulen that he'd just seen a familiar address.

"Are you Oben Özbek?" Vermeulen said.

This time the jaw muscles didn't move. The old man just shook his head. "No, I'm not."

"Well, it must be a case of mistaken identity. I have no business with you. You've gone through my pockets, so you know I work for the United Nations. Detaining me will cause you serious trouble. So let me go."

"I ask you again. What do you want from me?"

"I don't know who you are," Vermeulen said. "I

gather you live in that apartment building. But so do many others. I wasn't looking for you."

"Who were you looking for?"

"That's confidential."

The old man cleared his throat. "Mr. Vermeulen, I'm not playing…"

"Since you know my name. It's only fair that you tell me yours."

The old man's eyes flared in anger. "Don't interrupt me."

He raised his hand and the driver stepped forward and smacked Vermeulen across the face. It wasn't a hard blow, more like Tippi Hedren slapping the hysterical mother in *The Birds,* but given his battered state it was more than enough. He stifled a moan.

"Tell me who you are looking for."

"Okay, you made your point," Vermeulen said, breathing hard. "Can I have some water?"

"No water. Tell me who you are looking for. Maybe you get water then."

His delaying tactics exhausted, Vermeulen resorted to his fall back—tell as little of the truth as possible. "I'm looking for Oben Özbek, the president of Turk-Oasis."

"Why?"

"They received UN funds to rent cars, but they spent more money than they were allocated. We need to find out why. Can I have my water now?"

The old man raised his hand again and the driver left the room.

"Why were you looking for the president at the apartment building?"

The trick with telling just a little of the truth is knowing when to stop.

"Well, I went to the office address we had for TurkOasis, but they had vacated the space." So far, so good. He was only saying what could easily be verified. "Then I searched the internet and found the other address on their website. I went there to find an office, but it was just a residential complex."

The driver came back into the room carrying a glass of water. He lifted it to Vermeulen's lips and tipped it. Vermeulen gulped as best he could, coughing and sputtering, half the water running down his chin and onto his shirt.

"You didn't find what you were looking for?"

Vermeulen sat there like a drooling dog, furious that he was still tied to the chair and couldn't wipe his face. "No, I didn't. This is getting ridiculous. Will you please untie me. I don't know you from Adam and you have quite a nerve holding me here. You are causing an international incident. And you won't get away with it."

The driver stepped forward and slapped him again. As much as Vermeulen was prepared for it—he turned his head in anticipation—he gasped when the hand hit his face again.

"What do you know about TurkOasis?" the old man said.

"Nothing. They've hidden their tracks very well. Are we done here?"

The man got up and left. The driver took the man's chair, turned off the lights and closed the door.

Vermeulen remained seated, listening, watching. A door slammed. Did they leave again? This time, though, the slit of light under his door didn't disappear. One of them must have stayed behind. It better be the driver since he had Vermeulen's phone and keys.

THIRTY MINUTES LATER, Vermeulen stood up. He had to do something. Getting out of the room via the balcony seemed the logical answer except that'd be hard with his hands tied to the backrest of the chair. None of the tricks for defeating zip ties worked when your hands were tied separately. He'd have to use the chair as a weapon. He used his butt to fold up the seat, grabbed the chair and tried a few swings. Not very effective. With his arms behind him, he could lift the chair only a little. It would hit the knees of any attacker. Not enough to incapacitate someone as big as the driver. The solution, when it finally dawned on him, was too simple. He put the chair flat on the ground, which put it right under his butt. Now all he had to do was move his legs back through the gap formed by his arms and the chair on the ground. An easy move for a gymnast, which he was not. The first leg the hardest. He just couldn't get it past his wrist. The ties cut hard into his skin. Once it was through, the second was easier. He still needed a rest when he was done. The strain had made his head throb again. But at least the chair was now a real weapon.

He kicked the door several times.

"Hey, open up. I got to piss."

Banging the chair against the door made even more of a racket. He raised the chair over his head and pressed against the wall next to the entry.

A moment later the door swung into the room. A hand reached for the light switch. It was the driver's. Vermeulen held back. Hitting the arm would just make the man angry. Vermeulen needed him incapacitated. The light came on.

From the driver's perspective there were two places his captive could hide, either on the other side of the door or squeezed against the wall on this side. Behind the door was definitely the worse place since it left the initiative to the driver. All the man had to do was slam the door all the way open and hit whoever was hiding behind it. But human nature being what it was, a lot of people, including inexperienced bureaucrats, would choose that spot because the gut instinct is to hide from bad guys rather than confront them. Vermeulen hoped that he'd played the dumb bureaucrat convincingly enough to fool the driver.

Sure enough, the man took a step inside to give the door a hard push, which was all Vermeulen needed. The chair came crashing down on the man's head. It was a vicious blow. The man fell to the floor like a sack of potatoes.

Vermeulen squeezed back against the wall, ready for anyone else who might be out there. Everything was quiet. He eased into the hall. There was a short corridor that ended in a living area. Three doors led to other rooms. He searched them quickly. They were all empty. Nobody else was in the apartment. Either the old man was running an amateurish operation, or he was caught short-handed and was drumming up the rest of his crew. In either case, Vermeulen had to get the hell away from this place.

The kitchen was off the living area. He found a knife and was finally able to cut the ties. Massaging his wrists, he ran back to the driver and took his phone, keys and wallet from the man's pockets. He also had a pistol in a shoulder holster and the key fob for the fancy Mercedes. Vermeulen took both. He had no intention of using the car. He wasn't so sure about the gun.

Outside the apartment, he looked for an elevator. There was none. He followed the corridor until he found the emergency stairway. Better to avoid whatever reinforcements the old man might be bringing up the main stairs.

The adrenaline rush that powered his attack on the driver had given way to the throbbing pain again. He needed painkillers and an icepack. For another, he needed to find a place to hide. The old man orchestrated the cash card scam. He wasn't going to stop now. He had two million reasons to eliminate Vermeulen.

At the ground level Vermeulen stopped because he felt dizzy. He leaned against the wall and tried to get his head straight again. A concussion was nothing to mess with. After a few deep breaths, he pushed open the exit door. The surroundings looked familiar. He'd been held at the very address he'd investigated that afternoon.

There was no sign of the black Mercedes. He walked to the nearest thoroughfare and took a taxi back to his hotel. Slumping in the back seat, he sorted out what he'd learned. He was inclined to believe the old man's assertion that he wasn't Özbek. But who was, if not the old man? Someone even higher up? Gaby told him that he'd registered several companies. That seemed to indicate that he was in charge. Which made the old man something like the manager. Of course, that could have been a lie, too.

The cab dropped him at his hotel. Even though he was starving and the Big Yellow Taxi was still open, he fought the urge to eat first and hurried to his room where he packed his things as fast as he could. Downstairs, he checked out, put his bag in the rental car and drove the few yards to the burger place. He was the last customer. They locked the door after him.

TWENTY-THREE

CEYLEN FOUND THE door to the apartment open and his driver slumped against the wall, massaging his head. He didn't bother to ask what had happened. The bent folding chair told the whole story. It was his own fault. He'd let his disdain for bureaucrats get in the way of sound judgement. Vermeulen was indeed an elephant, not an ant. His nephew was no match for a man like that. He was big, which intimidated people, and he could drive, which was important, but he was as stupid as a donkey. If he weren't his nephew, he wouldn't have gotten this job.

A curse on family obligations. At least his sister has the smarts to pursue this life, if not the maturity yet to succeed.

"Make me a coffee," Ceylen said.

"My head hurts."

"If you hadn't been so stupid, it wouldn't. So get to it."

The nephew heaved himself up and trotted into the kitchen.

Family or not, he has to go. Inexcusable to be knocked out by someone tied to a chair.

Ceylen went into the living room and sat down. What to make of Mr. Vermeulen? He showed initiative, dug deeper when he was suspicious, didn't wait for approval from above, and he knew how to find information. All worrisome traits. Even more so because the cause of the investigation—a hundred thousand overcharged for cars—was not one he'd expected pushback on. That was mere pocket change in light of the value of the whole contract. Unless...

The nephew brought him a cup of coffee. The old man let it sit for a moment. He closed his eyes, breathed in the aroma and exhaled a moment later. Only then did he sip from the cup. The hot liquid burned its way to his stomach. It was a good burn. He took more sips. When the cup was empty, he knew what to do next.

First, Vermeulen wouldn't remain at his hotel. He'd be looking for nondescript lodging no more expensive than where he had stayed. Gaziantep had too many of those and he hadn't involved the local boss in the operation. So he couldn't call on outside help. The only option was to watch the UNHCR office. Vermeulen had to go back there. A couple of his men there should be able to keep track of him. Second, he needed to know if the car rental overage was indeed the only thing under investigation. If Vermeulen was sniffing around the cash card scam, then the need for intervention became a lot more urgent.

Eliminating Vermeulen as soon as possible would be the best solution. No dangling threads that could come back to bite him. Under ordinary circumstances, he'd have an assassin in place at the UNCHR office the next morning. But the circumstances weren't ordinary. Vermeulen was with the UN. A dead UN employee in southern Turkey would create an international nightmare. The place'd be swarming with cops. There'd be pressure on the government in Ankara to find the killer. President Erdoğan himself would get involved. That kind of scrutiny was bad for business at any time, but the next week was particularly sensitive. As long as the convoy was in transit, any hint that something was wrong in southern Turkey would be a disaster. Once in the warehouse, he'd breathe easier.

The better approach would be to find out what exactly Vermeulen knew. The only person who could help there was Balbay. So far he'd left the administrator alone. The cash card scam and the fake NGO had been cheaper and safer than bribing or threatening Balbay. It was time to have a personal talk with the man. As usual, patience was the key to paradise.

He took out his phone and speed-dialed a number. When the call was answered he said, "I need the mobile numbers for Bilek Balbay and anyone in his family." What good was operating a mobile phone shop as a front, if not to tap into the customer databases.

A half hour later a text message arrived. It was Balbay's mobile number and two other numbers. The note indicated that the two other numbers were registered to female names at the same address, most likely the wife and a daughter. Useful should Balbay demonstrate more spine than the old man expected.

At two in the morning he inserted a new SIM card into his phone and dialed the number. The phone rang for a long time, then rolled over to voice mail. He redialed. Again, the phone rang and rang. At the last moment a sleepy voice answered in what was more a croak than a word.

"Yes, Bilek. It's rather late or early, depending on your perspective, but there is an urgent matter I have to discuss. I suggest you get up and let your wife sleep in peace. This might take a while."

"Who is this? Are you out of your mind? D'you know what time it is?"

"It's two in the morning. Now get up."

He could hear a bed spring creaking, rustling noises as Balbay went somewhere private.

"Who are you?" Balbay said finally.

"I'm an old man who needs information. There is a UN investigator at your office looking at your books. Tell me what he's found so far."

There was a pause. Balbay was breathing into the phone. "This is confidential. Who are you?"

"I know it is confidential, if it weren't I wouldn't be calling you. So let me hear what he's found."

"This is outrageous. I'm going to hang up now and report your number to the police."

"Bilek, settle down. Reporting the number won't do any good. It won't exist by the time the police get around to checking it. I understand that telling me requires you to violate some rules, maybe even your personal moral code. I'm willing to compensate you for that. Would thirty-thousand lira be enough?"

There was silence on the other end.

"I see your conscience is a bit more expensive. I thought so. How about fifty-thousand lira? That sounds about right, doesn't it?"

The silence continued. It was a good sign. The fact that Balbay was holding out for more meant he could be bought.

"Fifty-thousand is more than fair, don't you think? So don't try to oversell yourself. It's the top price for the conscience of someone in your position. Are we in agreement?"

"No," Balbay said. "We are not."

"I must remind you, Bilek, that this isn't a game. I know where you live and I know you have a daughter. Wouldn't you rather enjoy fifty-thousand than forever look over your shoulder and worry about your child?"

"You leave my family out of this."

"I will, Bilek. But only if you agree."

There was renewed silence.

"Tell you what, Bilek. Tomorrow, someone will give your daughter a ride to school. She'll enjoy it. It's a nice car. Her friends will envy her."

"Leave my daughter out of this. I'll tell you what you want to know."

"Please proceed."

Balbay told him about the rental car overcharge and that they had followed up and found TurkOasis had rented cargo vans rather than cars. So far that matched what Vermeulen had told him. There was little chance Vermeulen had called Balbay and told him what to say.

"Good," the old man said. "That wasn't so hard. Was there anything else you need to tell me?"

This was the key moment. It all lay in the timing. If the "no" came too fast or after a long pause, the man was lying. Balbay's "no" fell in between. There was no obvious tell. Either the man knew how to lie or his "no" was genuine.

"Are you sure? This is a serious matter."

"Of course, I'm sure," Balbay said.

"I want to believe you, but I'm a suspicious person. So I think we'll give your daughter a ride to school tomorrow morning after all."

All the old man heard was a shriek on the other end. That's how blackmail works. Make a demand and lead the target to believe that fulfilling the demand will get him out from under the threat. So the victim does, and just when he's breathing a sigh of relief, you tighten the screw. It has nothing to do with the demand. It's all about power. The sap at the other end has to realize that he's completely powerless. Only then will you be certain to get the truth.

"So, Bilek, tell me again that there is nothing else Vermeulen is sticking his nose into."

A hesitation, then a croak, "There is."

"And what is that?"

"He's looking into the cash card contract."

"It would be nice if you could be more specific," the old man said.

"He knows that far fewer cash cards were ordered than the contract specified."

"Ah, that's what I needed to know. Has he asked about the warehouse?"

"Which warehouse?"

"The one where you store the mini-fridges and the hot plates."

There was a pause. "Why would he ask about that?" Balbay said.

"Well, if there's swindle in one part of the operation, why not check everything?"

"No, he has not asked about the warehouse."

"You're sure? Remember your daughter."

Balbay was reduced to a whimper. "No, I swear. He has not asked about the warehouse."

"Good. You see, Bilek, honesty is always the best approach. I'm sure your daughter would thank you for it if she knew. And remember the old saying *Keep the tongue in your mouth a prisoner*, otherwise your daughter will get a ride in a fine car and it won't be to her school."

He ended the call, turned his phone off, and removed the SIM card. He didn't think Balbay would call the police, but there was no reason to take chances. He told the driver to bring an ashtray and a lighter. He flicked the lighter and held the SIM card in the flame until the plastic melted.

VERMEULEN ATE HIS burger faster than he would have liked. The waitstaff putting chairs on empty tables was enough of a signal that lingering over his meal was not encouraged. Not that the place was worth lingering in. Too many neon lights, spelling out nonsensical phrases like "Save my education" next to a red "Love." Like all caricatures, the place captured the weirdness of an American burger joint of the 1960s; unlike a caricature, though, irony was completely absent. The booth made to look like a Checker cab wasn't meant as a joke. At least the burger was good and that made up for everything else.

Back in his car, he searched for one-star hotels on his phone. He needed a place at the outskirts of town. The old gangster was smart enough to know that Vermeulen would change hotels. That meant he'd put lookouts by the UNHCR office. A real problem because he still needed to get the printouts of the card recipients. But that was a problem for tomorrow.

He found what looked like a suitable place located near a highway interchange at the western end of the city. The two-story structure was so unremarkable he almost missed the turn-off. The lack of signage on the road was an added bonus. He checked in. His bed was hard but the shower was hot and that was all he needed.

TWENTY-FOUR

AHMADI SAT IN the passenger seat of a beat-up Volkswagen headed for Kilis. Erkin was driving. Kilis was just one of the cities covered in the survey, but since Ahmadi was more familiar with the town, Erkin had decided it'd be the best place for her to start. She was to serve as the translator. Once the sample of women had been interviewed, Ahmadi would likely come back to help in Gaziantep, which had a much larger refugee population.

Ahmadi read the questionnaire to familiarize herself with the procedure. Most questions were open-ended, meant to give the women space to answer as they wished. That also meant that the answers needed to be coded afterwards. More work for her. Erkin had told her they were aiming for two-hundred respondents in Kilis. They'd start out with the sample of women who'd contacted the women's center. From there, they'd widen their approach using the snowball method of asking each woman who else they should speak to.

As much as she appreciated Erkin and the center's help, the memory of her dead friend was foremost on Ahmadi's mind. She felt a little guilty that she'd taken this job under false pretenses, just a way to search for those responsible for Zada's death. But then she chided herself for even thinking that. The job needed to be done and her investigation wouldn't interfere. It'd be just another question she'd ask after translating the other ones. Her Turkish colleague might not even notice. A quick question in Arabic, nobody'd be the wiser.

They reached Kilis and the familiar sights boosted Ahmadi's spirits. Gaziantep was too big a city, Kilis was more her size. She could imagine a life here for as long as she couldn't go back home. It was also cheaper to stay here and she'd cleared with Erkin that she'd live in Kilis for the duration of the survey.

They reached the first address at the eastern fringes of the city. New construction in various stages of completion dominated the area. Some structures were mere concrete shells with dark holes for windows. Others were partially stuccoed or covered with a layer of bricks. The entire neighborhood had a bustling feel to it.

The house at the listed address looked like its owner had run out of money after completing the first floor. Piles of bricks were stacked on the concrete ceiling that cantilevered out from the wall to provide some shade. A new wall had been started upstairs, but looked like it had been abandoned some time ago. The ground floor was made of concrete blocks that hadn't been stuccoed. The two windows fitted poorly. The only adornment was the pink paint applied to the plastered entrance wall and the baby blue on the front door. Rust had broken through the paint like sores through skin.

Erkin knocked on the door and motioned for Ahmadi to stand next to her. The door opened and a woman wearing a black, full-length dress and a *hijab* appeared. She seemed to be in her forties. Ahmadi greeted her in Arabic and told her that they were from the Women's Center and wanted to ask her some questions. The woman seemed unsure.

"There's nothing to worry. We're not from the government. We're trying to find out what women refugees need. Just a few questions," Ahmadi said.

The woman grimaced. "My husband will come back soon. How long will this be? I'm cooking lunch."

"We could come back later."

The woman must have made a decision. "You can ask me in the kitchen. Better now than later."

They followed her into the stark apartment. There was concrete dust everywhere. The entire interior was unfinished. Unconnected wires were hanging from holes in the blocks where outlets and light switches were meant to go. Through a doorway they saw an equally bare room with a rug to soften the concrete floor. There were two plastic garden chairs, and a number of pillows. A little girl was sleeping on one and an older boy was sitting in one of the chairs, watching an ancient TV. The kitchen was bare except for a propane two-burner stove. A few groceries were piled in one corner. There were pots on each burner and the aroma made Ahmadi hungry.

"Go ahead, ask me what you want to know," the woman said.

They asked her where the family had come from and when they'd entered Turkey.

"We're from Aleppo," she said. "We tried to wait it out, but then things got worse. We left seven months ago."

"That must have been traumatic," Ahmadi said.

The woman shrugged, as if she no longer had the energy to recall that part of her life. She had gone to school, but got married and never had a job outside the home.

"Are there other members of your family in Turkey?"

The woman sighed and said, "Are you from Aleppo?"

Ahmadi nodded, not bothering to explain that she was actually from a small town south of Aleppo.

"Why do you even ask? You know what happened there. Yes, my sister's family is here, so are my parents. They left even before I did. My husband's brother and sister are in Turkey, too. Some are here. I don't know about the others. I haven't heard from them."

"What about services here. Like healthcare. Have you used doctors here?"

The woman became more animated. "Yes, it's very good. I took my children to the clinic for checkups and everybody was so friendly. Not like some of the Turks on the street. They did everything and even gave me pills for my boy's stomach."

"What about you, have you been to a gynecologist? Are you pregnant?"

The woman exhaled noisily. "Would you have a child while living here? I wouldn't. Anyway, I won't be pregnant again, so I don't need a woman's doctor."

The last questions were about living in Turkey. Ahmadi translated them and the woman became exasperated. "Of course we like it here. Nobody is shooting at us or dropping bombs on us. But it's expensive, and the Turks don't like us much. Once the war is over, we go back. I know everything we had is destroyed, but it's still home. We'll start over."

For Ahmadi, the results weren't a surprise. It fit with what she'd experienced picking grapes. But she understood the need to systematically gather data to tell aid agencies where and how to spend their money.

When they reached the end, Ahmadi asked who

else they should speak to. The woman suggested a few names. Before she turned to leave, she asked one more question. "Do you know Zada Homsi from Aleppo?"

The woman shrugged. "Can't say I do. Aleppo is a large city."

"What was that about?" Erkin said when they were outside.

"Nothing. Just checking if she knew someone I knew."

KNOWING THAT THERE'D be gangsters looking for him put Vermeulen on edge. He circled the block where the UNHCR office was located twice. Traffic wasn't too dense, but looking for suspicious people or cars while driving and keeping track of who was in front of you is not easy. He hadn't spotted any people loitering in the vicinity of the office. Cars were an entirely different issue. The fancy black Mercedes wasn't there, but he didn't think the old man was stupid enough to use it for surveillance.

After the third pass, he decided to find a spot to park and go inside. Vermeulen needed to get the address of the rental agency and find out what happened to the missing van and the list of the clients who were listed as having received cash cards. He should at least verify that a sample of the people didn't get their card before making grand accusations.

All of it felt like busy work. It wouldn't get him any closer to learning the identity of the old man. Or Oben Ösbek, for that matter. Instead of hunting the crooks, he was looking over his shoulder, because he was being hunted. Before entering the office, he decided not to tell Balbay about his abduction the night before. It didn't help the investigation and he didn't want to explain. The niggling pain in his neck was enough of a reminder.

Balbay muttered something in reply to his greeting, but kept staring at the screen of his laptop. Vermeulen shrugged and went to the temporary office and grabbed the printout of the recipients. If he tracked down twenty families who hadn't gotten their card, it should be enough evidence to convince his boss that UNHCR had been scammed. Still just busy work. Simply reporting on his conversation with Crescent Card should've been enough.

Back in Balbay's office, he said, "Can you give me the address of the rental agency? I want to follow up with them about the rentals and the missing van."

BalBay seemed deep in thought, and looked up as if surprised that there was someone in his office. "What?"

"The name and address of the car rental place."

"Oh. Right. Let me see."

He shuffled some papers. His silence seemed odd. Since they'd discovered the scam, Balbay had been solicitous, trying to help as much as possible. The motive may well have been self-preservation, but it still mattered. Being aloof as he was now wasn't his character.

"Ah, here it is," he said. "Green Rental. They have an office here and in Kilis."

"Does the contract say where the vans were rented?"

He peered at the contract in his hands.

"No. It doesn't."

"What about pickup location? Or were they delivered somewhere?"

More peering.

"Let me see," Vermeulen said, impatient now.

Balbay handed him the papers, avoiding eye contact. Something was off. The man wasn't at all like his usual self.

"What's going on? Anything happen since last night?"

"Uh, no. Nothing. Well, things at home aren't so well."

"You're probably spending too much time here. I know how that happens. The next thing you know you get an earful at home. You should leave early and take your wife out for dinner. You have kids?"

Balbay nodded.

"How many? Son, daughter?"

"One daughter."

Vermeulen saw that Balbay had difficulties keeping a straight face. And not because he was about to burst out in laughter.

"Everything okay with her? I have a daughter, too, and I know how much trouble they can be."

He plopped into the chair across from Balbay. "You want to talk about it?"

Balbay shook his head, the sorrow on his face replaced by panic.

"No, no. Everything is fine. No need to talk. You have what you need?"

Vermeulen looked at the contract. Some of the handwriting was illegible. He did see, however, that the scheduled pickup place was the branch in Kilis.

"I found the address I needed. Looks like I'll be taking another trip to Kilis."

"Oh, okay. Have a safe trip. Will you be coming back here?"

"I don't know what is going on, but if I didn't know better, I'd think you're trying to get rid of me."

"My apologies. I'm busy, there are other projects that need my attention. Stop by when you are done in Kilis." He turned back to his laptop.

Vermeulen stood there a full minute processing what had just happened. Balbay was really being weird. Something must have happened. Something that involved Vermeulen. Why else was he so eager to get rid of him?

Outside, he walked to his car, looking around for anyone following him. He started the engine and turned on the air conditioning. Had someone put pressure on Balbay? That would be a reasonable assumption. The look on Balbay's face when Vermeulen mentioned his daughter was fear. They could have threatened his daughter. Who? The old man? To get what? There wasn't a lot he could give away. Hell, Vermeulen had told him about the car rental discrepancy. The worst Balbay could have done was tell the old man that they knew about the cash card scam. That didn't matter anymore.

He took out his phone and dialed Balbay's number. When the man answered, he said, "Vermeulen here. Listen, Bilek. Don't worry. The safety of your daughter is the most important thing."

He hung up before Balbay could say anything. There was no need for a response. He started the car and eased into the traffic. After a mile, he merged onto the beltway and followed it until he reached the interchange with the Kilis highway. As he turned south, he noticed the same blue car that had been behind him since entering the highway taking the same exit. Either it was a tail or it wasn't. He didn't care one way or the other.

TWENTY-FIVE

DOING THE SURVEY WORK, as tedious as it was, put Ahmadi in touch with people who shared her fate. Meeting so many compatriots whose lives had been disrupted just like hers, who'd lost loved ones, made her feel less alone. An odd reaction, really. She'd expected the opposite, because she didn't buy into the idea that shared misery is easier to bear. Seeing the children bothered her most. Many seemed withdrawn, hiding behind their mothers' skirts well beyond the age one would expect them to.

As always, the women bore the brunt of the burdens of refugee life. They were expected to cook meals without proper kitchens, find groceries, keep track of what little money they had, and trade for what they couldn't get otherwise. It was the matter of fact manner in which many of them answered the survey that surprised Ahmadi. They didn't dwell on their misfortune, they'd taken charge. She felt solidarity with them, saw her own resolve mirrored in their daily struggle.

The only disappointment was the lack of information about Zada. None of the women she'd interviewed knew of her. One woman thought she remembered, but it turned out to be a different Zada. She told herself to be reasonable. The Kilis area was home to thousands of refugees. Even if many of them came from the Aleppo area, it was a stretch to imagine she'd find someone who knew Zada.

After interviewing ten women, Erkin suggested they break for lunch. They settled at a small restaurant. Ahmadi was happy to order her own food with her own cash. Finally a sign of normalcy.

"I'm surprised that seven of the women we've talked to hadn't gotten any money from the UN or the other NGOs," Erkin said after they'd ordered. "It was my understanding that a lot more had made it to those who needed it."

"How many do you think should have gotten some?" Ahmadi said.

"More than thirty percent, that's for sure. I'm on the email distribution list for organizations that support refugees and from what I read, the number should be around seventy percent, at least among those registered. There are always new arrivals, of course, but the women we surveyed all have been here longer than three months."

"The group of pickers I stayed with at that vineyard didn't get any cash either. They'd been here for a while. Some were registered. A friend of mine was. And she didn't get any money."

Erkin shrugged. "Bureaucracy, I guess. Getting money from the donors to the recipients always involves too many steps. The more middlemen there are, the more convoluted it becomes. Even worse, the NGOs compete with each other. I should know. Only when we get a grant or a contract, can we continue to pay our staff. The other organizations are in the same boat. Sometimes, surviving as an organization seems as important than the work we're supposed to be doing."

Ahmadi had never thought about it that way. It made

sense. The donors gave money, but individual groups or organizations distributed the money and supplies to those who were eligible. Some of the money given was used to pay the employees, like her own pay. The thought that she was making a living from money that was meant to help others disturbed her and she told Erkin as much.

"Oh. Rima, don't think of it that way. The people we serve don't get less because you get paid. Besides, this survey is used to determine what other services are needed for women refugees. So you are helping."

That assuaged her pang of guilt. Besides, it gave her an opportunity to find out what happened to Zada. Erkin might be sympathetic to her quest. Or she might be scared off by the fact that the police were involved. It was worth a try.

"This friend I mentioned," she said. "Her name was Zada and she was busy trying to make all our lives more bearable."

"What happened to her?"

"She was found dead."

"Oh. How sad. I'm so sorry. So you know what happened?"

"I don't. It was all very odd."

The arched eyebrows on Erkin's face told her to be careful.

"The last message I received from Zada was that she had found out something that would make our lives easier. She left the camp where we stayed and never came back. Then we got the news that she was dead. It scared me."

BY THE TIME Vermeulen reached Kilis, the blue car following him had settled about six car lengths behind him. It maintained that position even when other cars came between them. Since Vermeulen was sticking to the speed limit, those cars eventually passed him, giving him a clear view of the blue car. He couldn't tell if the driver was alone. The air outside was hot and shimmering.

At first, Vermeulen had worried about another attack, but the car following was about the size of his rental. A side swipe wasn't an option. He was being shadowed to make sure he didn't take an earlier exit.

He pulled off at the first Kilis exit and drove into a large gas station. He didn't need gas yet, but a full tank is always a good idea. You never knew when you'd need it. He pulled up to the pump and told the attendant to fill up. He took out his phone to search for hotels in Kilis. There were only four, including the one where he'd stayed before. It wouldn't take much to find him there. He was searching for inns and B&Bs when the attendant came to take his money. Vermeulen paid and parked by the mini-mart attached to the station.

As far as his phone was concerned, there were no other inns, pensions or B&Bs in Kilis. However, one of the options his search produced was an online vacation rental agency. Perfect and anonymous. No front desk manager who could be bribed to reveal the guest list. He entered the place and date and found four private rooms and one apartment for rent. The apartment had off-street parking which clinched the deal. The price was ridiculously low. Even paying the week-long minimum rental, it was still cheaper than three days in a hotel. He booked online, paid with his credit card and received an email that he could occupy the apartment in one hour. The message also contained the entry code for the gate. He went into the mini-market and bought a cup of coffee. Through the window he could see the blue car parked near the edge of the gas station. There was only a driver. A young man as far as he could make out. He hadn't seen him before.

Forty-five minutes later, he got back into his car, tapped the address of the apartment into his map app and drove off. All he had to do was lose the blue car.

The road into town was busier than the highway. The blue car pulled closer, two car lengths behind. Whoever was driving it had to know that he'd noticed the tail. If the driver maintained that distance, losing him wouldn't be as easy. It took finding the right moment and then acting fast.

That moment arrived sooner than expected. The road ended in a large roundabout. This was pretty much the best chance he'd get. He entered the circle and increased his speed, dodging cars both left and right. With all the traffic in the circle, the blue car had trouble keeping up. His tires squealing, he raced around the circle back to where he'd started. He waited until the last moment and swerved back onto the road that he'd come on. His front left tire hit a curb with a frightening sound, he yanked the wheel over, the rear fishtailed, pushing the car into a spin. He steered against it and managed to stay in the lane.

In the rearview mirror he saw the blue car boxed in by traffic, forced to go around once more. That gave Vermeulen enough time to make his escape. He cornered hard at the next intersection, entered a broad boulevard, shot toward the next crossing and dove into a dense warren of streets. He turned randomly left and right, his map app continuously recalculating the route to his apartment. After five turns, he felt safe enough to drive to the apartment.

When the electric gate closed behind him, he breathed out. So far so good. Except for his left front tire. It was almost flat. There had better be a jack and a spare in the trunk.

TWENTY-SIX

THE GREEN RENTAL branch where TurkOasis had picked up its vans was at the eastern outskirts of Kilis—a large parking lot and a single room office surrounded by a fence topped with barbed wire. A dozen vans were parked in neat rows. The only sedan Vermeulen saw stood next to the office. It was near closing time and Vermeulen hoped that the desire to go home would make answers to his questions more forthcoming.

The inside was as bare as an office could be, a desk, two chairs and a computer. This wasn't a place that catered to tourists or families renting a car for the weekend. Two men looked up as he entered, the younger one wearing blue overalls stained with grease spots, the older one wearing a suit. Vermeulen introduced himself and showed his UN ID. The man in the suit shook his hand with an expression of distaste as if he were the CEO of Avis having to deal with a petty customer complaint. So Vermeulen was more than happy when the mechanic ended up being the translator since the suit's English was less than rudimentary. He showed them a copy of the contract and both nodded. Yes, they had rented vans to TurkOasis. How many? Eight overall, but at different times. What about the missing van?

"It was in a wreck," the young guy said. "Pretty much destroyed."

"But you had insurance, right?"

The young guy shrugged and asked the suit. The answer sounded less than happy. The mechanic explained why.

"Insurance didn't cover everything. The renters were supposed to pay a share and they never did. We tried to find them, but the address was no good, so we lost money."

"Any idea what they used the vans for?"

The young guy shrugged again, asked the suit, who checked his watch and made like he was ready to lock up. The mechanic said they had to close now.

Vermeulen shook his head. This damn investigation had all the qualities of the molasses they made in Kilis. He was stuck in it and couldn't move in any direction. Meanwhile, the bad guys were on him like ants on a watermelon at a picnic. There had to be some traces left by the organization. You don't pull off a scam this big and just disappear. He knew there was no such thing as the perfect crime, but this one was starting to look like a close contender.

He thanked them for the information and went back to his car. The suit got into the sedan and drove off. The mechanic waited for Vermeulen to leave so he could lock the gate. Vermeulen rolled up to the gate, stopped and lowered the window. "I'm pretty sure you know how the vans were used, you had to clean them afterwards."

The mechanic looked to make sure his boss was gone, then motioned Vermeulen to lean closer. "I do," he whispered. "They were used for smuggling."

"You're sure?"

"One hundred percent."

"What makes you say that?"

"They reeked of petrol and diesel afterwards. You won't believe how much I worked to clean them up. I shampooed the seats, washed out the loading area. Unbelievable."

"They smuggled gasoline from Syria?"

"Sure, and they weren't the only ones. They drive across the border to the *Daesh* fuel depots, fill up and leave again. Sometimes, they stay in Turkey and fill up from pipes that come under the border."

"Wait," Vermeulen said. "The van that was in an accident? Was that on the Gaziantep highway? Last Sunday?"

"Yeah. That's what the police said. Good there was no fire. That would have been bad. They had to clean up a lot of petrol afterwards. A real mess. The highway was closed for a while."

"I saw that accident. It happened right in front of me."

"It did? You're a lucky man."

"It came from some dirt road and tried to drive up a berm onto the highway. Almost hit me, too."

The mechanic thought about that.

"That explains a lot," he said.

"What?"

"It explains why I had to replace the shocks on three of the vans after they came back. Those idiots must've raced them on dirt roads loaded like crazy."

"And they sell the gas around here?"

"Yeah, here, in Gaziantep. All over the place. Stations buy from them cheap. Make more profit that way."

"Any other smuggling?"

"Sure. Guns, ammunition, uniforms. Some legal, most not. War is good business."

"And your vans were used for that too?"

"I found loose cartridges in a couple of the vans. They must've rolled there and nobody cared to pick them up."

"What about the Turkish authorities? The police and military? Isn't supporting ISIS against the government's policy?"

The mechanic looked around, fear in his face. "You better not ask those questions. Nobody else does."

"Okay. One last question. Did you keep a record of the different drivers who checked out the vans?"

"Sure."

"Could I look at them?"

The mechanic shook his head. "The police came here to find the driver who crashed the van. My boss said that the papers had been stolen."

Vermeulen looked into the distance and slowly shook his head again. He couldn't catch a break.

"Don't worry. I remember that driver. He was a real jerk. I knew he was trouble. Had a pistol stuck in his pants, like the idiot wants to shoot his cock off. His name is Temir Korun."

He spelled out an address in Kilis and Vermeulen jotted it down on the gas receipt he found in the center console.

"But you didn't tell the police?" he said,

"They never ask me. Listen, I've already said too much. You better leave. I need to close up."

BACK AT THE APARTMENT, Vermeulen took his notebook and began sketching the new information he'd just received. The different boxes he'd drawn earlier weren't just odd coincidences. They were connected. Which changed the whole equation dramatically. He wasn't looking at a sham NGO that weaseled a couple million dollars out of the UNHCR. He was looking at a criminal network, complex and far reaching. Gun running, gas smuggling, cash card scamming, this wasn't some half-assed operation, even if his kidnapping seemed poorly organized and executed. It all added up to way more than his experience with the old man had led him to believe.

It also meant that he was in way over his head. The UN related crimes were probably minor compared to the totality of what the old man was doing. If he wasn't Özbek, who was? Maybe the old man was in charge of the entire operation, and Özbek was just running the fraudulent NGO and the sweatshop.

What if the *Selim Tekstil* was just a front? A few sewing machines up front for show and a lot of other things going on in the back. But they did hire that boy Tariq. So they were making something there. Why bother hiring refugee kids in violation of all kinds of labor laws when nothing of substance was being made?

He tapped the speed dial on his phone and called Gaby. He got her voicemail and asked if she could send him the list of the companies registered by Oben Özbek and where they had been registered.

The next person he called was Inspector Demirel. He wanted to find out more about the wreck last Sunday and if they had found the driver. No answer there either and Vermeulen left another message.

The final call was to Balbay. He was still in his office.

"Hi, Bilek, sorry to bother you again. On the drive down it occurred to me that I never checked on the warehouse with all the non-food items. Can you tell me the name of the company that you retained to manage it?"

"Just a second, I'll look it up. Why do you need it?"

"It may be nothing, but I'm not taking anything for granted at the moment."

"Hold on." Vermeulen could hear rustling papers over the phone. "Ah, here it is. The name *BenBek Lojistik*."

That name didn't mean anything to Vermeulen. "I'd like you to visit the warehouse tomorrow. Make sure that the mini-fridges and hot plates are still there. According to the inventory report, there should be several thousand. Call me when you've checked."

Vermeulen decided not to mention his earlier call. The less said, the better. Of course, he'd have to report that Balbay had been compromised. Balbay was quiet. Vermeulen clearly had just ruined his day, but, hey, that was his job.

"I can't. Not tomorrow. I've got appointments all day long," he said eventually. Before Vermeulen could say anything, Balbay added, "I'll go first thing Saturday. It shouldn't make a difference one way or another." He ended the call before Vermeulen could reply. Well, Saturday would be okay. One day wouldn't make a difference. Either the items were there, or they weren't. Nobody would cart them away overnight.

He showered and changed clothes. There was a washing machine in the apartment and he was tempted to run a load. He needed fresh clothes. But there was no dryer and he didn't know how to get his shirts ironed. The tourist brochures on the kitchen table included a map of Kilis. The apartment location was marked. It wasn't far from the center of the city. Another sheet listed restaurants in the vicinity. There were a lot to choose from. Unfortunately, there was no list of laundries or cleaners. He checked the map app on his phone and found one not too far from the restaurant he'd picked. He took his dirty clothes bag, stuck his phone in his pocket and left for errands and dinner.

TWENTY-SEVEN

THE CLEANER WAS still open and Vermeulen left his clothes. Communication was haphazard, but he managed to convey to the owner that he wanted his shirts ironed. Back on the street, he headed for the restaurant he'd chosen. He picked a table near the back and ordered from a waiter who knew enough English to explain the menu to him. The beer arrived not a second too soon. He finished half the glass in the first sip and sunk back into the chair. It had been a long day. His meal, roasted lamb, rice and an eggplant salad, came soon. He ordered another beer and started to eat. The meat was tougher than he expected, more mutton than lamb. But it tasted fine and made him eat slower.

The door opened and two women entered. The first one wore jeans and a blouse, and hadn't covered her brown hair. The second one kept a shawl over part of her hair. He did a double take. The clothes were different, but those almond eyes set rather far apart and the slightly off-center nose looked very familiar. It was Rima Ahmadi. Her reaction was the same. Vermeulen rose from his seat and stopped. Their last meeting had ended on a negative note. She might not even want to talk to him again. That worry was quickly dispelled.

"What are you doing here?" Ahmadi said. "I thought you weren't coming back to Kilis."

"Famous last words, I guess. It turns out, I still have work here, after all. What about you?"

"Thanks to Ayla and the Women's Center, I'm finally registered, and I have a job with the Center, too."

"Congratulations."

Ahmadi turned to her companion and said, "This is Mr. Vermeulen. He works for the United Nations. He helped me with the police..." She thought for a moment. "Oh my, that was only a week ago. It seems so much longer. Mr. Vermeulen, this is Ayla Erkin, she heads the Gaziantep branch of the Women's Center."

Vermeulen shook hands with Erkin.

"Would you like to join me?" he said. "Unless, of course, you have private business to discuss."

The two women looked at each other, nodded, and accepted his invitation. They seemed as ready for dinner as he'd been. After ordering, Erkin asked Vermeulen what his duties at the UN were. He explained the role of OIOS and his particular tasks in Turkey.

"And have you found something that needs attention?" she said.

Nothing like a direct question to get his attention. Not what he'd thought of when he invited them to join him. It was supposed to be dinner, not an interrogation. Unlike during his earlier encounter with Ahmadi, he now had real evidence of fraud. It wasn't public and he couldn't share it until he'd written his report and OIOS had publicized it.

"Did you ever receive a cash card?" he said to Ahmadi.

"Yes, I did. Just a couple of days ago. After I registered as a refugee. The Migration Management people sent me to an NGO to pick up my card."

"Which NGO was that?"

"A British one, Refugee Aid something."

"Can I see it?"

Ahmadi pulled it from her pocket. It looked like any ATM chip card, except it had the logo of the aid organization and UNHCR on it.

"Thanks. Did you know if your friend Zada ever had one?"

"None of the people I knew had one," Ahmadi said. "Now I'm thinking that this is what Zada was looking into when she was killed."

One of the persistent frustrations of his job were the limits to what the UN could do once OIOS had unearthed criminal behavior. When a crime was committed by a contractor, a peacekeeper or similar personnel, all the UN could do was terminate the contract and ban future contracts. Punishment of the crime was the responsibility of the country where the crime was committed, or the country of nationality. And there, as often as not, the trail disappeared in some bureaucratic quicksand. If he could establish a link between a murder and the fraud, there'd be added pressure for the police to do their job.

Ahmadi told Erkin more about her friend Zada. How, despite the difference in ages, they'd bonded over similar experiences.

"And you think she got in trouble over the cash cards?" Erkin said. Her face showed her incredulity. How could anyone get into trouble over something as mundane as a cash card?

"It's the only thing that makes sense," Ahmadi said.

"I'm pretty sure she's right," Vermeulen said. He let

that hang there, wishing he'd kept his mouth shut. But it was too late. The two women looked at him.

"What do you know about TurkOasis?" he said to Erkin.

She pursed her lips. "Hmm. Not much, really. They showed up maybe seven, eight months ago. The usual NGO bulletins suddenly carried their name, and the contracts they'd gotten. It was nice to see a Turkish organization getting in on the game instead of all the big European and American outfits."

"Why?" Vermeulen said.

"I was hoping they'd be around longer than the foreigners who jump on to the next disaster when the current one is no longer the big thing. Who wants to donate money for Syrian refugees after a year? They need a new disaster, South Sudan, Central African Republic, wherever, to keep their fundraising machines going."

"And did they?"

"I don't know. They've been quiet for a while now. Their name hasn't popped up in the newsletters the past couple of months."

"Did you ever meet anyone from the organization?"

She scratched her chin. "Now that you mention it, no. That's strange. Hmm. They probably were one of those outfits that subcontracted a lot."

"Did you know what exactly they did?"

Erkin grimaced. "Not really. Refugee work, of course, but I'm not exactly clear what specifically."

"Did they handle cash cards?" Ahmadi said. She had obviously caught on to Vermeulen's game of deflecting their questions with questions of his own.

"Does the name Oben Özbek mean anything to you?" Vermeulen said to Erkin, ignoring Ahmadi's question.

Erkin thought for a moment, then said, "No. It's not a common name. Was he involved with the TurkOasis?"

"That's the man who owns the textile factory where Tariq works," Ahmadi said. "What does he have to do with cash cards?"

"I didn't say anything about cash cards," Vermeulen said. "But yes, that name was mentioned in connection with *Selim Tekstil*."

Erkin stared at Vermeulen, then at Ahmadi, and back again. "What's going on here? Who is Tariq? You keep asking me all these questions and Rima is answering. I have no clue what we're talking about."

It was time for Vermeulen and Ahmadi to look at each other. The anger that marked their last encounter had vanished. And having an ally was a good thing.

Ahmadi explained their history, the police station, the phone call, the attack by the pickup, meeting Tariq who was sent to shadow Vermeulen, and finding the sweatshop where Tariq worked. Erkin looked like she was wondering what she'd gotten into by hiring Ahmadi.

"How did you find out it was owned by Oben Özbek?" Ahmadi said.

"I asked my daughter in Düsseldorf to check the company registers she had access to on her job. It turns out that Özbek is listed as the owner of several other companies. How about you?"

"I just asked the men at the factory." She grinned.

"Did you ever run across an old man with bushy eyebrows, hooded eyes and grimly set lips, wearing plain clothes?" Vermeulen said to Erkin.

"There are thousands of such men around here. Why are you asking?" Erkin said.

It wasn't a question Vermeulen wanted to answer. He'd decided to keep the kidnapping and questioning by the old man quiet for now. It served no purpose to have that story spread. It would taint his job in ways that weren't helpful. Once people thought he had a personal axe to grind, his credibility as a UN representative was gone. Better to play it safe.

"I came across a rather suspicious character who looked like that," he said. "Just wondering if he could be Oben Özbek. I have a different question, though. How deeply is the government engaged in the war in Syria? I heard of all kinds of smuggling going on with the police looking the other way."

Erkin's eyes widened. She put her index finger against her lips and looked around.

"Don't even say those words," she whispered, leaning in. "Erdoğan has spies everywhere, especially this close to the border."

Vermeulen couldn't help but check the restaurant too. It was silly. Nobody had stopped what they were doing. Conversations continued uninterrupted, nobody had taken out a little notebook or was whispering into a phone.

"You think I'm paranoid?" Erkin said. "Not so. People around here support the president. He doesn't even need spies. Ordinary folks will confront you if you're openly critical of Erdoğan."

"We could go to my place and talk there."

Erkin shook her head. "Doing the work we do is difficult enough. We don't need no more troubles."

"Did you just quote Bob Marley?" he said.

Erkin smiled for the first time since they met.

"I'll call you," Ahmadi said to Vermeulen.

TWENTY-EIGHT

BACK AT THE APARTMENT, Vermeulen received two calls.
The first one was from Inspector Demirel.

"I thought you were done with Kilis," the inspector said.

"I had hoped so, but things didn't turn out that way.
The accident that Sunday morning, did you ever catch
the driver?"

"Why do you want to know?"

"During my investigation, I found that a contractor of
UNHCR had rented vans instead of cars and that these
vans weren't used for the purposes their contract specified. There is a likelihood that the van that crashed on
the highway was one of those rented by the contractor."

Demirel said nothing. Since Vermeulen had nothing to add, he did the same. After a minute, the silence
turned into a competition. After two minutes, Demirel
blinked.

"Who is that contractor?"

"Did you catch the driver?"

More silence. Finally, Demirel said in a small voice,
"No, he disappeared. You were the only one who saw
him. By the time the uniforms arrived, he was gone."

Vermeulen waited a beat. "His name is Temir Korun.
See if you can pick him up."

There was a pause. "How do you know?" Demirel said.

"I talked to the mechanic at the rental place."

"Ah. I bet my men talked to the boss. Damn, I do have to do everything myself."

"Sometimes it feels that way, doesn't it?"

"Tell me about the contractor," Demirel said.

Vermeulen hesitated. He'd be in trouble if information was leaked before he filed his report. But Demirel's help would be welcome. It would all come out soon anyway.

"This isn't official yet, so don't repeat it anywhere, but it was a scam. An NGO set up for the sole purpose of defrauding the UNHCR. The name was TurkOasis. And guess what, its president is Oben Özbek, the same man who owns *Selim Tekstil*. I can't find any information about the NGO anywhere."

The renewed silence had a different quality, more like commiseration than competition.

"Where are you now?" Demirel said.

"Back in Kilis."

"D'you want to meet for a drink?"

"Sure. But there are people looking for me, so we can't be seen in a popular place."

"There are people after you? Who? The police?"

Vermeulen hesitated a moment. "No, not the police, it's not really relevant right now."

"Where are you staying? I hope not in a hotel."

"No, a vacation rental."

"Give me the address, I'll come there."

Vermeulen did so and ended the call. His phone rang immediately. This time it was Gaby.

"Hey, Dad, got your message. How are you?"

"Hi, sweetheart, great to hear your voice. I'm okay, mostly, stuck in the middle of a morass of fraud. And you?"

"Busy, as always, but it's a good busy. So, it sounds like this Oben Özbek is involved in whatever you're dealing with."

"He is. Özbek is the *eminence gris* around here. Somehow he's involved but nobody knows who he is. Things have gotten bad here. Worse than I'd anticipated."

"Be careful, okay? Usually when things go bad you get hurt."

"I am careful. But someone is after me and I don't know who he is. He says he's not Oben Özbek and I have no evidence to prove the contrary. But he's behind a major fraud. They ripped off at least two million dollars from the UNHCR."

"Really? Money that was meant for refugees? That's terrible."

"They created a fake NGO and got the contract for the cash cards, but kept most of the cash. There's other stuff going on, too. That's why I asked for the list of companies. Last week, you said something about money laundering. I figured they have to rinse that money somehow, so maybe there's a connection."

"I'll email you the list tomorrow morning. I don't have it at home. Listen, about the money laundering, I know you've dealt with financial crimes since before I was born. So just a heads up, the methods have changed a lot. The crooks no longer use cash businesses to make their loot look like clean earnings."

Vermeulen had to smile. There was a time when Gaby had hated his job at the Prosecutor's office in Antwerp, hated the fact that he spent more time at work than with his family. He remembered a particular moment a few months before the divorce, when she told him that she'd rather starve as an artist than become a lawyer. Back then, that remark had stopped their fighting for a moment because both remembered that Gaby had, only days earlier, proclaimed rather pompously that she'd decided she had no talent for art. The levity of that moment didn't last and she swore she'd never go near the kind of job that kept her from her family. And here she was, thirteen years later, still single, putting in long hours at her global logistics company, telling her dad about money laundering.

"I know," he said. "There aren't enough pizza shops in the world to launder the billions illegally earned every day."

"Right. Today it's done internationally, with offshore letterbox companies and more often than not facilitated by supposedly reputable banks. It's a huge game. I have to deal with it every day. Do these goods we're forwarding actually exist, or did we just send an empty container around the world and thus helped a crook launder his loot."

"Good, I'll keep my eyes open. How are things otherwise. Is there finally a man in your life?"

"Oh Dad, you keep asking that. I'm too busy for flings and I haven't yet met anyone who I can imagine spending the rest of my life with. You'll be the first one to know when that changes."

He doubted that very much, but didn't say so.

"Have you talked to Tessa?" Gaby said.

"No, not yet."

"Call her. Now. You're in trouble, I know. We talked the other day and she was worried that you hadn't called."

"I don't want her to worry, that's why I didn't call."

"Come on, Dad. You guys are living together. Call her."

"Okay, I will."

"I mean it, Dad."

His doorbell rang.

"Gotta go, someone's at the door."

He ended the call and went to the entrance door. A peek through the peephole confirmed that it was Demirel outside. He opened the door.

Demirel held out a bottle.

"Here. You have to try this before you leave."

Vermeulen took the bottle. The label said *Yeni Rakı Ala*. The liquid inside was clear.

"What is it?"

"The best *rakı* you can drink short of knowing a distiller and getting some *özel rakı*."

"But what is it?"

"It's booze. Turkey's finest. Like *Pernot* in France, only far better. You have ice?"

"I haven't checked the freezer yet."

There was ice and there were glasses and water. Demirel made a show of teaching him the proper preparation of the drink.

"Nobody drinks *rakı* straight. Most put cold water and ice in, some just ice and have the water on the side."

He fixed two glasses. When he poured the water, the clear liquid turned milky. They toasted.

At first the strong anise flavor seemed overpowering, but that sensation quickly faded and left only a cool feeling in his mouth that seemed to spread through his entire body.

"You like it," Demirel said. "I can see. Good. Turkey's contribution to world civilization. That and bureaucracy."

"I'm afraid others had their hand in that too."

"Sure, but the English language doesn't have the word *Byzantine* for nothing."

They drank more.

"So tell me," Demirel said. "Who's after you?"

CEYLEN WAS GLAD to be back in his office in the back of the TekCell shop in Kilis. It was his home base, from where he ran his organization, where he received supplicants who needed help, a quick loan, or a conflict settled. Gaziantep always felt like he was just visiting. Kilis was his city, even though his organization and reputation reached far beyond even Gaziantep. In Kilis he got things done without having to rely on men who worked for those who owed him favors. Every time he called in a favor from a local boss, he owed something in return. He'd always made sure his account had more credits than debits. You don't become a godfather by owing others.

The office was quiet. The shop had closed. The idiot of a nephew was waiting in the car. He looked at the map of southern Turkey on the wall. Fifty years ago, he'd started carrying heroine across the border. A tiny node in the network that funneled drugs to Germany and the rest of Europe. Today he controlled this section of the network.

When Kilis became its own province in 1994, he made sure the new government bureaucrats knew his generosity. By then he was known as a community minded man, because he believed in the proverb that he who's considerate in prosperity will not be afflicted in adversity. First, he donated school books, then computers to the local school, endowed a scholarship at the local university, financed summer vacations for poor kids. It was another way to launder his ill-gotten profits through legal fronts and the recipients became his supporters. The politicians liked his benevolence. It made up for their own bungling.

Heroin was the mainstay of his operation, even today, but he never ignored new opportunities. After the Soviet invasion of Afghanistan, he added weapons to the mix. The continued unrest kept his profits flowing. When the civil war started in Syria, he was the closest source and he crashed in. Now the guns made the counterfeit drugs from India, fake shoes, and cigarettes mere afterthoughts.

Of course, he'd also attracted attention from the authorities. There were always some who couldn't be bribed. He'd made sure that their impact was limited by those on his payroll. Occasionally, the balance shifted against him. There were campaigns to clean up public life, honest politicians, muckraking journalists. A strategic death, sometimes overt, sometimes covert, usually kept those efforts in check. The past couple of years were different. The rise of *Daesh* had weakened his network. Sure the money was still flowing, but negotiations were hard. Fanatics are impossible to accommodate. They only take and never give. Reciprocity is alien to them. Even some of his men had gone over. Fools. Little did they know that they were joining a criminal operation far less forgiving than the mafia. Already, one had begged to come back after displeasing one of his black-clad commanders simply because he looked at the man's "bride."

The presence of *Daesh* had also increased official scrutiny of all happenings at the border. Which was bad for his network. Once the pressure from NATO to control and keep track of who and what crossed the border had filtered down to local officials, the result was confusion. Some flipped a hundred-eighty degrees and refused any bribe whatsoever. Others just got greedier. Once solid arrangements suddenly were up in the air, depending on the whim of the moment. Add to that the military maneuvers and you had a dicy situation.

But there were also upsides. Supplying weapons was the most important one. The demand was insatiable. Funny how men who wanted to turn the clock back to the stone age had a pressing thirst for the latest gadgets as long as it could kill their opponents. He saw that opportunity right away and was among the first to get in. His largest shipment yet was en route. Lots of bribes had been paid. Important politicians were looking the other way. So were the cops he'd paid off.

The refugees were the other upside. They provided cheap labor, they needed money and would pay usurious rates because they thought the loan was only for a short time, and it brought a lot more money to the region. The cash card scam set up by his niece was one way to cash in. She'd done well until that godforsaken UN investigator stumbled onto the scene. Now it threatened his entire operation. A measly two million dollar scheme undermining the weapons deal worth a hundred times as much. He couldn't let that happen.

The eyes of the world were on Turkey and how it dealt with the refugee crisis. Erdoğan's government used it to demonstrate to the world its humanitarian qualities. Turkey was leading the world in refugee set-

tlement and support, and didn't want to miss an opportunity to show off. It was also a useful bargaining
chip when it came to the European Union and potential
membership. All this was at stake if Vermeulen publicized his findings. The government would ignore any
previous arrangements and make an example of him.
That's why he should have asked for help in Gaziantep
instead of going it alone.

Part of it was his goddamn vanity. He didn't want
to admit that he couldn't deal with a single bureaucrat
on his own. But there also were obligations and promises he'd made. Cutting in the local boss would've cost
him. Now that reasoning looked stupid. If he'd thought
about it rationally, he'd have called for help the moment it became clear that Vermeulen was an elephant.
There is no right way to do a wrong thing. How often
had he preached that to his men? And yet, he'd ignored
his own advice.

Well. Tomorrow would be different. Vermeulen
made a mistake coming back to Kilis. His men were
scouring the city. They'd barely missed him after the
manager of the van rental had called. It wouldn't be
long before they'd find him. They knew every hotel
and every guest house in Kilis.

TWENTY-NINE

"AN OLD MAN?" Demirel said. "Describe him."

Vermeulen started with the bushy eyebrows and sunken eyes and the plain clothes, the grim lips and the bent posture. "He's got a really fancy Mercedes-Benz and a driver."

"Ah. Just as I thought. You've been tangling with Mehmed Ceylen."

Demirel finished his *rakı* and poured himself another one. He pointed the bottle at Vermeulen, who nodded. Their glasses refilled, Vermeulen said, "And who is Mehmed Ceylen when he's at home? He's not by any chance Oben Özbek, is he?"

"Who? No. He's the local mob boss extraordinaire." He raised his glass. "A toast to Valentin. You survived an encounter with Ceylen." They clinked glasses and drank. "There are quite a few who can't claim the same."

"Why is he still around?" Vermeulen said.

"Like all mob bosses everywhere, he's an expert of the arm's length approach. We have no evidence that links him to any crime, even though we know he's responsible for them. He's paid off who needs to be paid off, his crimes rarely affect the local community, but a lot of peoples' livelihood depends on his goodwill. You really were alone with him and his driver in Gaziantep?"

"Yes, they held me in an apartment."

"How'd you get away?"

"I hit the driver upside the head with a folding chair I was tied to. The whole kidnapping was of such amateurish quality. If he's really such an important mob boss, why didn't he do this right?"

"Either he was surprised and really did improvise or he didn't want to call on the Gaziantep boss. Maybe that fraud you uncovered cut out the local crooks. That'd be enough reason for bad blood. It had to be something like that because men of his position usually don't get involved with the dirty work. How did he find out about you?"

"I think he saw me outside an apartment building. I'd gone there because that address had popped up on an old version of the TurkOasis's website. It was removed later. So I went there, but there was no office in that building. I had a coffee at a ground floor café. He and his driver walked right by me. I remember thinking that he was probably visiting a mistress, but then he came back out again too fast. He must have been surprised seeing me there. So does that mean there is a crosshair on my back?"

"You better believe it. Right now, you are the only one who can put him behind bars. They're out looking for you right now. How safe is this place? Did you speak to anyone about it?"

"Just you. The entire reservation process was online."

"Good. That means it will take some work to find out where you're staying."

Vermeulen finished his drink. Demirel followed suit

and made to pour another. Vermeulen held up his hand, but Demirel ignored it. Vermeulen added water.

"There are a couple of other names I want you to check on," Vermeulen said. "This Oben Özbek and Yesim Yaser. They were listed as president and vice president respectively for the NGO. Do those names mean anything to you?"

"Yesim is the old man's niece, the apple of his eye."

"He doesn't have any kids of his own?"

"No, but he relies on his brother's family. Yesim is being groomed for a top position. Probably going to be the first female mob boss in Turkish history. Her older brother turned out to be a dope. Definitely not management material."

"And what about Özbek?" Vermeulen said.

"No idea. Never heard that name."

"Are there cops in the old man's pocket?"

"Sure. His generosity extends far and wide."

"Like who? How high up?"

"Hard to tell. Think of that attack with the pickup. Obviously someone must have called him from the police station. That's how they knew to follow you. My money is on one of the cops who brought you in. How high it goes, I can't tell you."

"So you could be on his payroll too?"

"Sure. He paid for the *rakı*. Do you think I could afford such a nice bottle on my inspector's salary." He paused a beat. "Come on, man, I wouldn't be sitting here drinking with you. I'd have called him as soon as I knew your address and one of his goons would have shot you right through the eye when you looked out the peephole."

That comment made Vermeulen swallow. "So why are you, a Turkish cop, helping me?"

"I've wondered about that too." Demirel downed more *rakı*. "Maybe I'm just a nice guy. But seriously, I wouldn't mind getting a few things cleaned up around here. The problem with mobsters like Ceylen is that they slowly corrode the bonds of our community. It starts with a bit of graft here, a small bribe there. Nothing big enough to worry about. But it sets the tone. It lowers the expectations that people have of themselves."

He poured more *rakı*. Vermeulen shook his head, but Demirel filled both glasses anyway.

"You see," Demirel said, his words slurry now. "Mine is a foolish one-man battle against corruption. But then fighting foolish battles is in my DNA."

"How's that?"

"My last name. It's Demirel, right? Well, my father changed it from Demirer, because it was a Kurdish last name. He didn't want his sons to be labeled enemies in their own country. The Armenians taught us what happens after you've become the designated enemy. Those who survived are in exile now. The Kurds are still fighting. As to our future, I'm not holding my breath."

They were both quiet.

"It's not foolish," Vermeulen said after a while. "Justice is never foolish." Maybe it was the booze talking, but he knew he'd met a kindred soul, a man who kept doing his job, all evidence of futility notwithstanding. He raised his glass.

"To justice."

Demirel raised his and said, "Or what little bit of it we might achieve."

They downed the liquor.

Demirel looked at his watch. "Shit, I better go home."

"Is there someone waiting for you?"

The sad smile on Demirel's face was enough of an answer.

"Don't forget to check on this Oben Özbek," Vermeulen said. "His name has popped up way too often."

"What? Is having a mobster on your tail not enough trouble for you?" Demirel stroked his mustache. "Where else have you seen that name?"

"In addition to being with TurkOasis, he owns several companies."

"That's all? Not a lot to go on. Lots of people own several companies."

"He owns a sweatshop here in Kilis," Vermeulen said.

Demirel raised his eyebrows. "How do you know that?"

"Long story, but my daughter works for a global logistics company in Düsseldorf and she looked him up. Apparently, he also owns a slew of other companies. My daughter thinks it's a scheme for tax evasion."

"Example?"

"Well, that sweatshop. The morning after that pickup incident, I noticed that a young boy was watching me. I took him to lunch and Rima talked to him. He's a Syrian refugee and works in a sweatshop called *Selim Tekstil*. That's why I asked my daughter and, according to the Turkish Business Registry, Özbek is the owner."

Demirel rubbed his mustache again and got up. "Honestly, I don't know what to do with that information. It's late and I drank too much *rakı*. I'll be in touch tomorrow. In the meantime, be extremely careful where you go. A blond man like you sticks out. When you go out, don't come straight back here. Make sure first nobody is following you."

Demirel grabbed the *rakı* bottle and left, leaving an air of sadness behind.

Vermeulen poured himself a large glass of water. It wasn't going to dilute the alcohol he'd already drunk, but at least he wouldn't wake up with a parched mouth. Not that he was going to bed.

Instead he dialed Tessa's number. If he calculated the time difference correctly, she should be drinking her afternoon tea just about then. She answered after four rings.

"Pronto?"

"Hey, are you in Italy?"

"No. I just felt particularly Italian today."

Vermeulen chuckled. Tessa was the daughter of Zambian parents, born not far from Ndola. There was nothing Italian about her.

"Are you still in Turkey?" she said.

"Yes."

"I expected you home a couple of days ago. What's taking you so long? And why didn't you call?"

She sounded stern, there was no trace of humor. It sobered him faster than a bucket of cold water could have.

"The whole job turned into a nightmare," he said.

"But you had time to call Gaby?"

"That's because I needed…" He stopped, realizing he was digging his hole deeper. "I'm sorry, I should've called much sooner."

"That's right. You don't leave on a three day assignment and only call a week later. I thought you'd fallen off a cliff."

"No you didn't."

"How do you know?"

"You called Gaby."

"Yeah. If it weren't for her, I would've thought that. You know what that means?"

"Uh…what?"

"That you'll have to do some serious making-up when you return."

"I'd love nothing better."

"And when, pray tell, will that be?"

"I don't know. Sorry, I really don't know."

Tessa let out an exaggerated sigh. "Why don't you tell me about it?"

And he did.

By the time he was done, it was well past midnight. Telling the whole story in one sitting helped him shake off his listlessness. Tessa's standoffish demeanor stopped the moment he spoke about the pickup attack. She promised to do some research on organized crime in Turkey and coordinate with Gaby on finding out more about Oben Özbek.

"Your job is to find evidence that clearly ties the mobster to the fraud," she said. "Otherwise it'll be just your word against his. Sweet dreams."

THIRTY

FIRST THING THE next morning, Ahmadi called Vermeulen. She remembered one thing that he could help with.

"Good morning. I hope it's not too early to call," she said when he answered.

There was a pause. Since he didn't say anything, she continued.

"I'm still looking for who killed Zada. I haven't told Ayla everything. She might not let me work for the Women's Center if she knew what I'm doing. So far, I haven't had much luck. We've talked to almost twenty women yesterday, but nobody even knew Zada, not to speak of having seen her. It's very disappointing. Last night, I thought of Zada's phone. The police still have it. Maybe you could ask the inspector to give it to me? There must be information on it that could help me."

"Thanks for remembering that," he said after a while. "The phone could be very useful. Not sure he'll give it to you. It's not like you are family. Maybe we can look at the messages and the call log."

"Are you okay? You sound strange."

Vermeulen said something about not sleeping well.

"I don't really want the phone," she said. "It's the information on it I want. I think you have a better chance of getting it than me. I have to go now. Ayla is waiting for me. Let's talk later this afternoon, okay?"

"Okay. I'll contact Demirel about the phone."

Ahmadi left the apartment and got into the car with Erkin. The job of finding and interviewing female refugees could be tedious. Understandably, the women weren't eager to participate. They thought Ahmadi and Erkin were from the government. When Ahmadi explained that they were from the Women's Center, the next question invariably was about the service the center offered. Erkin told her to say that participation in the survey would lead to better benefits, which Ahmadi thought was a bit of a white lie. There was no assurance that the European Union would give more money for refugees after they got this survey.

After three interviews, Erkin told Ahmadi that she would return to Gaziantep. "You know what to do. There's no need for me to tag along. If you need transport, take a taxi, but make sure you get a receipt. I'll call you tonight. You can probably meet a lot of people over the weekend. I'll come back on Sunday afternoon and see how far you got."

She dropped Ahmadi at the next stop and left. Ahmadi was relieved. She didn't have to hide her search for Zada's killer any longer. The next two stops were no different from the previous ones. More suffering, more despair, and less hope that the war would ever end. She noticed the sullen nature of the men she saw. Without work, they must have been feeling useless. Of course, they could've been helping the women, but that was beyond what they could imagine.

The woman who answered the door at the third stop showed the same reticence she'd encountered with the previous interviewees. Three children ranging from toddler age to early teens stole peeks at the visitor from behind a curtain that separated the living area from the entrance.

The woman wore a headscarf. She had suspicious eyes. Ahmadi told her that the survey was intended to improve services to refugees. That changed the woman's attitude and she answered the questions without hesitation. When they came to the section of what difficulties her family faced, the answer was depressingly predictable.

"Food is so expensive here," the woman said. "My husband has no work and my kids need food. We appreciate the help but it's not enough. Whatever you can do to help us, please do it."

"We'll try," Ahmadi said. "What other problems do you have here?"

"The language. It's a big problem. I can't even talk with people here. I want to tell them that we are grateful, but the Turks don't talk much with us. The only people we meet are other Syrian refugees."

"How about language classes. Would you go to one?"

The woman looked pensive. "I don't know. My kids learn some Turkish in school. That's good. They can talk to the grocer and explain what we need. Me, I'm too old to learn."

Ahmadi shook her head. The woman was thirty-seven. "You are not too old. We all can still learn."

"*Shokran,* my child. But when do I go to class? I cook, I clean, I wash. There is no washing machine, you know."

At the end of the interview, she asked again about Zada. The woman raised her eyebrows.

"Zada from Aleppo?" she said.

Ahmadi sat up. "Yes, she's a little shorter than me and forty years old."

"Long hair?"

As quickly as she'd perked up, the disappointment set in. "No, short hair. Thanks anyway."

But the woman wasn't done yet. "Ah, wait. I remember a Zada with short hair. I was having tea at a friend's apartment. There were several of us and one brought her. She asked about getting money. We showed her our cash cards. She said she hadn't gotten one."

Ahmadi's heart started pounding. "When was this?"

"Oh, two weeks ago."

"Did she say what she was going to do next?"

"She was going to visit the different places where we picked up our cards and ask why she and her friends weren't getting those cards."

"What kind of places?"

"They're all over town. I went to an office in the provincial government building. Others went to a bank. One actually got hers at a TekCell shop."

AFTER TALKING TO AHMADI, Vermeulen sat on the edge of the bed and took stock. On the bodily front, things weren't looking good. He hadn't had a hangover this solid in a long time. *Rakı* had shot to the top of the list of liquors to be avoided at all cost. He shuffled to the bathroom, drank water and looked into the mirror. What he saw didn't inspire confidence. He stepped into the shower and tried several water temperatures. Lukewarm turned out to be the most soothing. He stood under the water for ten minutes. Once the cobwebs in his head turned less opaque, he lathered up, washed his hair and spent another ten minutes under the shower. The headache remained, its edge dulled a bit.

He made coffee with an ancient moka pot that must have come over from Italy before WWII. Mercifully, the coffee grounds were much fresher. A cup of thick black coffee and a couple of pills were all he could get down before he went back to bed and dozed with his eyes closed. *Goddamn it.* What in the world made him drink so much of that weird booze?

Ruminating on these and other thoughts, he stayed in bed for another hour until the pain killers had bullied the headache into a tiny corner of his brain and he no longer had an excuse to keep from working. He dressed and checked his laptop for new messages. There was an email from Gaby. It contained the list of currently active companies registered to Özbek.

There were a total of six. Two were registered in Romania, two in Turkey, one in Qatar, and the final one on the Caribbean island of Nevis. When he saw the name *BenBek Lojistik,* his stomach clenched. According to Balbay, that company operated the UNHCR warehouse. The mob had infiltrated the entire UN operation here. He called Balbay, but only got his voice mail. He left a message telling him what he'd just learned and asked him to call back right away.

Gaby had pasted the basic information for each company under the respective names. Özbek was indeed listed as managing director of all the companies. The surprise was Yesim Yaser. She was listed as the vice president for each entity. Demirel had been right. She was definitely being groomed for bigger things.

The geographical distribution of the companies struck him as odd. Vermeulen searched online to find

additional information that would explain the connections. A ding announced a new email from Gaby.
According to her research, the Nevis company, Oboz
Investments, had lent thirty million dollars to one Romanian firm and twenty-two million dollars to the
other. The only reason Gaby knew this was because
both Romanian firms had defaulted on their loans. Her
employer subscribed to various newsletters that kept
track of such defaults. His stomach tightened again.
What was going on here? Özbek lends money to himself and then doesn't pay it back. Such transactions
were always a red flag. He looked out of the window
and shuddered involuntarily. This whole thing looked
much bigger than the cash card scam.

Reading the rest of Gaby's message, his worst fears
were confirmed. The Turkish companies, *Selim Tekstil*
and *BenBek Lojistik*, had guaranteed those loans. Another red flag. He'd seen *Selim Tekstil*. It was a hole-in-
the-wall sweatshop. He'd be surprised if the inventory
of that shop amounted to more than fifty thousand dollars. How could that tiny outfit guarantee loans in that
amount? The answer was obvious. It was a facade, a
mere conduit to funnel dirty cash to where it could be
laundered.

He called Gaby who answered immediately.

"What are the implications of those loans," he said.

"I think they are straightforward," Gaby said. "The
companies that guaranteed the loans are on the hook
for the total amount when the borrower defaults. Like
when parents co-sign a loan for their kids and the kids
don't pay it back, the parents are liable."

"Do you speak from experience?" He meant it as a

joke, but the moment he said it, he knew it didn't sound like one.

Her voice was icy when she replied, "Yes, Mom did co-sign a loan for me and, no, I didn't default. You weren't around, Dad, remember?"

And if I hadn't found you in that heroin squat and gotten you into rehab, you'd be dead. But he kept his thoughts to himself. "I'm sorry, sweetheart, that was a thoughtless thing to say. Please forgive me."

"Okay, this time." She sounded mollified. "Back to the loans. The first default, the thirty million loan, was certified by a judge back in March. The second default is in court as we speak. It should be certified any day. What's the deal with those Turkish companies? Are they legit?"

"Nope, they're not. Yesim Yaser is the niece of the local mob boss and, according to a local cop, the apple of his eye. Word is the boss is grooming her as his successor. This Oben Özbek is also listed as the president of the fake NGO that operated the cash card scam. I don't know him, but I'm sure none of this is above board."

"What're you going to do next? You know as well as I do that this is way beyond your job description," she said.

"I know. But if I can give the police the evidence they need to arrest those guys, maybe the UN can get some of its money back. I'll talk to my police contact. He's got access to the registration system. Maybe we can find them. Thanks for your help, without you, I'd be traipsing in the dark."

"You're welcome. And, Dad? Don't say dumb stuff. Bye."

Was there ever going to be a time when he and Gaby could forget the past? Maybe not. His headache flared up and he drank another glass of water.

Then he dialed Demirel's number. All he got was a busy signal.

THIRTY-ONE

INSPECTOR DEMIREL INSTANTLY regretted lifting the phone receiver. It was the Superintendent's secretary. She only called to patch through the Superintendent and since she didn't like Demirel, she wouldn't lie for him and tell the Superintendent that he was out. He had good reason for not wanting to talk with his boss. Not only did he feel a bit shaky after the boozy evening with Vermeulen, but his boss, who rarely cared about whatever cases he was working on, only called when something cropped up that had the potential to make him look bad. Which meant not speaking to him was the best way to get work done. Answering the call only meant he'd have to deal with whatever had attracted the Superintendent's attention, while also continuing to work on his cases.

"Yes, Superintendent, what can I do for you?"

"Inspector, I have a rather delicate situation at my hands. It involves some United Nations employee. Vermeulen, I think. Have you heard anything about this?"

Demirel's mouth went dry. "A United Nations employee? There are lots of them around. The High Commissioner on Refugees has an office in Gaziantep. His representatives are in and out of the refugee camp at the border."

"Yes, I know." The Superintendent sounded impatient. "I don't mean any United Nations employee, I'm referring to this Vermeulen person. Apparently, he is some kind of investigator. I wish I had been informed of his visit, professional courtesy is not what it used to be. So have you heard about him?"

"Yes." Demirel's heart beat increased. Leave it to the Superintendent of all people to get wind of Vermeulen's investigation.

"And what is that." The Superintendent sounded annoyed now.

"He's looking into how the UNHCR is spending its money." *Play it cool.*

"So I've heard. Have you met him?"

His heart pounding now, Demirel hesitated a beat. *Calm down.* He turned his head, took a breath, then said, "Yes, I have."

"Inspector, why do I have to drag every word out of you? What aren't you telling me?"

"Superintendent, I'm rather busy with a murder investigation and I'm simply too stretched to worry about a UN employee. The man seemed cordial and straightforward. I wished him good luck with his work and we left it at that."

"So you haven't heard anything about him sticking his nose into local contractors and such?"

"All I know is that he was in Kilis to visit the official camp and then went to Gaziantep. No idea what happened there."

"Apparently he's back in Kilis. I got a call from a local businessman who complained that this Vermeulen is interfering with his work for the UNHCR. If you hear anything about it, or if you learn of Vermeulen's whereabouts, let me know."

"Will do, Superintendent."

Demirel hung up and let out a big breath. This wasn't

the place he wanted to be in. He'd never lied to the Superintendent. Sure, he'd reported carefully edited versions of events, but he never outright lied to him. This was different. The Superintendent acting on a call from a "local businessman?" That could only have been Ceylen. Which raised all kinds of questions. The Superintendent had risen to his post not because he was a good cop, but because he'd invested in the right relationships. Was the mob boss one of those? He couldn't fathom the Superintendent being in the pocket of Ceylen. The man didn't have the intellectual acuity to be a cop on the take. Would he really believe that Mehmed Ceylen was just a local businessman? Demirel couldn't fathom that either. Maybe he'd underestimated the Superintendent.

These musings weren't just hypothetical. The information Vermeulen had given him the night before was enough to open a case against Ceylen. The Chief needed to sign off on that. Damn.

His phone rang again, an outside call.

"What was that stuff you brought last night," Vermeulen said. "It gave me the worst hangover."

"You'll get used to it. I could bring another bottle tonight. I guarantee, tomorrow you'll notice the difference. But that's not why you called, right?"

"Good guess. I have two questions. First, the phone you found with Zada Homsi? Her friend is asking for it. She considers herself to be as close to 'next of kin' as anyone here. I guess she wants it as a memento of her friend."

"I might consider that, but the case is open. So until we close it, we'll have to hang on to it."

"Of course. Is there a chance she could just check it, see if there are some pictures, etc., on it?"

"Come on, Valentin. You know how this works. Her death is suspicious, and until we get the autopsy results, we can't let anyone handle the evidence. Once we know how she died, we'll take it from there."

"You haven't got the autopsy results yet? It's been a week."

"And this isn't New York City. We don't have a pathologist here. Autopsies are done in Gaziantep."

"Got it. Sorry, I didn't mean to sound pushy. I hope you'll let me know when you have the results. The second question is about a P.O. box number. Is there a way for you to find the address of someone who rented it?"

"Sure, if I have a warrant."

"Is there an unofficial way to get that information?"

"Do you have a name?"

"Oben Özbek."

"Oh, that mystery man you've mentioned. I can just query MERNIS, the Central Registration System. If he's a Turkish citizen, his ID number, address and other personal information is in there. There's one caveat. All MERNIS queries are logged, so I have to be able to justify the query. How this is related to your case?"

"Özbek is the president of the fraudulent NGO and he owns a string of companies. I just learned that one of them manages an UNHCR warehouse. I got the local official checking, but I wouldn't be surprised if they stole everything in it. The other companies are probably also engaged in illegal activities. You might as well start an inquiry. Consider my report last night an official complaint. That way your queries are covered."

"Yeah, from your lips to God's ears. I'll need my boss to sign off and he just called me about you, telling me that a local businessman has complained about your interference."

"Shit."

"My words exactly. I'll get back to you. In the meantime, stay low."

AHMADI'S LAST INTERVIEW before lunch was near the city center and she decided to take her lunch break there as well. After the turmoil of the past months, the simple act of entering a restaurant, ordering, and paying for the meal made her feel almost normal. Strange how something so mundane could become so special after having been deprived of everything. The delight had the dark lining. She was alone now. She didn't have anyone in the world to share a meal. Whatever aunties, uncles and cousins she had were either dead or scattered around Europe.

Waiting for her order, she figured it was this loneliness that made her dig into Zada's murder. Zada had been all alone, too. Nobody cared about what happened to Zada. Just another dead refugee. She wasn't going to let that happen. Would anyone care that much about her when her time came? A depressing thought. Hell, no. That's a long time off. She'll have a new life then. With new friends and a new family. *Yeah. Right.*

Her food came. She ate. The meal was unremarkable. Even pretend optimism couldn't hide how low she felt.

After lunch, she walked down Cumhuriyet Caddesi to the TekCell shop the woman had mentioned. It was the closest and the least likely place to find a clue. Afterwards, she'd check at the government building and do more interviews.

The TekCell shop sat next to other cell phone shops

touting competing companies and phones. There were shops like these on almost every block. It was as if all Turks did was buy cell phones. She opened the door and walked into the cool store.

Inside was a long counter and several vitrines displaying the latest smart phones. Posters advertised different plans. A young man stood behind the counter, tapping on his phone. He wore a white T-shirt with the black letters NEFRET emblazoned on it. A middle-aged man with a grizzled beard approached her.

"Merhaba," the bearded man said. He continued in Turkish saying something obnoxious because she could see the young man cringe behind the counter.

"Afedersiniz!" she said. *"İngilizce konuşuyor musunuz?"*

The T-shirt guy behind the counter said, "No problem, I speak English."

The bearded man made a face and went to sit on a chair near a back door.

"Do you need a phone?" the young guy said. "We have some good models back here. Not expensive."

He pointed to a display case in the rear.

"No, thanks. I have a question. I was told that refugees could get cash cards here. Is that correct?"

His smile disappeared and was replaced by a long-suffering expression as if he'd had enough of refugees already.

"Not anymore. That's stopped some time ago. Did you get a text to come here?"

"No. I'm not looking for a card. I'm looking for a friend, who came here to ask about the cards. Her name is Zada Homsi, short hair, about my height, around forty years old."

He perked up but tried to hide it with a shrug. "We had a lot of refugees coming in."

Ahmadi didn't buy the act. "She came in early last week."

The young guy spun around and said something to the bearded man, who jumped up, opened the back door, stuck his head in the crack, then turned back and shook his head. The T-shirt guy hurried to the entrance and locked the door.

Ahmadi's gut told her that this was bad. She ran after the T-shirt guy and reached for the deadbolt lever. He blocked her. She banged on the glass and screamed for help. Outside, faces turned. Before she could hit the glass again, a hand clamped over her mouth from behind. The bearded man grabbed her arm. That gave the young one the space to push himself away from the door and take her other arm. They talked to each other in clipped sentences. From their faces, she could tell they were more frightened than aggressive. That eased her fear a little. They weren't going to rape her. That meant her investigation of Zada was on target.

Together the men maneuvered her to the back of the shop and sat her on the chair. It was still warm from its previous occupant. The older one unplugged the extension cord that connected a display case and used it to tie her hands behind the backrest of the chair.

"We wait," was all the young guy said.

THIRTY-TWO

VERMEULEN DECIDED TO stay close to his apartment and bought a few groceries at a small shop around the corner rather than finding a restaurant. Demirel was serious when he told him to lay low. There were people out there looking for him, probably lots of people, and, with his height and blond hair, he was an easy mark.

Carrying a plastic bag of groceries, he walked past the gated entrance to his apartment, just in case someone was watching him. At the next corner, he stopped suddenly and turned around. The street was busy, but he saw no furtive movements, no one turning around, no one stopping in mid stride. He crossed over to the other side and walked back the direction he'd come. None of the faces on either side of the street looked familiar. He hadn't seen any of them since he left his place. A passage to a courtyard offered the next opportunity to dodge a tail. He turned into it and found a small alcove for mailboxes to his right. He waited for five minutes. Nobody familiar passed in front of the alcove. He went back to the street, hurried across it and punched the code on the keypad by the gate.

While eating a sandwich with hummus, tomatoes and cucumbers, he mulled over the corporate connections Gaby had uncovered. A Nevis outfit lends money to a Romanian company. That loan is guaranteed by a Turkish firm. The Romanians default on the loan.

That meant the Turkish guys were on the hook for that money. They'd have to transfer the funds to Nevis. Straightforward as far as that went.

It wasn't clear how any party in this transaction made any money. Sure, the Romanian branch got their hands on several millions. At the same time, the Turkish side had to cough it up again. The money could've been sent straight from Turkey to Romania. But then the Nevis leg of that stool made no sense at all. Gaby had mentioned tax avoidance as a motive. He couldn't see how that would work. Money was transferred from Britain to Romania and afterwards from Turkey to Britain. There was a black hole in the middle. What happened to the money in Romania? Drugs? Guns? All were possible, but how did the Turkish side of the deal profit? And what role did the Qatari operation play?

He got up and made himself coffee. While the moka pot percolated, he unwrapped a baklava from its plastic package and put it on a plate. When the coffee was done, he settled back at the table and ate his dessert. The baklava was sticky with honey and the pastry had gotten soggy in its packaging, the downside of not buying fresh goods. He gobbled it down and cut the cloying sweetness with the coffee.

What would I do with millions of stolen dollars? He tapped his fingers on the table. They were sticky from the honey. He got up to wash his hands. As the water ran over his hands he remembered Gaby's earlier point. The biggest challenge for all criminal enterprises was laundering the money, make it appear legitimate. What if the loan from the Nevis firm to the Romanian one was just on paper? What if the money was never transferred? The Romanian default triggered the liability of the Turkish company, which then sent the corresponding amount to Nevis. The funds would be beyond the reach of the Turkish authorities. In Nevis, that money would be considered a legitimate payment for the defaulted loan. The paper trail was there. The dirty money had been washed. All it took was a judge in Romania to certify the default. That didn't sound like an insurmountable obstacle.

He called Gaby again.

"That entire setup is to launder money from Turkey," he said when she answered.

"Hi, Dad, good afternoon, and how are you?… Just kidding. For a moment I thought my boss was calling me. Money laundering, huh? I think you've got it. Just as I assumed. Question is, what're you gonna do about it?"

"Isn't that always the question? Not only do I have to prove that the money was stolen from UNHCR. I'll have to show what happened to it. The first part is easy. The second part? Probably impossible. It involves three jurisdictions. Suarez—you remember my boss—has no interest in ruffling that many feathers."

"So, write your report, pack up and leave. Stop in Düsseldorf for a few days. Better yet, call Tessa and ask her to join us. We'll have a grand time. My company owes me plenty of vacation days for my overtime."

It sounded tempting, very tempting. She was right. There was little more he could do but write his report and submit it. And, for once, Suarez would agree with him.

"Let me think about it," he said.

"Do. But not too much, before you stumble onto yet another twist and change your mind. I can get time off immediately. Just call me when you're boarding the plane."

He ended the call and dialed Balbay's number. Still no answer. He repeated his message and ended the call. It was time to draft an email to his boss, explaining the rough outlines of the case and promising to submit his report soon. After that, he'd book his ticket and leave.

His phone rang. It was an unknown caller. Against his better instincts, he answered.

"Valentin, they are holding me." It was Ahmadi. Her voice was shrill. "Zada's killers, they have me. You have to help. Please."

His stomach clenched. It was the phone call he didn't need, but couldn't ignore.

"Are you hurt?" he said.

"No, she's not hurt," a man's voice said. It sounded like the mob boss Ceylen. "It's up to you to make sure it stays that way."

"Okay, okay. What do you want me to do?"

"Where are you?"

"I'm at a café." He almost didn't hesitate before telling the lie. Whatever came next, he wanted to make sure the place where he was staying remained a secret.

"No, where are you staying?"

"A small guesthouse at the north end of town."

"The address?"

"I can't pronounce it. Just tell me what you want me to do."

"What's nearby?"

"A mosque." Vermeulen figured there were plenty of mosques so he'd be safe.

"The name of the mosque?"

"I don't know. Tell me what you want."

There was a moment's hesitation. Vermeulen listened for background noises. There were none.

"Come to the old mosque on Cumhuriyet Caddesi, right by the provincial government. A car will be waiting there. Be there in twenty-five minutes. I don't have to tell you not to speak with anyone."

"I know the protocol."

He ended the call and dialed Demirel's number. The phone rang forever and rolled over to voicemail.

"Demirel. Ahmadi, the woman you interrogated last week, has been kidnapped. The gangsters threatened to hurt her unless I come to the old mosque by the governor's office. I sincerely hope you get this message in the next few minutes because I have to be at that mosque in twenty minutes. If you don't see me there, it's too late. In that case look for *BenBek Lojistik* or *Selim Tekstile*. They probably will take me to one of those places."

He left all personal items, credit cards, passport and driver's license in the apartment. The place was rented for a week and he had the code memorized. The last thing he did was call Tessa. He didn't want to, but knew he owed her that call. The phone rang and rang. It was early morning in New York. At the last moment, a sleepy Tessa said, "This better be good. You know what time it is?"

"I'm about to meet a mob boss who's kidnapped the refugee woman I told you about and threatened her life unless I meet them. I wouldn't have gotten you up for anything less important."

"Are you out of your mind?"

"No. But the man wants me and having him torture Ahmadi wouldn't change that situation."

"Call the police. The UN. Anyone."

"I called the police inspector I know. He didn't answer his phone but I left a message. Listen, I have to go. I've got little time to get to the rendezvous point."

"What's the inspector's name and number."

Vermeulen gave it to her.

"Don't go, Valentin."

"I have to, but don't worry. I'll be all right."

He synced his phone with his laptop, turned his computer off and reset his phone to factory settings. This time they weren't going to get any information from his phone, especially not the calls to Demirel and Tessa.

The gate fell shut behind him. The mosque wasn't far. It'd be easier to get away on foot. He took a deep breath. What could possibly go wrong? Everything. But he'd been in tighter spots before.

THIRTY-THREE

VERMEULEN SLOWED AS he neared the mosque. It wasn't as much a conscious decision as his body's survival reflexes telling him that Tessa was right. He wanted nothing more than to agree with that sentiment, except, no matter how he'd spun the situation, he couldn't think of any other way to help Ahmadi. Overwhelm the driver who was waiting for him? Problem was, once he put the guy in the trunk, he didn't know where to go. He could grab the driver's gun and make him drive to where they held Ahmadi. Nah. No good. Nothing like the confined space of a car to make well laid plans go awry. They'd grabbed her only to get to him. The only option was to do what they demanded.

He was standing in the shadow of the provincial government building. Across the square stood the Kara Kadi mosque. There was no cover. They could see him approach. There could be a rifle already aiming at his head. He had nothing to offer them except his silence. What better way to assure that than a sniper's bullet from across the square. He wasn't so stupid as to believe that his surrender would secure Ahmadi's release.

There was no sign of Demirel. No cops at all, except for a patrol car parked near the entrance of the city hall, to the west of the provincial government. Had Demirel told the cops to stay clear of the area? Was he waiting in hiding, ready to follow them and grab the whole nest of gangsters? Even in that scenario he and Ahmadi were dispensable. He'd never heard of a police force that would forgo a coup like this in order to save innocent lives. Sure, they'd make a halfhearted effort, maybe even bring in a hostage negotiator—did they even have those in Turkey?—but in the end, they'd storm the place and hope for the best.

He made himself walk across the square toward the mosque. It was a slow march, without a plan B, driven by that moth-eaten notion of chivalry that Ahmadi should not suffer in his stead. His only hope was a silly belief in his ability to improvise.

There was no sniper waiting across the square, just the black Mercedes and the same driver he'd knocked out a couple of days ago. The man patted him down and took his phone, the only thing in his pockets. He wasn't even rough about it. After that necessity, he opened the rear door and invited Vermeulen to sit. Either he'd forgotten being knocked out with a chair, or he was used to getting beaten up, figuring it came with his job. Which would explain his dimwittedness.

A third option was that his boss had impressed on the driver to behave. A hint of a silver lining, because if the goal was to kill him, there was no need for a courteous prelude. There were good reasons to make a deal with him. A dead UN investigator would bring unwanted attention. Even bribed cops would have to pretend to make an effort. Ceylen wouldn't want this much attention.

The conversation would be tedious. First the empty choice between accepting dirty money and death. Then the offering up of a sacrificial lamb, the driver, if Ceylen was smart. He'd heard it more often than he cared to remember. In the end it would come back to death. By that time, he very much planned to be somewhere else.

He settled into the back of the car. It was truly a luxurious ride, something he'd missed the first time around because he was unconscious. The driver took him toward the western outskirts of Kilis. The residential areas were well behind them. Some of the empty land around them had already been surveyed for new construction. A few solitary trees stood in the fields, looking forlorn as if they'd escaped from a forest but had gotten lost afterwards. A wrecked semi tractor stood next to a warehouse a little farther down the road.

The warehouse turned out to be their destination. It had seen better days. The letters *BenBek Lojistik* were barely legible above a large gate. The driver approached the rear of the building with a sweeping turn. He came to a stop. The rear door of the Mercedes was perfectly aligned with the double doors that led into the warehouse. At least he was good at something. He tapped the horn once. The door opened and Ceylen stepped out.

The boss talked to the driver who handed him Vermeulen's phone. His raised eyebrows told Vermeulen that he'd expected more. Ceylen opened the car door. "Follow me."

THE INSIDE OF the warehouse looked exactly like a shell company's location. A dilapidated semi trailer stood near a corner, its many tires flat. A row of industrial-strength shelves, empty, except for a dozen nondescript boxes, occupied one side of the space. A forklift with a stack of empty pallets on its tines was left near the center, as if quitting time had come early. On both sides of the entrance were offices. It was clear that this was not a going concern. No cargo had been handled here in a long time.

Ahmadi wasn't anywhere in sight. Besides Ceylen, there were two beefy men carrying submachine guns, leaning casually against the wall. If this was the nerve center of their criminal operation, they sure kept staff at a minimum. Ceylen gestured toward the row of offices with his left hand and put his other hand behind Vermeulen's back. A casual gesture as if they were about to begin a meeting.

Ceylen opened a door to the left. The room contained several file cabinets against one wall. A desk and a chair stood by the outside wall. A window displayed the arid landscape outside. On the other wall hung a picture of President Erdoğan. Ceylen sat down in the chair. Which left Vermeulen standing there facing them. So much for courtesy. At least they hadn't shackled him. Yet.

"Before we get started, I want to make sure we understand each other," Vermeulen said. "Whatever you want from me, Ahmadi has nothing to do with it. Unless you let her go, I won't cooperate. So, let her go now. I won't say a word until I have received a text from her that she's safe."

Celyen gave him a perplexed look. "We aren't here to negotiate." His voice was colder than ice.

Vermeulen swallowed, his mouth suddenly as dry as the dust on the concrete floor. "There is always something to negotiate."

The look in Ceylen's eyes changed from mystified to stony. "The only thing I want from you is your silence. And I already know how to obtain that."

The bluntness of the threat made Vermeulen's blood pulse in his ears. He managed to keep a calm voice. "To quote the Rolling Stones, 'You can't always get what you want.' This is one of those situations."

Ceylen's brows arched. "You haven't submitted your report yet. Balbay told me so."

Sensing a shift, Vermeulen said, "You assume I would've told Balbay. I know he was compromised. I bypassed his office and sent the report straight to Ankara, copy to New York."

The calm confidence of Ceylen's demeanor was gone.

"You're bluffing," he said with barely concealed anger.

Vermeulen smiled. "Whatever makes you sleep easier. All I know is the report is in the two inboxes where it belongs."

Ceylen called someone. Two different guys, with submachine guns slung over their shoulders came into the room. They were just as beefy as the others. They grabbed Vermeulen's arms, zip tied the wrists behind his back, and marched him to the neighboring office. There, they pushed him onto the floor and tightened a larger zip tie around his ankles and left him on the concrete. The door slammed shut again. Other doors opened and closed. The last sounds came from the metal door to the outside.

The big question was why he hadn't been killed yet. If all they needed was his silence, a well-aimed bullet would have gotten them that.

Instead they had lured him here.

His death, as sad as it sounded, wouldn't make a big splash. There would be a UN inquiry followed by a report and a note of condolences to his next of kin. That'd be the extent of it.

Not that anyone outside the UN knew that. The lack of knowledge about the organization surrounded it with a strange aura. The United Nations. Not an outfit to be messed with. He loved exploiting that misconception, waving his ID as if he had more powers than presidents. Nothing could be further from the truth. But, more often than not, that trick worked.

He bet that it worked on Ceylen, too. If they were afraid of an investigation into his death, it meant that they hadn't wrapped up whatever they were doing. And that meant there was still time. And as long as there was time, there was a chance to get out.

THIRTY-FOUR

THE EARLY CALL had launched Tessa into emergency containment mode. Valentin was doing something exceedingly stupid. He needed all the help she could provide. First, she called the number of that police inspector. There was no answer and she left a message urging the man to call her back.

Next, she called Gaby, and got another request to leave a message or call a different number. Tessa did that and was informed that Gaby would be unavailable for the next thirty minutes. She dug into research on the Turkish mafia. There was plenty of material to dig through, but much of it focused on the past. She found accounts of famous gangsters like Alaattin Cakici, the Black Sea mobster who supported the fascist Grey Wolves, and Dündar Kılıç, also from the Black Sea area who often and quite successfully ran his organization from behind bars.

Of more interest was the move of Turkish Cypriots to London. Valentin had told her about the money laundering. She'd have to verify that with Gaby, of course, but she was pretty certain. The trend in transnational crime was to wash money as quickly as possible to make it available for legitimate purposes, profit coming from the quick turnover of capital.

Since the attacks of 2001, global financial regulations had tightened dramatically to prevent the flow of money to terrorist groups. It was much harder to buy luxury apartments in famous cities with dirty money. Transnational gangsters adapted by mingling the illegal with the legal. Shell entities in the Caribbean were particularly useful to launder the cash. No wonder the majority of high dollar real estate owners in Manhattan hid their true identity behind limited liability companies with inventive names.

When Gaby called her back, Tessa filled her in on Valentin's situation.

"He what?" Gaby said.

"He went to meet the mafiosos because they had taken a refugee woman hostage to get to him."

"He didn't call the police?"

"He did leave a message for an inspector he knows. But he sure didn't wait to speak to him. It's his goddamn stubbornness."

"You're telling me? What do we do?"

"I have a call in to the inspector in Kilis. We need to find the links between those companies, what corrupt actions they are involved in and more. Once we have that, we put some fire under the police there."

"Okay. I'll get on it right away. I'll email you the list of companies I've collected. And then I'll look for more info."

A few moments later, Tessa had the same list of companies Gaby had sent to Valentin earlier that day. One of them, Oboz Investments, caught her attention because it was registered on the island of Nevis. A tax haven. No taxes, no transparency, plenty of secrecy.

On a whim, she searched the major real estate transactions on the *New York Times* website. As she worked her way backward, she noticed there was an obvious correlation between the purchase price and the likelihood of a corporate buyer. Going back month by month was tedious, but watching the prices at which units sold was mesmerizing. With each new record, a hundred million dollars for a penthouse was the highest so far, she felt compelled the find a new one with an even higher price.

A half hour later, conscious of wasting precious time, she found what she was looking for. April 2015. Oboz Investments had purchased an apartment in a new tower off Columbus Circle for the not insubstantial amount of thirty million dollars.

She dialed Gaby again.

"Guess what? One of the companies, the one listed in Nevis, bought a fancy apartment here in the city. Thirty million dollars."

She could hear Gaby suck in her breath. "That's exactly the amount of one of the defaulted loans."

"What loan?" Tessa said.

"The Nevis company has made loans to the two Romanian companies, thirty million dollars to one and twenty-two million to the other," Gaby said. "Those loans were guaranteed by the Turkish firms. And guess what?"

Tessa was getting antsy. "The Romanians defaulted, right? It's the Russian Laundromat all over again. The guarantor pays and gets the dirty money laundered. How many of the Romanians have defaulted?"

"Both. No surprise, as you already guessed. But here's the deal. The default in the second loan hasn't been certified yet. I just read on a blog that the judge in the latest proceedings has postponed his ruling. So the twenty-two million loan isn't in default yet."

Tessa pursed her lips. "And?"

"You know the Russian Laundromat. The judges are paid off. The rulings certifying the defaults are a foregone conclusion. There's never a postponement. So either the case has landed with a judge who isn't in the pocket of the gangsters, or he's holding out for more money."

"Why does that matter?"

"Because it's Friday evening here. That means no ruling until Monday morning the soonest."

"What does that have to do with Valentin?" Tessa said.

"Come on. You know Dad. He loves to pretend that he's some global super cop, what with his UN ID and all."

Tessa smiled. That was her man all right. "Sure," she said. "I've seen him do it many times… Oh, I see. You think the gangsters were taken in by that?"

"Right. And their latest transaction is held up. The laundromat is stuck, the money is still in Turkey. The last thing they want is attention. And if Dad did his thing, they'll think his death will attract a lot of attention."

"I get it. So you think they'll keep him alive for the weekend?"

"I sure hope so. I don't even want to contemplate the alternative."

Tessa throat tightened. She swallowed. "Neither do I," she said much quieter. She took a deep breath. "I'll call the inspector. That has to be our best chance."

VERMEULEN HEARD THREE short taps against the wall to his right, followed by three taps with pauses and ending with another set of three short taps. S-O-S. He maneuvered his body to that wall. Tapping with his hands bound didn't work. Besides, he'd forgotten most of the Morse code he'd been taught during his days in army intelligence. There was a vent in the ceiling. Chances were it was connected to a similar vent in the neighboring office.

"Can you hear me?" he said, louder than a conversation would be but not shouting.

"Yes," a voice said. It was Ahmadi.

"Are you hurt?"

"No. I'm tied up and lying on a cement floor."

"Me too."

"They killed Zada."

"How did you find out?"

"Doing the survey, I met a woman who'd met Zada. She told Zada where she and other refugees picked up their cash cards. One of those places was a TekCell shop in the city center. I went there and asked. They never let me leave."

"They made you call me?"

"I'm very sorry, but I couldn't do anything about that."

"Don't worry about it. I was in their crosshairs anyway. They had kidnapped me once already, but I got away."

"Oh."

"We'll get out of here, too. Don't doubt that for a moment."

"How?"

That, of course, was the rub. Preaching optimism was no substitute for actually getting out. "We'll figure something out," he said, sounding braver than he felt. "What's in your office?"

Ahmadi didn't respond right away. He heard faint sounds. She was moving around.

"There isn't a lot," she said. "There are file cabinets against the wall, a desk on the window side and a chair."

"Our quarters are depressingly similar."

"What?"

"Never mind. Wait a moment. I'll try something. If it works, I'll tell you what to do."

Vermeulen maneuvered himself into a kneeling position. He bent forward and raised his tied hands behind him. The muscles in his shoulders popped with a sharp pain. For once, he thought that the yoga classes Tessa had urged him to attend would've been a good idea. He brought his arms down on his sacrum as hard as he could. The wrists strained against the tie that bit into his skin. Nothing happened. He tried again, this time raising the arms a little higher and pressing his wrists apart as he swung them down. The zip tie broke with a snap. Good to know that this trick wasn't just an internet spoof.

Getting the tie off his ankles wasn't much harder. He simply tied his shoe laces together and used them to saw right through the ties.

"Are you still there?" he said.

"Yes."

"Here's what you do. Get into a kneeling position. Bend slightly forward. Raise your tied hands behind you as high as you can and slam them against your sacrum, you know, that bone between your hip bones, while pressing the wrists apart."

"What?"

"I know, it sounds crazy, but just do it. First kneel. Can you do that?"

A pause. Then, "Okay."

He heard a faint slap. "Ouch. That hurt."

"Sorry, yes, it does, but try it again. A little higher and press your wrists apart."

There was some commotion on the other side of the wall.

"I got my hands free. These things aren't very strong."

"Good. Do your shoes have laces?"

"Uh, no. Just straps."

"Don't worry. Look around, see if there's something you can use to cut them. Even just rubbing them against something rough will do the trick."

While she was doing that, he checked out the room. The file cabinets were locked, as were the drawers of the desk. The window to the outside was not operable. Of course, he could throw the chair through it. But the noise would attract attention. From what he'd seen of the landscape around the warehouse, there were no hiding places.

The inside of the warehouse offered better options. There was the old trailer, the forklift and the shelves. So far he'd seen four men with automatic weapons. The driver and Ceylen would carry guns as well. Although those two were probably gone. So, he and Ahmadi against four armed guys.

Pretty bad odds.

But not necessarily so. The psychological factors were important. The four guys weren't worried. Not about a woman and a bureaucrat. Two of them were probably slacking off somewhere, watching stuff on their phones. One could well be on a food and beer run.

The only worry was the one guy who pretended to be guarding them. And he wasn't doing a great job. He hadn't noticed Vermeulen and Ahmadi talking through the vent.

The toilet trick had worked once already. It would do so again. Like most people, gangsters didn't relish having to put up with the results of untended bodily functions. So getting to use a toilet was usually not hard. All he needed was something hard to hit the guy. He scanned the room again. There was nothing obvious.

THIRTY-FIVE

INSPECTOR DEMIREL HAD spent the morning finding out more about Oben Özbek. There were none listed living in the region. The ones living in the rest of the country didn't claim to be the owner of a sweatshop in Kilis.

He sat up. Vermeulen had told him that Özbek was listed as the owner of *Selim Tekstil*. He switched to the company registration portal and, sure enough, found the company and Oben Özbek listed as owner and director. How could this be? He took the ID number listed for Özbek in the company listing and plugged it into the personal registration system. The query returned nothing, or, rather, the system told him that the number didn't exist and wondered if he had made a mistake entering it. He tried again, same result.

That didn't make sense. The whole promise of MER-NIS was that all information centrally stored would eliminate duplication of efforts and errors. And yet, here he looked at a name of a business owner who didn't exist. Someone could have made a mistake entering the number, so he compared the faulty ID with the ID numbers of the Özbecks he'd found. None of them was off by just one digit. Definitely not a typo. He'd follow up with Vermeulen later.

The rest of the day he spent chasing down leads on Temir Korun, the driver of the van full of smuggled gasoline. The spectacular accident had gotten a lot of attention. His superintendent wanted results. The search of MERNIS had yielded an address, but, not surprisingly, the man wasn't home when he got there. The neighbors didn't offer much help. Nobody had seen him since that Sunday when he crashed the van.

Using the picture he'd gotten from the online copy of Korun's ID card, he visited gas stations around Kilis. At first the response was blank stares. Only after he assured the attendants that he wasn't interested in smuggled fuel, did some acknowledge that Korun had indeed delivered to them at one time or another. The best lead he got was from a young man who told him that he'd seen Korun at a bar a couple of days ago. He stopped by the bar on his way back, but didn't learn anything new.

Finally back in his office, he first heard Vermeulen's message. He shook his head. Was that man crazy? He checked his watch. It was too late to tell him not to go. The next two messages came from an international number. He listened to a woman's voice identifying herself as Tessa Bishonga, Vermeulen's partner. She said something about a massive money laundering operation involving Oben Özbek and companies all over the world and asked that he do everything he could to find Vermeulen. The two companies registered to Özbek should be the starting place. Her second call only added urgency.

She wanted him to mount a manhunt that required a lot of cops. Right at the beginning of the weekend. He'd have to get the Superintendent's permission first. How'd he explain the search after he'd lied to him about not knowing Vermeulen's whereabouts? Come clean and tell his boss that he'd gotten drunk with Vermeulen? Not an option. He could play the messages from Bishonga for the Superintendent, but how would he explain that she had his number?

No matter the angle, he couldn't explain away the fact that he'd lied to his boss. That meant disciplinary proceedings, assignment to desk duty, or worse. None of it would help Vermeulen. Which left only one option, do it on his own. He checked for the addresses of the two companies Bishonga had mentioned. The sweat-shop lay just outside the ring road to the south of the police station. The freight warehouse was farther out and to the west. The map told him that the warehouse was a better place to stow hostages. Unlike the sweat-shop, there were no adjacent buildings.

He stopped by the dispatch room. The man at the desk looked sleepy.

"I need four uniforms for backup," Demirel said.

The man sat up, shook his head. "What?"

"Four men for backup."

"Not gonna happen. It's Friday evening. Five units are out dealing with accidents. The remaining are wran-gling drunks. Nobody's free."

At that, a tall policeman walked into the room. Demirel remembered him from a week ago when they brought Vermeulen and Ahmadi to the station. The cop told the dispatcher that he was back from an accident. His partner was filing the paperwork.

"Come with me," Demirel said. "I need backup to check something out."

"What about my partner?" the tall cop said.

"Is he ready to go?"

"Nah. He's slow with filling out the forms."

"Okay, then it's just the two of us. It's urgent."

"Where are we going?"

"Checking out a warehouse. It's probably nothing, but I'd rather not go without backup. Your gun loaded?"

The tall cop checked his Yavuz 16 and nodded.

Demirel was already at the door. "Let's go," he said.

THE WAREHOUSE LOOKED like one of those structures the Kilis economic development committee loved to hold up as an example for what was preventing the city from becoming the economic hub of southern Turkey. In the eyes of the business boosters letting property rot away was worse than not building. Demirel knew a few of those people and knew why they were barking up the wrong tree. Letting a building fall apart was often useful, and not just for tax purposes. The shabbier a place looked, the less attention it attracted. Which allowed for new uses that did better without too much scrutiny.

The tall cop seemed fidgety.

"Why are you so nervous?" Demirel said. "We're just checking out a warehouse for suspicious activity. If there's anything going on, we'll wait for reinforcements."

"It's getting dark and we are walking into an unknown situation. I signed up for traffic patrol, not gun fights. Who told you about this anyway?"

"I got a call. Didn't sound like much, but we have to follow up."

The cop nodded.

Demirel parked near the front of the building. There were five loading docks along the length of the wall. The gates—a yard or so above ground level—were closed. The rubber bumpers below them had rotted in the sun. No trucks had been loaded or unloaded there for a while. Dirt covered most of the broken asphalt around the loading docks. It had been smoothed by the winds of several winters. There were no other cars visible.

He stopped near the front of the building and got out. Fresh tire tracks led to the rear.

"Doesn't look like anything's going on here. I'm going to the rear. Go around the other side. It's better to be spread out."

Demirel turned and walked to the building. On his way, he pulled his Yavus 16 from the shoulder holster and pushed the safety lever up. He hoped that the tall cop had done the same thing. The short side of the warehouse only had a row of vents mounted well above his head. When he reached the next corner, he peered around it and saw the cars that had made the tracks in the dirt, two black SUVs. No one stood outside. The cars stood in front of a double door, half way down the length of the warehouse. There were windows on either side of the doors.

He turned around and called the station on his way back to the car. When the dispatcher answered, he requested two more units for backup. The dispatcher didn't sound encouraging but promised to send whoever was available. When he got back to the front, he found the tall cop leaning against his car.

"Did you check out the other side?" Demirel said.

"Yeah. Nothing there. I came back."

The man was lying. He'd been too lazy to walk around, otherwise he'd have seen the SUVs.

"There are two SUVs in back. That could mean up to eight men," Demirel said. "I've called for backup. In the meantime, I'm going to check out the windows back there, see if I can get a peek inside. Cover me."

The tall cop made a face, but didn't say "No." Demirel walked back to the corner he'd just left. The sun was setting fast. He inched along the wall toward the entrance, the pistol pointed straight ahead. About halfway toward the door, he stopped and turned. The tall cop had remained at the corner. Demirel waved for him to follow. The man took small steps forward as if he expected the bad guys to pop up from the dry dirt in front of him.

"I'm going as far as the first window," Demirel said when the cop had finally caught up with him. "Keep an eye out for anyone approaching. If you see anything at all, whistle."

He was pretty sure that the cop would run to the car and drive away the moment he heard the slightest noise. So be it. He eased toward the window and peeked inside. Nothing. Blinds were lowered all the way down. Light seeped out between the slats. The next window proved equally opaque.

The double doors came next. They weren't covered with blinds. He knelt to the side of the door. In his experience, people examined their environment first at eye level before letting their gaze wander lower. He counted on that moment to pull back in case someone was there. He peered around the door frame. On either side of the entrance were offices with solid doors. The short corridor led to a large dark space. He got up and took three long steps past the door and tried the window on the other side. Its blinds were all the way down. The blinds of the last window hung askew and left a triangular view into the room. He saw Ahmadi sitting on the ground working on her ankles which seemed to be tied. Oddly, her wrists weren't. He resisted the temptation to knock on the window. Nothing else to do but go back to the car and wait for the reinforcements.

At the double doors, he again squatted before peering around the edge of the door frame. The corridor was still empty. He rose and made to take his three steps. After the first one, the office door opened and a man came out. He wore all black. A submachine gun was slung over his shoulder. Demirel froze. The man stopped at the opposite office door. His lips moved. He was saying something through the door. Demirel couldn't hear anything.

Demirel remained frozen. No way he could move now. The man with the gun said something else, laughed, and turned to go back to where he'd come from. Unfortunately for Demirel, his luck ran out that very moment. The man didn't turn towards the dark interior, he turned towards the door. He stopped. The moment of recognition lasted only as long as it took for the guy to assess the situation. Demirel saw his eyes widening, his nostrils flaring, the hand reaching for the submachine gun. All of which took only a fraction of a second. Enough time for Demirel to fire two shots. The glass of the door shattered. The man and his submachine gun turned into a mosaic. Shards sailed through the air like icicles. The man's body swayed when the bullets hit him. He did not fall like the bits of glass. He stumbled backward. The submachine gun's muzzle rose.

Fire again! Now! Demirel's brain was screaming. His arm didn't obey fast enough. The man pulled the trigger and his submachine gun blasted at an incomprehensible rate. A gale of lead surrounded Demirel, the individual bullets almost visible as they drilled through the air. He looked up where most of the bullets flew and missed the three that hit him in the chest. He tumbled backward. The image of the shattered door grew fuzzy. His index finger, having a life of its own, tightened around the trigger once more. He didn't hear the shot. The man sank to the floor, mirroring Demirel doing the same outside.

He grasped his chest. His blood flowed over his hands, warm and viscous, and smelling like sheet metal. There was a shout, "Don't shoot." The volley of shots that followed the cry was the last thing he ever heard.

THIRTY-SIX

VERMEULEN EYED THE CHAIR. Nothing special about it.
A cheap swivel chair on five casters, the seat fabric
worn from long use, and the backrest off kilter. It was
too bulky to use as a weapon. The desk matched the
chair in terms of shabbiness. It did have one redeeming
quality—four metal legs. They were screwed into the
pressboard sides. It wouldn't take much effort to wrench
one off. The only question was the noise. If he made a
big racket, the one guard who wasn't distracted would
show up too early. But he had time, and with time, taking the legs off wouldn't be noisy.

The desk was surprisingly light. A good thing, too.
He'd imagined it full of paper files behind the locked
doors. Turning it so its top was on the floor was easy.
He grabbed one leg and started pulling. Not too hard
at first, just enough to see if there was any play. There
was plenty of it. He pulled a little harder. The pressboard creaked a little. Maybe side-to-side movement
would loosen the screws that kept the leg attached. He
pushed left and right to no discernible effect.

Decision time. One hard yank and get it over with,
or keep pulling and hoping the pressboard would give
without a racket. Since time was precious, he grabbed
the leg and pulled it all the way to the floor. The wood
groaned like a rusted door hinge, the screws popped
out and he held the leg in his hands. A solid weapon.

Luring the guard was the easy part. What happened after the guy opened the door was trickier. He could press against the wall and hit the man as soon as he stepped in. But, and that was a big but, would he step into the room? Vermeulen went on the assumption that these guards were better at their job than Ceylen's driver had been in Gaziantep. They expected him to be lying on the ground, tied up, and the desk standing as normal. Guards worth their salt would know something was off when the room wasn't like they left it. They'd stay outside the door and try to get him to come outside. All of which meant that he had to be back on the floor.

The downside to pretending that he was still tied up was that the guy would be standing over Vermeulen, giving him a tactical advantage. On the other hand, the surprise would be on Vermeulen's side. He decided to go that route. He righted the desk and kept it balanced on three legs by shoving the chair into the place of the missing leg. He kicked the door hard several times and laid down on the ground so that the guard could open it. The zip tie over his ankles should fool the guard enough to come closer and within reach of the desk leg he held under his back.

The response to his kicking the door took a long time. He was about to kick the door again when a voice on the other side of the door said, "What you want?"

"I need to piss," he said.

"So, piss."

"How? I can't even unzip my pants."

"Piss your pants. You dead soon. No need clean pants."

Damn. That guy was definitely smarter than the driver. And it left Vermeulen without a strategy to get out.

"Come on," he said, now pleading. "I know I'm going to be dead, but at least let me die with dignity."

Silence. Then, "You need piss, do it."

That's when two gun shots boomed through the air. One of the submachine gun responded sounding like a sewing machine running on a thousand volts. Vermeulen jumped up. The cavalry was there. Demirel had come. He opened the connecting door to the next office. Ahmadi had cut the ties around her ankles.

"They're here to get us. Get down, you don't want to get hit by a stray bullet," he said and they hit the floor.

THE SHOOTING STOPPED ABRUPTLY. Vermeulen heard someone shouting outside. The MP5 fired again. Then it was silent. He sat up. This didn't sound like the cavalry coming to save them. Who'd been out there? Whoever it was, it hadn't ended well for them.

"We need to get out of here," he said.

Ahmadi stared at him with wide eyes that said, "How?"

Vermeulen pulled up the blinds. The window was operable, but looked like it hadn't been opened in a long time. There was a clamp that held the movable section in place. He tried it. It was glued shut with grime. There were no tools around that could have helped. So he pushed it as hard as he could. It snapped open.

"Where should I go?" Ahmadi said.

"Get away from here and hide. Once the coast is clear, find your way to Kilis."

He grabbed a piece of paper from the desk and wrote Gaby's phone number on it.

"If you need help getting out of Turkey, contact my daughter. She lives in Germany. Now go."

She put the paper into her bag and wiggled through the tight slit outside.

"Hurry," he said, "they are coming."

Ahmadi hesitated a moment, turned and looked at him. "What about you?"

"Go. Stay out of sight."

She dropped to the ground outside. He lowered the blinds. The door opened. Two of the gunmen barged in, their eyes were wide with adrenaline. One of them smashed the butt of his gun in Vermeulen's side. A red lightning shot through his midsection, and he folded like a pocket knife. He searched for something to hang on to. The cord operating the blinds was the only thing close. He grabbed it and tore the whole contraption off the wall as he hit the ground. His vision turned muddy. The clatter of the blinds hitting the floor masked the angry voices of the two men. One of them turned Vermeulen on his back.

"The girl?" he shouted. "Where?"

The pain still dominated his brain, so he didn't reply. A grinding sound told him that they opened the window wider. Next thing he knew, they yanked him up and dragged him through the door, past the neighboring office and out the front door. Vermeulen tried to focus. He saw one of the gunmen on the floor, the shattered glass all over the place, the door with its jagged shards.

Outside, lay another body. He recognized the jacket. It was Demirel's. His heart sank. His last hope was dead. No ticket to Düsseldorf, no spending time with Gaby and Tessa.

THIRTY-SEVEN

THE BACKUP DEMIREL had requested—two cars, four policemen—showed up a half hour later. They found Demirel's car, then the tall cop, and, finally Demirel. The squad leader, a short wiry man, whose blue uniform seemed tailored for his body, looked at the carnage, and didn't disturb the scene. He radioed in his assessment and a half hour later, the old warehouse was swarming with police. Crime scene techs in white Tyvek coveralls and blue booties had put up halogen lights and combed the old warehouse and the ground outside for evidence. A mobile lab was ordered in from Gaziantep.

An hour after that, the superintendent arrived, angry because his dinner with a spunky redhead who was not his wife had been interrupted. He listened to the reports and walked around the scene until the techs shooed him away. He stopped to chat with the occasional officer, patting them on the back, telling them to buck up, they would find the animals who killed their colleagues. He retreated to his car, where he tried to assess how this whole thing might come back to bite him. Of course, Demirel was to blame. His lone wolf attitude, his ignoring orders, his not sharing his intel with his colleagues were well known. Most didn't like him. At least that's what he thought. But a dead cop was a dead cop. The ranks closed and speaking ill of the deceased was frowned upon. He was one of us. That's all that mattered.

What had Demirel been working on? That dead refugee woman. Yes, that was it. Damn refugees. Nothing but trouble. And did the department get more personnel? Of course not. What could they do with the limited resources? So, the dead refugee woman. He'd have one of the other inspectors check to see how far he had gotten. It wasn't at all clear what that case had to do with this shootout. Had he found the men who killed the refugee? Maybe. And then he went straight to them rather than wait for backup.

There was also the man's strange reaction to his questions about the UN investigator. Demirel was usually straightforward, but during that phone conversation he'd been evasive. He definitely knew more than he let on. But what he knew was anyone's guess.

Two dead policemen was bad news. There was no brushing that under the carpet. His men would be out for revenge. There'd be a manhunt and he had to look like he was out in front, leading the posse. He got out of the car again. Time to exercise some leadership.

One of the inspectors walked by and he stopped the man.

"What have you found so far?"

"We think Demirel and the gunmen surprised each other. He got a couple of shots off before he was hit. Then they went for his backup. That guy didn't even fire his gun. It looks like there were holding one or more hostages. We found broken zip ties. That would explain why Demirel was here in the first place. He did request backup. We think he was exploring the lay of the land when he surprised one of the gunmen. The fingerprints will tell us how many people were here."

The Superintendent nodded. "Do you know what cars they were driving?"

"There are recent tracks from three cars. On the basis of the tire impressions we can say that there was one sedan and two SUVs. The sedan was large, probably a luxury vehicle, given its wheelbase. The SUVs are anyone's guess."

"Any witnesses nearby?"

The inspector shook his head.

"So, no solid leads?" the Superintendent said.

"No. Nothing until we analyze the casings and the fingerprints. We may get to the SUV brand via the tread pattern, but that will take a while."

The Superintendent sighed. It was going to be a long night.

AFTER AHMADI CLIMBED through the window, she'd crawled away until she heard voices and flattened herself to the ground. There was more shouting inside. Steps crunching on broken glass. Something—or someone?—being dragged across the dirt. A car door opening. She resisted the urge to look up. The angry voices were too close. One SUV started and raced away, followed immediately by the second one.

She waited a couple of minutes longer. There was only silence. She raised her head. Nothing. The crickets restarted their chirping. She stood up. Turned around. The body, illuminated by a light from inside the warehouse didn't shock her. She'd seen enough bodies over the past years. No time to find out who it was. Getting away from this place was more important. She walked around the building to the road. Kilis was to the east of her. The glow of its lights defined the horizon.

The way back to the city was long and quiet. She kept her pace moderate. There was no place she had to be. When she saw the red and blue lights of police cars coming in the distance, she left the road and hid behind a shack. Ten minutes later, when nothing else appeared she went back on the road. It wasn't long before the next cavalcade of police vehicles approached. Again, she hid and let them pass. By the time the final police car, a larger sedan, raced by, she had reached a built-up area with other people on the road. No need to hide anymore. Other than the gangsters and Vermeulen, nobody knew she'd been at the warehouse.

A small restaurant catering to nightshift and early morning workers had an empty table where she sat to rest. She dug through her bag and found that the kidnappers hadn't taken her money. She ordered coffee and eggs. The smell of coffee and food revived her, but didn't change the fact that it was five in the morning and she didn't know what to do next. Part of her wanted to go to her room and sleep. Make the ugly world go away. But she knew she couldn't. The men still had Vermeulen. He'd helped her escape. She owed him.

None of that altered the fact that she couldn't go to the police. She had a healthy distrust of public authorities born from her experience in Syria. Maybe Turkish police were different, but her short interaction with them didn't give her any reason to think so. Admitting that she'd been at the warehouse made her a witness, or, worse, a suspect. They wouldn't let her go, they'd lock her up. Talking to Ayla in Gaziantep wasn't a good idea either. The Women's Center wouldn't want to be dragged into this. It could mean the end of her job.

No matter how she approached the problem, she arrived at the same conclusion. She was alone. Again. Which reminded her of the last time she felt so forlorn. Was it really only last Monday when she'd sat on the bench in the park? When Deniz Nazaryan had stopped and helped her? Of course. Nazarayan was just the person she needed. A lawyer could help with the police.

The gangsters did take her phone, so she had to find a public phone. The waitress pointed outside. She dug through her bag and changed a bill for some coins. Outside, she took Nazar's card and dialed her number. It was not even six in the morning. But this was an emergency. Worst case, she could leave a voicemail. She didn't have to. Nazaryan answered, albeit after many rings.

"Hi, Deniz. This is Rima Ahmadi. I'm sorry to be calling so early, but I'm in trouble."

THE SUV HADN'T missed any of the potholes as it raced away from the warehouse. Vermeulen was half lying on the rear seat of the SUV. Every jolt reminded him that the strike from the gun butt had bruised at least one of his ribs. The pain was manageable, though, which was a good sign. A broken rib would've put him out of commission. The goons had been in such a hurry to get away from the warehouse, they hadn't noticed that he wasn't tied anymore. Or, if they had, they didn't think it mattered. He had an entirely different opinion about that. He raised his head a little to look out the window. It was all dark. They were still some way from the city.

As soon as they reached it, they'd have to slow down. That'd be his moment.

The moment didn't come and he realized that they weren't driving to Kilis, at least not taking the most direct route. Which made sense since that's the way the police would come. It made him wonder where they were headed. The fate of Zada Homsi came to mind. Were they driving towards the border to kill and dump him there? Not if his earlier calculation was correct. On the other hand, once the police had uncovered their operation all bets were off. Whatever reason they had to keep him alive might no longer be important.

The SUV took another corner far too fast. His head bumped against the door, making him glad that modern four-wheel drives were build for comfort rather than ruggedness. In an old Land Rover, his head would have hit metal instead of fabric. The sun rose. For a while, it seemed as if they were just driving around. The two crooks up front were talking with each other incessantly. They sounded worried, which would explain why nobody had made a call yet. That should have been the first order of business. Maybe Ceylen didn't abide failure.

The driver slowed for another turn. Vermeulen raised his head again. He could see buildings. Good. Hopefully, they were back in Kilis. The car didn't speed up again and drove at city speeds. His chances were about to improve. It was only a question of time before they'd come to a stop light.

That took quite a bit longer than he'd expected. The guy in the passenger seat finally made a call that took a long while. An hour later, the car finally came to a stop. Vermeulen was prepared. He hit the unlock button, pulled the door lever and propelled himself out of the SUV. He managed to contain the damage the asphalt could do to his shoulder by rolling to the side. The strategy was lost on his ribs, which protested loudly. There was no time to entertain complaints from body parts. The passenger door flew open. Vermeulen pushed himself upright. They were at an intersection with cars and pedestrians around. On his side stood shops, most of them closed. A small kiosk stood at the street corner, selling newspapers, cigarettes and candy. The gunman jumped out of the car, the submachine gun in his hand. Vermeulen dove behind the kiosk. He heard the gunman shout. People on the sidewalk screamed. They took shelter in doorways, dove to the ground, ran across the street.

The kiosk was made of plywood. About as useful against a bullet as the newspapers in its window. Vermeulen was about to find out if Ceylen still needed him alive.

THIRTY-EIGHT

THE NEWS OF the police raid had set Mehmed Ceylen on edge. He sat in the living room of his mansion at the eastern outskirts of Kilis and watched the sun rise over the fields and woodlands. Ordinarily, those sunrises in the picture window calmed him, got him ready for the day. This morning, the magic didn't work. A confluence of imponderables had created a situation that was a genuine clusterfuck. First came this UN man Vermeulen, who wasn't happy to leave well enough alone. Totally unpredictable. Second, the idiot judge in Moldova, who'd decided to grow a spine and demand more money. Maybe not as unpredictable in principle, but the timing certainly was. Third, Demirel, one of the cops not on his payroll, who gets himself killed at his warehouse. Again, totally unpredictable. Even honest cops don't just risk their lives for nothing. Finally and worst, the warehouse was off limits for the foreseeable future. Just when the transport was about to arrive. The delivery needed to be redirected immediately. He made the call.

"Immediate change of plans. The trucks cannot go to the Kilis warehouse. The place is now off limits. Redirect the delivery to the Gaziantep warehouse. Yes, I know we've only leased it for the UN, but it's almost empty and this is an emergency. We need to get the cargo off the road. Call me as soon as the trucks arrive."

He needed some breakfast. The help was off for the

weekend and his wife never emerged from her bedroom before noon. So he went to the kitchen and took matters into his own hands. Fresh coffee came first. He rinsed his favorite coffee pot, the one with the mosaic inlays and the long wooden handle, added fresh water and put it on the burner. While the water heated, he ground the beans as fine as possible. He checked the water temperature with his pinky, waited a minute longer, then spooned the coffee grounds into the water. Two spoons of sugar followed. While the coffee grounds hydrated, he heated the frying pan, added butter and got eggs from the basket on the counter. He turned down the heat under the coffee. After the butter had melted, he chopped a couple of tomatoes and tossed them into the pan with garlic paste. The coffee was ready for stirring. He whipped the spoon in the pot until dark foam rose. He let it simmer, cracked the eggs into the pan and waited for them to set.

He took his food back to the picture window and had a sip of fresh coffee. That cleared his head. The warm food comforted him. Things were never as bad as they first seemed. It was only his mind that made them so. Change the attitude and get a better perspective. Take Demirel. Yes, his death was bad. The cops, even those on the take, were upset. One of theirs was dead. They'd be out for blood. For now, it meant a lot of bribes wasted. But wait a week or two until their greed comes back and they'll line up again. Which would be as good a time as any to remind them of their obligations.

The upside of Demirel's death was that his investigation would stop. He'd become dangerous. Ceylen's informant at the central registration administration had alerted him when Demirel's MERNIS searches showed up in the log. He'd found out that the Oben Özbek listed in the business register didn't exist. That had always been his first tripwire. It told him it was time to make preparations.

His second tripwire was someone connecting him with *Selim Tekstil* and *BenBek Lojistik*. When that happened, it was time to disappear. So far that wire hadn't been tripped. He'd taken a lot of care to keep that connection secret. The man he'd bribed to enter the fake ID when he registered the two companies was dead. The money transfers were all made from the same branch. The two people in charge would be dead as soon as the last transfer was complete.

He'd made one obvious mistake, letting his niece talk him into this cash card scam. She'd wanted a big project of her own, something big enough that gave her credibility in the eyes of his men. He'd understood that and wanted to give her a leg up. Still, it was far from easy. Yesim was a fire cracker and he was happy to put her in charge of the scam. Trouble was, she was also very beautiful. Her flirty ways distracted the men working with her and it made her seem less serious when negotiating with others. The more he got to know her, the more he worried. She had none of his patience.

At least his men had dealt with the situation at the warehouse and were on their way into the city with Vermeulen. They should be at the safe house any moment. Sure enough, his phone rang. The confirmation.

"You got away clean?" he said.

"Yes."

"And Vermeulen? Everything under control?"

"No. He got away. We're after him."

"Where is he?"

"Somewhere on İstiklal Caddesi. He jumped from the car at an intersection."

"He jumped? Why wasn't he tied up?"

"We didn't know he'd untied himself. We had to get away from the warehouse as fast as we could."

"Find him, but don't make a scene."

Ceylen ended the call and dialed the manager of his cellphone shop. His man answered almost immediately. Another early riser.

"Can you trace Vermeulen's phone and find out where he's been in the past few days?" Ceylen said.

"Hm. It's a foreign registration. We'd have to contact his provider and for that we'd have to have the phone's IMEI number. That's a problem. His provider won't just give us that information because we ask. They usually require a police request, maybe even a search warrant."

"But he's used it in Turkey, wouldn't the Turkish roaming provider know where his phone is? Can't you just approach them?"

"Only if we know who the roaming partner is, and for that I need his provider."

"I think I can find that. Let me call you back."

Ceylen redialed the number of his crew leader.

"I gave you Vermeulen's phone at the warehouse. Do you still have it?"

"Yes."

"Who is his service provider?"

There was a pause that dragged on longer than Ceylen wanted. Being patient was a virtue that seemed extravagant in the current circumstance.

"Okay," his man said. "It is called American Mobile."

"Thanks."

He called back his manager and told him the provider's name.

"Good," the man said. "I'll see what I can do. If Tek-Cell is the roaming partner you'll have the information within the hour."

So FAR, no shots had been fired. The gunmen didn't want to cause a public stir. It gave Vermeulen a small window to escape. With his back pressed against the kiosk, he sorted out his options. There was a narrow alley between two buildings. It was tempting, but he didn't know where it led. It could end in a courtyard and then he'd be trapped. The alternative was running along the street. It wasn't too busy, so the gunmen could follow him easily. At the same time, the street was public and, at the moment, that was his best insurance. He made a dash for the cross street.

The gangsters didn't miss a beat and were after him with only a few yards between them. The cross street had a median. It connected to a large roundabout. Nothing but open space. No place to hide. He'd need to keep running. And he was in no shape to do it. His lungs were already complaining.

He crossed the street to the tiled expanse at the center of the roundabout. Passers-by got out of the way. Whatever it was, they didn't want to get involved. The black-clad men could be cops. Best not to tangle with them. Vermeulen kept feeling guns trained on his back. A crazy notion, really. If they wanted to shoot him, they'd have done it already.

A group of teenagers with skateboards practiced their jumps and skids on the smooth surface. One of them gave him a thumbs-up. Vermeulen would have smiled if not every fiber in his body were screaming for him to stop running.

There was a scream behind him, followed by a thud. Another thud followed. He turned his head and saw the two gangsters on the ground. The skateboarders scattered fast, skating in all different directions. They must've tripped them. Vermeulen kept running. Across from him, a black SUV stopped. It was the third gunman. He'd driven on to intercept him. Vermeulen zigged ninety degrees to the right. The SUV tried to back up, but the cars behind it honked. The driver had no option but to go around the circle.

Vermeulen reached the edge of the tiled center and dashed into the traffic of the roundabout. More honking. He vaulted over the hood of a small car, dodged a second one and reached a small copse that served as an island between the traffic circle and an access street. He ducked behind the trees and bent down to fight back the nausea. His side ached with a stitch. He gulped for air. This wasn't the place to stop. He needed to keep going.

Through the greenery and across the access street, he saw the skateboarders. One of them waved to him. He raced across the asphalt. There were eight of them and they surrounded him like a protective cordon. The one who'd waved, a lanky kid in black jeans and T-shirt, said something. He had a hint of beard and longish black hair.

"English?" Vermeulen said.

"Sure, man. Come with us. We know a spot."

They led him into an alley to a rusty metal door. Two of them pulled at it. The gate groaned open a couple of feet. They all filtered in and the last pulled the door shut again and slammed a heavy bolt across the steel frame.

Vermeulen was still panting.

"Thanks," he said. "I needed a place to hide. Did you trip the men behind me?"

Two of them nodded.

"Another thanks. Without that, they would've gotten me."

"Were they cops?"

Vermeulen shook his head.

"Gangsters. They'd kidnapped me."

"Why? Who are you?"

"I work for the United Nations."

There was a spark of recognition in the eyes of the lanky kid with the black hair.

"We thought they were police," the lanky kid said.

"That why you helped me?"

He nodded with a grin. "Police are always after us. And all we want to do is skate. So we have solidarity with people running from the police."

"Thanks again."

Since the goons had only taken his phone, he still had his wallet. He fished it out and said, "I have to make a phone call. Could one of you buy me a cheap phone?"

One of the skateboarders nodded. He had reddish curls and was shorter than the others. Vermeulen gave him what in his mind was more than enough money and told him to buy as much air time as he could.

"I can't stay here," Vermeulen said to the lanky kid, who nodded.

"You need different clothes," he said. He turned and spoke to one of his friends. That one disappeared into the house to which the courtyard belonged.

"His old man is at work, his mother split, that's why we hang out here."

A few minutes later, the kid came back with a pair of trousers, a blazer and a cap. Vermeulen changed right there and rolled his clothes up to take to his apartment. The borrowed clothes were on the small side, but they'd do. The cap made the most difference because it hid his blond hair.

The gang left the courtyard and scouted the surroundings. The lanky kid stayed with Vermeulen. Ten minutes later, the scouts returned. Three reported seeing the gangsters searching in the vicinity but more toward the east.

"Okay, man," the lanky kid said. "Where do you want to go?"

Vermeulen gave him the address of the rental apartment.

"Good. We take you there on safe streets."

As they left, the redhead came back with a phone. It looked fancier than Vermeulen expected, but he saw that the kid had gotten three hundred minutes of air time. That should be enough.

THIRTY-NINE

A PHONE CALL woke up Yaser early on Saturday morning. The call came from her uncle. No surprise there. Nobody else would dare wake her up on the weekend. Since she discovered the money transfers that proved Ceylen paid for her father's assassination, she was filled with cold hatred. The kind that was calculating, scheming. As much as she wanted to kill him right then and there, she knew the real revenge would be having him see her take everything from him. Such a plan needed careful consideration. She had taken first steps, but that didn't constitute a plan. In the meantime, she played along.

"Yes, Uncle. What can I do for you?"

"I have a delicate job. We're looking for a man who's escaped us. His name is Valentin Vermeulen. He works for the United Nations and is serious trouble. It is crucial that you find him. On the basis of his phone records, we know he stays somewhere near the *Pirlioğlu* mosque. There is no guest house or hotel listed in that area. So we don't know where he stays. You must find him. If he gets away, it puts our entire operation in jeopardy. That means you too. I'll send you his picture."

"Sure thing. What do I do when I find him?"

"Call me. That's all. Don't talk to him. Don't even let him see you."

"Okay."

She ended the call. Seconds later her phone buzzed and the picture of Vermeulen arrived. Middle aged guy, blond, his face somewhere between coarse and rugged. Not really her type. But the fact that he worked for the UN made her pause. The flicker of an idea floated just at the edge of her consciousness. *Let's find the man first.*

She fired up her laptop and searched for online agencies that offered short term rentals. There weren't that many. Kilis wasn't a tourist destination. She checked each and looked at the locations offered. One of them, a vacation rental company, had an apartment near the mosque. She smiled. Another reason why her uncle needed to go. He was too old school. She knew tech in a way he couldn't even fathom. That hint of an idea became more concrete. She called the TekCell shop. Nobody answered. Good. A stop there and then on to that apartment. *All right, Mr. Vermeulen, let's see how useful you are.*

AHMADI LAY ON the sofa in Nazaryan's apartment and gazed lazily at the curtain rippling in the breeze. She had slept a little since her early morning arrival. Nazaryan had been kind enough to hold back with the questions until Ahmadi had recovered from what she called "the ordeal."

Ahmadi had been tired, for sure, but the civil war had robbed her of any squeamishness when it came to spilled blood. A calloused shell encased that part of her that used to abhor violence. As far as she was concerned, it was a good thing, the only way forward. Occasionally, a small voice, deep inside, warned her that this hardness would scar her for good and told her to soften again. She pushed that voice away. *Some other time. When everything was back to normal.* To which the small voice usually responded, *As if.* By then, she was usually tired of arguing with herself and something else demanded her attention.

At noon, Nazaryan brought a lunch of hummus, pita bread, pickled vegetables and lamb *köfte.* Ahmadi wolfed it down without any conversation. Finally, she wiped her mouth with a napkin, looked up and said, "I need a lawyer."

"What happened," Nazaryan said.

It took a while to tell her all that had happened. The disappearance of Zada, meeting Vermeulen, the interview at the police station, the job with the Women's Center, finding the woman who had met Zada and following the lead to the TekCell shop, her detention and her escape at Vermeulen's expense.

When Ahmadi finished, Nazaryan took a deep breath, breathed out slowly, looked at the young woman and said, "I think a lawyer is the last thing you need. You need a safe place, preferably far away from here."

"Where can I go?"

"Go to Germany, Sweden, anywhere. It's not safe for you here."

"I sort of realize that. There's nothing you can do to help me?"

"I'm a real estate lawyer. I don't know how to protect you from the kind of gangsters who kidnap you."

"What about the police?" Ahmadi said.

Nazaryan grimaced, then shook her head. "I don't trust the police. You are obviously involved in something. According to the news, two policemen were killed last night. Right now, they want revenge, anyone caught up in this mess will be detained. The last place you'll want to be is jail."

"Can't I stay here?"

Nazaryan hesitated a little too long before saying yes. "Let's say for a couple of days. In the meantime, I'll find out what's happening. Maybe there's a way you can testify and help them find the cop killers. I'll also talk to a colleague who's better equipped to handle criminal issues."

Ahmadi sighed. She was asking too much. "I really appreciate your kindness. Maybe staying here isn't a good idea after all. I'd better leave town. I still have my room in Gaziantep. Nobody knows about that except for Ayla. I could just go there."

The relief in Nazaryan's face was palpable. "Yes, that's a better idea. Even though Gaziantep isn't very far, it's a different world. Funny how that works. I can drive you there now. You stay out of sight and I'll do some investigating. Don't worry about Ayla. I'll talk to her after I drop you off. I'll explain to her what happened. You can even do survey work in Gaziantep. It'll get you out and doing something, better than sitting here cooped up with nothing but bad memories."

She drove Ahmadi to her room so she could pack her things.

"I'll be back in a little while," she said.

THE SKATEBOARDERS MOVED around Vermeulen the way body guards protect VIPs. Not so close as to be obvious, but close enough to let a careful observer know their man wasn't alone. Before coming to an intersection, two of them would skate ahead and check the cross street and give the all clear sign. Vermeulen couldn't help but smile. There was a delightful innocence about the seriousness with which they performed their task. Adults sometimes don't get how kids in their mid-teens can be very focused when they set their minds to it.

They knew the streets inside out. It was also clear that they chose their streets because they were more suitable for their skateboards. They didn't talk much to Vermeulen, but there was a constant patter between them. The lanky kid, who was definitely their leader, would occasionally ask a question about living in America and his job at the UN. That was the extent of their communication. By the time they reached the neighborhood where his rental was located, it had become afternoon. Vermeulen recognized the surroundings and stopped.

"We're getting close to my apartment," he said. "Can you all go ahead and have a look around?"

"What are we looking for?" the lanky kid said.

"Anything unusual. You have a feel for the street. Are there police? Cars parked with people inside doing nothing. People loitering, looking like they have no place to be."

"Okay."

They went ahead. The location of his rental was still secret. The false information he gave to Ceylen the day before hadn't been questioned. So the scouting was not really necessary. Still, better to be cautious than run blindly into a trap. He thought of calling Tessa, but decided to wait until he was safely behind the gates of his apartment.

The skateboarders drifted back to where he waited. The erratic quality of their maneuvers made for excellent cover. The lanky kid skated toward him at a rather high speed. At the last moment the front of his board kicked up, he made a quick one-eighty turn on the rear wheels, jumped off, and grabbed the board that seemed suddenly suspended in mid-air.

"We saw nothing suspicious. There were a few people on the street, but they were all going places. The parked cars were empty, except for one, a BMW Z4. A young woman sits behind the steering wheel. She's hot. And she's doing stuff on her phone."

"Did she notice you?"

"Of course, kids with skateboards are always noticed. We didn't come back the same way we went. I don't think she suspected anything."

"Thank you. You've been great. Really. Is there anything I can do for you?"

The lanky kid beamed with pride, but he shook his head. "You were in trouble, and we helped you. Next time you hear someone complaining about kids with skateboards, tell them what we did."

"I'll do that. For sure. Good luck to you."

"We'll bring you to your place. Let's go."

They proceeded as before. When they neared the apartment, the lanky kid pointed to the silver BMW parked on the other side.

"That's the woman. She's still there."

Vermeulen caught a glance and did a double take. He'd seen that face before. The mess of curly hair, the oblong face with a clear jaw line and a small pointed chin. It was the face from the website, Yesim Yaser, vice-president of TurkOasis. She seemed to pout as she looked at her phone. She looked up before he could turn away. Their eyes connected only for a split second, but Vermeulen saw the flash of recognition.

FORTY

VERMEULEN LOCKED THE gate and the front door after him. Having the perpetrator of the card fraud waiting outside his supposedly secret apartment spooked him. Hell, he'd barely escaped from her uncle's kidnappers. How could she have found his place? He didn't have his phone anymore, so they couldn't have traced that. The elation he'd felt after escaping from the SUV fizzled. Trouble just kept finding him.

First, he had to call Tessa. He registered the new phone, loaded the credits and made the call to New York City. Tessa answered after several rings.

"It's me. Different phone, but I'm okay."

He could hear her exhale.

"Ahmadi and I got away," he said. "First I helped her escape from a warehouse and, later, I got away after they tried to ferry me to a different place. So, no reason to worry anymore. At least for now."

"What do you mean? Get the hell out of there. Make your way to Düsseldorf and be done with this mess."

"I will, I promise. But Yaser, the woman who ran the fake NGO and the card scam is parked outside."

"Did she recognize you?"

"Yes."

"Any idea what she might want from you?"

"She's the niece of the mobster who kidnapped me. It's pretty clear what she wants."

There was a pause. "Then why hasn't she done it already?"

"Hmm," he said. "I wonder of she's on a different page than her uncle. I mean, why else show up without the goons?"

"So what's the plan?" she said.

"I'll book the ticket and get a taxi to the airport in Gaziantep. Once I'm past security, even the mobsters won't be able to get to me. So, the only obstacle is getting out of here unseen."

"You want me to book the ticket?"

"Nah. I got my laptop here."

"And how are you going to get away?"

At that moment, the doorbell rang.

"Hold on," he said.

The patterned glass in the front door didn't give him a clue as to who stood by the gate. He went back and tried to find a window that would give him a better view. He couldn't see anyone.

"Who's there?" Tessa's voice came from the phone in his hand.

"No idea. I can't see the gate from the house." What he could see was the BMW on the street. It was empty.

"I think it's Yaser," he said.

"What are you going to do?"

"Talk to her. As long as she's outside the gate, she can't do anything."

"Don't. Just book your flight and get out of there."

"How can I leave with someone at the gate?"

"You still have your rental car. Just get in and ignore the woman."

"I don't think that's an option. So far, every crook I've encountered here was armed. Driving away in a hail of bullets doesn't strike me like a good choice. I'll put the phone on speaker, so you can hear everything."

He opened the front door. Sure enough, Yaser stood at the gate. She looked even more striking than what he'd seen of her through the windshield. Her jeans and T-shirt were fashionably close-fitting and she was holding a large envelope.

"Mr. Vermeulen," she said. "I have a proposition for you. Could you buzz the gate open?"

"Why don't you tell me about it through the gate?"

"Because it's complicated and confidential. It would only take one call right now and in less than fifteen minutes you'd be surrounded by a large number of men with guns. I'm offering you an alternative."

"You're the vice president for the sham NGO and other companies owned by Oben Özbek. Why should I even listen to you?"

"Okay. To show you I'm serious, let me share this bit with you. The Oben Özbek listed as the owner of those enterprises doesn't exist. They are all owned by my uncle Mehmed Ceylen. He's been running a massive money laundering operation to clean the money from his illegal weapons deals."

"How do I know you weren't sent to put a bullet through my skull?"

"I left my jacket in my car. As you can see there's no way I'm hiding a gun."

She turned around. Her snug T-shirt revealed no telltale bulges. Her jeans were skin-tight.

"Pull up your jeans legs," he said.

"You don't know much about women's fashion, do you?" She tried to roll up the hems, but didn't get far.

"I think I'll let her in," Vermeulen mumbled loud

enough for Tessa to hear him and pushed the buzzer. The gate opened and Yaser came inside. He made sure she pushed the gate shut again. Inside the apartment, Yaser chose the most comfortable chair and examined Vermeulen.

"You don't seem too surprised," she said.

Vermeulen sat down opposite her and put the phone on a side table.

"I know about the money laundering," he said. "The gun running is new information but that doesn't change anything. All I care about is the UN getting reimbursed the two million dollars you stole, so that the refugees get the aid they need."

"Oh. How did you find out?"

"I have my sources. Why don't you tell me about your proposition."

"Why don't you turn off the phone. I'd rather not have someone overhear our conversation."

"And I'd rather leave it on. I will need a record of what we talked about. If it's any help, the person on the other end is not in Turkey."

Yaser shrugged. "Okay. It won't make much of a difference. My proposition is simple, help me bring down my uncle and you'll get to leave Turkey alive."

"That doesn't work for me on so many levels, I don't even know where to start."

"You're not in a position to negotiate. One call and you go down. But listen first. I'm glad you already know about the money laundering. Didn't you ever wonder where the money that needs laundering comes from? The two million from the UN is mere petty cash. It was my project anyway. My uncle didn't even want to do it because it was too small."

"So did you kill Zada Homsi?"

"No. I didn't. But she got in the way and was a risk."

"So you had her killed?"

"Yes, but that's not why I'm here."

Her dismissive reference to a murder she'd ordered sent a chill ran down Vermeulen's spine. Yaser was bad news. He had no interest in anything she might have to offer. Oblivious to his concerns, she opened the envelope and took out a sheaf of papers, held together by a paper clip.

"Here," she said. "Have a look at these."

Vermeulen took the papers and examined the one on top. It was a spreadsheet printout, each row with a description and a price. It was the description that made the hair at Vermeulen's neck tingle. He was looking at a shopping list for some deadly military hardware. Five hundred AK-47 rifles, a hundred cases of matching ammunition, Humvee-mountable fifty caliber machine guns, hardened steel armor for Humvees, more ammunition. He flipped the page. Two hundred shoulder-launched antiaircraft missiles, all the hardware to support these apparatuses. The next pages listed artillery shells, mortar rounds. He stopped reading.

"What is this?"

"It's the last order from *Daesh*. You call them ISIS. It's in transit right now. As far as I know, a convoy entered Turkey from Georgia a few days ago. It should be close by now."

"How did it get to Georgia?"

"I don't know everything. Our company in Qatar bought the hardware with the proper end user certificate. There are plenty of Qatari billionaires who want *Daesh* to win. From there it came by ship via the Suez

Canal and the Black Sea. They didn't unload this stuff in Turkey, since that would imply complicity, so they ship it to Georgia and then truck it through Turkey."

Vermeulen stood up and paced. He'd forgotten that Tessa was on the phone.

"Does the government know about this?" he said.

"What do you think? Of course. Nothing of this scale happens in Turkey without Erdoğan knowing."

"How can they allow it? I mean Turkey is a NATO member, and NATO is fighting ISIS."

"That's why the mob is doing it, plausible deniability. Come on, you must know that Erdoğan is an opportunist. He'll support anyone who'll fight the Kurds, including *Daesh*. The last thing he wants is a Kurdish state on the other side of the border."

"Why are you coming to me?"

"My uncle is in way over his head. He's leveraged like crazy on this deal. It's a stupid deal even with the amazing payoff, because he'll be at the mercy of the government. Anytime they want to turn the screw, all they have to do is threaten an investigation. He let the money blind him."

"Why do you care?" Vermeulen said, sitting down again.

"Because I have no interest in having him gamble with and lose my patrimony. And for what? A bunch of crazy fanatics who want to put me in black burkas and rape me at their leisure. He's playing with fire. I don't want to get burned. My uncle is a holdover from the past. Erdoğan's market reforms have turned much of what used to be illegal legal. Why be a loan shark when you can charge crazy interest rates with legal loans? Sure, drugs are still a profit center, but once legalization spreads in Europe, that will diminish, too. I have good ideas how to restructure the business. But he won't listen. So I'll have to take matters into my own hand."

"Ah. Biting the hand that fed you. Not very gracious."

"He also had my father killed. Is that enough of a reason?"

The edge in her voice made the hair on his neck stand up. "What do you want me to do?"

"Smuggle these papers out of the country. Give them to someone at NATO or the UN. The moment this becomes public, his life is over. I want to see him publicly humiliated. After that, it gets personal. I'll push him out and take over what's left."

"What's in it for me? As I said outside, my non-negotiable condition is that the two million dollars are returned to the UNHCR. That shouldn't be hard, with you being the vice president of the companies. Once I see that the money has been transferred, I'll leak the information about Ceylen."

Yaser made a show of thinking over his proposal. "No. I can't agree to that. I will have given up a substantial chunk of money without any assurances that you will release the information about my uncle. As I said, without me, you won't get to the airport alive."

"And one call from me to Ceylen and you go down," he said. He didn't have Ceylen's number, but she didn't know that. "I guess we're at an impasse. I have things to do. Please leave."

Yaser didn't move from her chair. "Why the hurry? We've barely finished the opening round. I'll return half of the money to UNHCR, you leave and release the dirt on my uncle, and I'll transfer the rest."

"Nice try. But I don't trust you to live up to your promise."

"But you expect me to trust you?"

"I'm not the criminal in the room. I didn't order a poor woman killed because she asked questions. I'm not the one proposing to get rid of my uncle. I'm just the investigator trying to stop the fraud you committed. I think I'm ahead on the trust meter."

Yaser shook her head. He could tell that this wasn't going the way she had planned. Before she could say anything, Tessa's voice came from the phone. "Take the documents, book your ticket, and get to the airport."

"What about making sure the money is returned to UNHCR?"

"I don't think there is any way you can assure that will happen," Tessa said.

"Well, how about that," Yaser said. "Whoever this is on the phone, you should listen to her." She got up, walked to the phone, and said, "Thank you for talking sense. Why are all men so stubborn? So, do we agree?"

Vermeulen nodded. He took the phone off speaker and walked into the kitchen. "Are you serious?"

"No. I just want you to get the hell out of there. Forget the UN money. That's not coming back. You are between two warring mob factions and if you don't want to get ground to pieces, you play along until you are at the airport."

"Okay."

Back in the living room, Yaser's phone rang. She answered. "Yes, I'm looking for him. I have a lead, but so far, no results. Where are your men looking? By the mosque? Yeah, me too. I'll be in touch the moment I know more."

She ended the call and looked at Vermeulen. "That was my uncle. His men are combing this neighborhood. They have your picture and they know what car you rented. The only way out of here is in my car. Book your flight and let's go."

Vermeulen opened his laptop and booked a flight to Düsseldorf for that evening. Unfortunately, there was no direct flight, but Izmir seemed far enough away to be a safe stopover.

FORTY-ONE

AHMADI DAWDLED AS she was packing her things. As logical as it was to go to Gaziantep, the feeling in the pit of her stomach told her that she was betraying Zada. She was running away instead of bringing her killers to justice. The phone shop was the key to the case. That's where Zada had gone and that's where she'd disappeared. The men who'd detained her there probably didn't kill Zada, but they knew who did. The men who'd taken her to the warehouse could have been the killers. They were ruthless. There was nothing she could do to them to avenge her friend.

She shared Nazarayan's aversion for the police. She didn't know much about the Turkish police, but the cops in Syria were to be avoided whenever possible. So she was inclined to believe Nazarayan. On the other hand, the time at the police station—was it really just a week ago—hadn't been so bad. The inspector wasn't friendly, but he also hadn't harassed her. Maybe Nazarayan was wrong about the police. They didn't know she'd been at the warehouse where the gunfight took place. She'd made sure that nobody saw her when she walked back to Kilis. She could go and give her statement. After that, it was in their hands. Maybe the killer would never be found, but at least she'd done what she could to make it happen.

She stopped folding a skirt. Better to do it now. Nazarayan would be back soon to give her a lift to Gaziantep. If she hurried, her friend wouldn't even know she'd talked to the cops. She put on her scarf and left.

The Kilis police headquarters was like a wasp nest that had been poked with a stick. Cars were coming and going, policemen hurried in and out, dispatchers were hollering, radios squawked with the voices of cops. She heard the name Demirel several times and wondered if the Inspector was even at the station. Others shouted something about black cars. It had to be about the shooting at the warehouse. That put her on edge. If they ever found out that she'd been there, she wouldn't leave the station in the foreseeable future.

A policeman brought her to Demirel's office, but Demirel didn't sit in his chair. In his stead she saw a fat older man in a fine suit, who had beads of sweat on his forehead. In front of him lay three piles of papers. He pointed to a chair but kept sorting through the papers in front of him. One of the dispatchers came to the door and said something about a black car and a traffic jam near İstiklal Caddesi. Ahmadi had no idea where that was.

"Excuse me," she said in English. She needed to avoid any chance of misunderstanding. If the policeman behind the desk didn't understand English, they'd have to get a translator.

The fat man raised his index finger but didn't look up from the papers he was rifling through. Another cop came to the door. Apparently kids with skateboards had chased an American. The fat man told them to find the kids and went on to the second pile, just examining one document at a time. She was getting antsy. Why was this man ignoring her?

"Excuse me," she said, a little firmer now. "Inspector Demirel, please."

The man looked up, not so much angry as agitated. "Sorry dear, you've come at a bad time. Major crisis, just wait."

At least he spoke English.

The first dispatcher came back reporting that the kids had been found, but not the American. *Was that Vermeulen they were talking about?* He'd been so kind, letting her escape first and get away from the people who'd killed Zada. Maybe he'd gotten away, too. That made her feel better. Another dispatcher came in the room and said that two of the skateboarder kids had been caught. She couldn't understand all of it, but it sounded like they'd been with Vermeulen. Next thing, the fat man went to the map on the wall and marked several streets with push pins. Then he told the dispatcher to send the police cars to those streets. At the center of the shape made by the streets was the symbol for a mosque.

Finally, he sat down and looked at Ahmadi.

"Inspector Demirel isn't in. I'm the Superintendent, can I help you?"

"I'm Rima Ahmadi. I spoke with the Inspector a week ago. My friend Zada Homsi, she was killed eleven days ago. I have more information."

The superintendent shuffled through one of the piles in front of him and found several pages stapled together. He scanned the pages and looked up again.

"Yes, I see. What would you like to report?"

"Can I speak with the Inspector, please? He knows the case."

"I'm afraid that's not possible. You can speak to me, I'm his superior."

Ahmadi hesitated. Not that she'd trusted the inspector, but at least she knew he'd treated her with respect. His boss had ignored her for the better part of fifteen minutes. Well, better to get it over with and get away from Kilis.

"I know who killed Zada," she said.

The superintended raised his eyebrows, but didn't miss a beat. "You do? Please tell."

Ahmadi explained how she had been looking for anyone who'd seen Zada, how she'd found a woman who'd told her about the cash cards and where to get them, how she'd gone to the TekCell shop, where two men detained her. "I'm sure these men know who killed Zada."

"How did you get away from these men?"

Ahmadi looked down. "I escaped," she said after a long second.

"Yes, I understand that, but how? From the shop? Did they take you somewhere else? Did someone help you?"

She felt the heat rising in her. She wasn't good at lying, but she had to.

"I got away. That's all I can say."

The superintendent didn't seem satisfied with her answer. His eyes became harder.

Hoping to steer the conversation back to the gangsters, she said, "Are you going to arrest these men?"

"Before I can order their arrest, I need to know more about this entire matter."

"Didn't the inspector tell you about this case?"

The superintendent pointed to one of the piles in front of him. "That's all I have. But tell me. Is there a UN employee by the name of Vermeulen involved in this? He accompanied you when you came in the last time, did he not?"

The mention of Vermeulen's name shocked Ahmadi. Her face froze. She was so bad at lying. The superintendent definitely didn't believe her. "Listen," he said. "Inspector Demirel was killed last night. We are looking for his killers. We know it has to do something with this Vermeulen. So, if you know anything at all, tell me, or you'll be in big trouble."

"And if I tell, I'm in big trouble too," she said.

"No, you won't be. I promise."

She knew he couldn't make such promises. So she shook her head. He tried again.

"If you didn't do anything illegal, you'll have no trouble. Did you?"

"No, I'm a registered refugee and I've not broken any law."

"Good. So tell me what happened."

"They took me to a warehouse. They made me call Vermeulen, and he came." She continued the story until her escape and her walk to Kilis. She did leave Nazarayan out of her story.

"Do you know where Vermeulen stays in Kilis?"

"No, but I saw him at a restaurant and it was close to the *Pirlioğlu* Mosque."

The superintendent got up, went to the map and pointed to the center of the square made by the pins. "That's right here." He picked up his phone and said something about searching for Vermeulen by the mosque. There was something else. All she heard was TekCell. But that was enough. He was acting on her information. That's all she'd wanted. She rose to leave.

"Please sit," he said. "We must wait."

"I can't wait," Ahmadi said. "I have to go to Gaziantep. I have a job there."

"Sorry, we need you to identify the men once we catch them."

"How long will that be?"

The superintendent just shrugged. "You can wait in one of the interview rooms. The dispatch crew can get you some coffee."

He picked up the phone again and barked something into the receiver. A cop appeared in the door and took Ahmadi to an interview room. He closed the door on his way out. There was no door handle on the inside.

FORTY-TWO

VERMEULEN BACKED HIS rental car out onto the street. He wanted to make sure the agency could retrieve it. The accountants at the UN would be very unhappy to have the cost of a car added to his per diem.

While Yaser drove her silver Z4 into the parking space, he went back inside, ostensibly to get his luggage. But he took a detour into the bathroom where he pulled the envelope with the arms deal information from his briefcase and photographed each page.

His skin felt damp. This was the crux of the plan that hadn't even formed yet in his mind. Half way through, he heard Yaser calling him.

"I'm in the restroom. Be out in a minute."

He turned on the water. Being tense didn't help his photography skills. Twice he had to delete a photo because it wasn't sharp. When he was done, he emailed the photos to himself and to Tessa, then deleted his email account from the phone. He flushed.

Outside, Yaser waited, talking on her phone. She put her hand over the microphone and said, "You are too young to have an old man's bladder."

He didn't bother with an answer and lugged his suitcase downstairs to load into her trunk. His blood was rushing in his ears. He felt like a goal keeper staring at a loose ball in the penalty box. If the other team got there first, they'd score. Trouble was, there was more than one team and he was all alone.

She slipped into the driver's seat, still talking on her phone. Apparently, getting her own crew to run interference wasn't as easy as she promised. At one point she was shouting, a moment later her voice could have frozen the Mediterranean.

He was starving and the next meal he could anticipate was airline food. But he figured that asking for time to go make a sandwich would be pushing it.

"It's all set up," she said finally. "Let's go."

"You'll return the money to UNHCR?" he said. He didn't know why he even asked. She was going to do no such thing.

"Of course, as soon as I know you've given the documents to the right people. Check with Balbay. He'll confirm it."

That was no assurance. Balbay would tell him anything he was told to say.

"I believe you said you were going to transfer half now and the other half after I deliver the information to the authorities."

Yaser looked at him with an air of pity. Tessa had read the situation right. The money was gone. Getting out of here alive was his only job. She backed onto the street.

"Wait a moment, I have to close the gate," he said.

"Don't you have a remote?"

"I left it inside. I'm checking out."

She groaned and stopped. He got out, punched the code on the pad and the gate slid shut. He looked down the street and saw a black SUV round the corner at the end of the block. Damn, they're here already. He hurried to the BMW and slipped into the passenger seat.

"The goon squad is coming, we better get away."

She looked back, saw the SUV and stepped on the accelerator. The tires squealed as she shot down the street.

"Really?" he said. "Couldn't you have made it a little less obvious?"

"That's how I drive."

He turned and saw the SUV speed up behind them.

"Well, now they are following us," he said.

"You didn't have to close the damn gate."

"And you didn't have to take off like a bat out of hell."

"A bat out of hell? Is it an American idiom? I like it."

He shook his head. Yaser took the next right entirely too fast. The passenger side tires lost contact with the pavement for a moment. The centrifugal force threw him against her. Her perfume was sweet but not cloying. Not that it had any calming effect. She swerved into a left turn which threw Vermeulen against the door. It was worse than a ride at the fair.

Behind them, the SUV had dropped back some, but it was still following. Maybe they weren't sure a speeding car was worth pursuing. Which made sense if their job was trolling the streets, staring at a picture of his face. On the other hand, they might have spotted him closing the gate. Blond hair wasn't all that common in Turkey.

Yaser continued to drive as if she were qualifying for the Monte Carlo Grand Prix. At least she was good at it. He glanced over and saw her relaxed and smiling.

"A bat out of hell," she said. "Cool. That's me all right."

Next thing, she slammed on the brakes, sending the car into a crazy skid. Vermeulen saw why. Another SUV was heading straight for them. They'd called in reinforcements.

Yaser turned the skid into a right turn and raced into a narrow alley. Problem was the alley was full of people and things. The people scattered frantically. The things were left behind. She hit a kid's bike. It flew against a wall. An old man had dropped his cane and they broke it into pieces. Vermeulen looked back and saw that the SUV was stuck at the entrance of the alley. Yaser must have noticed too because she slowed down but it didn't stop her from mangling a trike.

Before he could celebrate, he saw an SUV block the other end of the alley. Yaser swore under her breath. She rolled to a cross alley and turned left, but the alley dead-ended in a wall.

Yaser looked over her shoulder. "Ah, there's the way out." She jammed the stick into reverse and squealed backward, crossing the alley they had come on and shooting down the narrow cobbles. Vermeulen had never backed up this fast, certainly not in a narrow alley with stone houses that loomed only a foot away on each side. By the time his brain had registered how mad she was, she'd swerved into a street. She blew through a stop sign and barely missed a police car careening past them with sirens wailing.

"I think I'd rather take a taxi," Vermeulen said, somewhat queasy. "Let's drive until we see one we can flag down. That'd be my safest way to the airport."

"What? You don't like my driving? I lost the guys, didn't I?"

"Yeah, but that's at best temporary. They know your

car. I bet there aren't many silver Z4s driving around Kilis. How many black SUVs does your uncle have?"

"My uncle can mobilize any number of cars, depending on which favors he calls in. And not all of them will be black SUVs either."

"That makes my point even stronger," Vermeulen said. "If you want your documents out of the country, I need to be in a different car."

"Correction, we need to be in a different car. I'm not letting you out of my sight until you get into your airplane."

"I see. I guess our distrust is mutual."

"I'm not going to have you sell me out to my uncle to get your stupid money back."

They reached Yavus Sultan Selim Cadessi. The street led straight to the Gaziantep highway. There was more traffic. Yaser turned and headed south. She saw an empty taxi and maneuvered to cut it off. The driver honked furiously. She jumped out, large bills in hand, and yelled back at him. The negotiations took only a moment.

"Put your stuff in his trunk," she said.

Vermeulen hustled over with his things. Yaser parked her BMW and joined him in the cab. All Vermeulen understood was *havalimanı*. He hoped it meant airport. The driver, infected by their edginess, stepped on it. They hit the interchange with the D-850 in less than ten minutes and merged onto the northbound lane.

Vermeulen started breathing a little easier. That lasted about five minutes. A black SUV inched past the taxi in the left lane. It had almost passed them when it fell back. He could barely make out the face behind the tinted window, but it was staring at him.

"They're onto us," he yelled.

Yaser looked past him, saw the SUV and swore in what must have been very colorful language. The driver turned around, mouth agape. She yelled at him, he yelled back. He pointed to the speedometer, she yelled some more. He didn't speed up. The SUV stayed next to them. Vermeulen knew in his bones what was coming next. There were only two options. They'd shoot him right there, or they'd push the car off the road, make it stop and then shoot him. He scooted over to Yaser's side of the back seat, moving out of easy target range. Good thing the taxi was lower than the truck. It'd make the first option more difficult.

"They're going to ram us," he said. "Tell the driver to be prepared for that."

Yaser translated. The taxi driver looked at the SUV, at the road ahead of him, and shook his head. Vermeulen could see the driver's face in the rearview mirror. He'd regretted accepting this fare a hundred times already. Not even the large bills Yaser had waved before his eyes could make up for getting his car smashed up.

The driver slowed down. The SUV matched the speed. The goons must have been looking for the right spot to make their move. The black car sped up and pulled ahead. *Here it comes.* Vermeulen braced for the inevitable impact. But the SUV just kept going, pulling ahead fifty feet, then a hundred. *What's going on?* There was a sound coming from behind. When the SUV was five hundred feet ahead of them, Vermeulen recognized the howl of a police siren approaching fast. Two police cars passed them at breakneck speed, the wail dropping an octave as they passed. The SUV was far ahead, but the police cars were catching up.

"It looks like this is our lucky day," Yaser said. "Why are the cops after them?"

"Your uncle's men killed two cops."

Yaser looked back at him, her forehead creased. "Really? How stupid. Man, that's a lot of bribes down the drain. My uncle must be livid."

"Your uncle is in trouble no matter how you spin it. And you just lost your bargaining chip. With the police after your uncle's men, you have nothing to threaten me."

Yaser pulled a silver pistol from her purse. "Don't count on it."

The cab driver saw the gun in the rearview mirror. His eyes widened. This had to be the worst day of his career.

"I am," Vermeulen said. "You're not going to shoot me in a cab going seventy-five miles per hour. You won't shoot me at the airport, what with all the security there. I'm going to get on my plane and I will tell the police everything, including your role in it."

That's when a Christmas tree's worth of brake lights lit up in front of them. The driver slammed on his brake. The traffic slowed to a crawl and came to a stop. A police officer was putting down flares guiding the traffic to the left lane. There had been an accident. As they inched forward, merging left eventually, they saw a car rolled over just by the breakdown lane. It was one of the police cars. The other stood just past it, one of the cops working on getting his colleagues from the wreck. The black SUV was nowhere to be seen.

"How quickly things change, Mr. Vermeulen."

FORTY-THREE

CEYLEN PACED IN front of the picture window looking out at the dry earth. The updates from his men were sporadic. He hadn't heard from his niece either and she'd promised to call once she'd found his whereabouts. Finally, one of his men called.

"We just saw them," he yelled over the roar of road noise.

"Them? Who?" Ceylen said.

"Your niece and the UN man. They were in the same taxi."

"You saw Yesim and Vermeulen in the same taxi?"

"Yes, sir. They were sitting in the rear together."

"Where were you?"

"We're on the Gaziantep highway. We were driving right next to them."

"Is that where you are right now?"

"No, there are two police cars following us. We had to speed up."

"Police? Where did they come from?"

"We saw a lot of them near the mosque. They may have picked up on us."

Ceylen scratched his head. None of this was making sense.

"Okay, Tell me from the beginning."

The man told him how they'd been cruising the neighborhood of the mosque, looking for a sign of Vermeulen, how they'd seen him get into a silver BMW, which took off very fast.

"Did you say silver BMW? What model?" Ceylen said.

A Z4, the man said, which then took them on a chase of the neighborhood until it disappeared. A little later they found the Z4 parked and assumed that Vermeulen must have switched cars. Next thing they saw the two in the back of a cab on the Gaziantep highway.

Ceylen was shaking. His niece, his apprentice and future heir, had made some kind of deal with the UN man. He had no doubt that they were headed to the airport. Where else?

"Get to the airport," he said. "Hurry. Make sure that UN man doesn't get on a plane."

His man on the phone told him they would, now that the cops were taken care of.

"What did you do?"

"We stopped really hard. The cop following us swerved to avoid us and rolled over. The other car stopped to help. So we're clear."

"No, you are not. If they were following you, they have called in your plate numbers. Now you're really wanted. There'll be more cops. You can't be caught in that car. Ditch it at the airport, long-term parking is best."

"What are we going to do with the UN man?"

"Don't worry about him. Reinforcements are on the way. Meet them at the Departures entrance. And make sure you get my niece."

Ceylen dialed another number. His phone rang awhile before Temir Korun answered.

"Where are you?" Ceylen said.

"Fifteen miles south of Gaziantep."

"Okay, what did you load today?"

"Premium, high octane. At least that's what they promised. You never know."

"Change of plan. How far are you from the airport?" Ceylen said.

"I'm on the 27-27. Just south of Sazgin, maybe ten minutes to the airport connector."

"Okay. When you get near the airport, park the van far enough away to still be visible and implement the emergency procedure. And, don't get caught."

There was a pause.

"Emergency procedure? Really? Why? There's nobody after me."

"Do it. The less you know the better."

THE TAXI SPED up again after passing the crash site, but the slow down had caused the traffic to bunch up. Vermeulen couldn't see the black SUV anywhere. There could be more. He was certain that the men in the car had contacted Ceylen, who'd sent more of his goons. Once they exited to the airport spur, the cordon of cars around him would thin. And there'd be an SUV waiting for him.

"How are we going to play this?" he said to Yaser. "With your uncle's hit squad around, I don't think I can just waltz into the airport."

Her phone rang. She looked at the screen and grimaced. Despite her obvious misgivings, she answered. *"Alo, amca. Ne's yukarı?"*

She didn't say anything for a while. Vermeulen heard a male voice shouting but couldn't make out any words.

"Yes, we're in a cab together," she finally said, continuing in English, presumably for his benefit. "Why? Well, he wanted the two million dollars back. I asked what he'd be willing to trade for it. His offer was satisfactory and we've come to an arrangement. What? It's not my two million dollars? I beg to differ. The firm is in my name, Özbek doesn't exist. His offer? Would you believe it? He's got access to some serious intelligence. He knows every detail about your money laundering strategy. In exchange for the return of two million dollars, he promised he'd keep quiet. I thought it was a good deal. You don't agree?"

There was more shouting at the other hand. Yaser smiled. Vermeulen didn't believe she was as calm as she pretended to be. Her fingers were fiddling with the seam of her jeans.

She spoke again, this time in a conspiratorial whisper. "I'm not stupid, uncle. Of course, I know that. What? No, of course not. Uncle, relax, I have it under control. But you could help a lot if you'd call off your men. We want this to go smoothly. Okay. Thanks. We'll talk soon."

"Well," she said. "It would have been nice, but he is livid. He didn't come out saying it, but I think he knows what I'm up to. I'm sure he didn't fall for my story. So, be prepared to make a run for it. The good news is that his men can't have a shootout at the airport. Even he can't afford that."

Vermeulen shook his head. If only he'd not answered the door. If only he'd left as soon as he could. If only…

The taxi left the highway and merged onto the airport connector. The access road divided again, the straightaway headed to the terminal building and the exit turning into a minor road. Vermeulen saw a van parked not far away, off the side of the road. It looked a little like the van that had cut him off and caused the massive gasoline spill last Sunday. Obviously, it wasn't, but seeing it rattled him nevertheless.

The driver stopped at the checkpoint and Vermeulen looked ahead again. They were waved through. Good. He would be on that flight to Düsseldorf.

VERMEULEN GOT OUT of the taxi at the international departure entrance. There wasn't a pressure wave or a loud bang that made him look back. Just a whooshing sound and a sense that something had happened. He saw a large cloud of black smoke rise to the sky. Below it huge flames obscured the horizon. The flames raged about where he'd seen the van parked by the side of the road just a few moments ago. So it was one of the gas smugglers. Except, the van that had crashed on the highway a week ago hadn't caught fire. Why this one? It was just standing there.

Wailing sirens interrupted his thoughts. Airport fire trucks raced toward the inferno. Three ambulances and more police cars followed suit. He saw an armored vehicle bringing up the rear. Its crew must have been waiting for a moment like this.

So, a terrorist attack, at least in the eyes of the authorities. He wasn't so sure. Something about that van, parking where it had, made no sense. A truck bomber would have tried to get as close to the airport as possible, would have smashed through the checkpoint and right into the departure entrance. That van had stopped where it wouldn't do any damage. The fireball must've had a different purpose.

That purpose revealed itself quickly. Armed police

trotted towards the departure and arrival entrances and took up positions outside. A long announcement came over a loudspeaker. He looked to Yaser.

"They just closed the airport," she said. "All departures are cancelled until further notice. I bet this is my uncle's doing."

"No doubt. One of those gas smugglers."

"Goddamn it. How are we going to get you inside?"

Yaser was fiddling with her key fob, pacing, trying to spot the guys from the black SUV. Vermeulen didn't want to be affected by her nerves. Always better to ask someone in charge. He walked to the door for international departures and saw a couple dozen tourists huddled around a man in a suit and a yellow security vest.

"I'm sorry, ladies and gentlemen, all I can say is that departures are halted for now," he overheard the man say. "Once we get the all clear, flights will resume."

"What about the 6 o'clock flight to Izmir," Vermeulen said.

The man in the vest shrugged. "I don't know."

"Can I check in anyway, even if the flight leaves later?"

"Sorry, no check-in until flights operate again. Is Izmir your final destination?"

"No, I'm going to Düsseldorf."

"Sorry. You may miss your connection."

Vermeulen shrugged and walked back to the curb. Yaser was still looking for the goons. He tapped her on the shoulder. She spun around.

"Listen, I need to get away from here. What are the other options?" he said.

"A taxi?"

Vermeulen looked at the taxi stand. The airport closure had caused a rush for taxis. Only three cabs waited, no match for the number of tourists who stood in line.

"Any other option?" he said.

"We'll take the shuttle bus back to Kilis."

FORTY-FOUR

AHMADI WAITED TWO HOURS in the interview room before deciding that she'd had enough. She knocked on
the door. Nobody answered. She knocked again, louder.
On her third attempt, she kicked the door. That got a response. A uniformed cop opened the door and seemed
surprised to see her.

"Toilet?" she said.

The cop looked flustered.

"Klozet?"

His face brightened and he led her along the hallway
to the toilets. The station was still as busy as an ant hill
after a shower. Uniformed officers were answering the
phones, others coming in and hurrying out. Officers in
civilian clothes were shouting orders.

She did her business in the toilet and waited. She
wasn't going back into that interview room. By now
Nazaryan was probably in a tizzy with worry.

She opened the door quietly and just a crack. The
cop who had brought her stood at an open door across
the hall and gossiped with someone inside. She eased
out of the toilet, gently closed the door and walked in
the opposite direction.

The officers behind the dispatch console didn't pay
any attention to her so she walked toward the exit. The
desk officer near the entrance looked at her expectantly.
She smiled and said *"Hoşça kal."* He smiled back and

said *"Hoşça kalin."* She opened the door and stepped outside into the early evening.

The sidewalks were busy with evening shoppers. It slowed her progress, but it also hid her should the police decide they wanted her after all. She knew that her quest to find Zada's killer was over. She'd done what she could. The next step was to get back to Gaziantep and continue her work for the Women's Center. After that, who knew? Maybe Nazaryan was right. Maybe she should try to go to Germany. Many Syrians were going. She'd seen the newspaper photographs showing relieved refugees being welcomed at train stations. Or she could go to Ankara or Istanbul, big cities like Aleppo, where there were opportunities. Anything was better than staying here and waiting.

Almost to Nazaryan's apartment she heard a child's voice say, "Rima." She looked back and then forward again and saw Tariq. He stood rather forlorn in a corner, a sign advertising cell phone plans hanging from his neck.

"Salam, Tariq. Kaifa haloka?" she said.

"'aadee," he said.

She could tell he was doing worse than "so-so." He looked miserable.

"You're no longer working sewing uniforms?"

"No, they fired me. Because I didn't do my job right. This is all I could find. The pay is very bad, but my mom needs the money."

"Does she get any support from anyone?"

"No."

"I think I can help you. Come with me."

When they reached Nazaryan's apartment, she told Tariq that they'd be talking in English.

She rang the door bell. The door flew open as if Nazaryan had waited by it.

"Rima! Where have you been? What happened? I was besides myself with worry. Are you okay?"

"I'm very sorry, but yes, I'm fine. I went to the police to tell them where they can find Zada's killers. But the inspector I had spoken to earlier wasn't there. He'd been killed and the superintendent wanted to keep me there as a witness. It took me until now to get away."

"How did you get away?"

"They are so busy finding the men who killed the inspector, I just asked to go to the bathroom and then walked out. Easy."

"But they'll notice and will be looking for you."

"I can't help them any more than I already did. I'm leaving, they won't find me."

"Who's the boy?"

"This is Tariq. I met him earlier when I was with Vermeulen. He was working in a sweatshop until they fired him. He and his mother need help. Where in Kilis can they go to get cash assistance?"

"Come inside, both of you."

She brought them to the living room and asked if they wanted anything to eat or drink. Both said yes and Nazaryan brought them each a glass of water and a plate with pistachios and dried apricots. She disappeared again and came back with a card.

"Tariq, take this to your mother. Tell her to go to this address on Monday. They will get her registered and help with food and money."

Ahmadi translated. Tariq took the card, shook Nazaryan's hand quite formally and said, *"Shokran."* He turned and gave Ahmadi a big hug.

"Can we bring you somewhere?" Ahmadi said to him.

Tariq shook his head, "I walk back to my mother. It's not far. Where are you going?"

"Away. I don't want to be here anymore. I want to go to Germany. They welcome refugees there, I saw it on TV."

Tariq smiled. "I want to go to Germany, too. They have great soccer players."

"Maybe you will. Good luck."

She gave him another hug. He opened the door, stepped outside and walked away. After ten steps, he turned and waved once, then continued on his way.

"Do you still want to go to Gaziantep?" Nazaryan said.

"First, I'm so sorry. I wasn't thinking right. I thought I was running away from my duty. But nothing came of it. I hope you can forgive me."

Nazaryan looked at her beneath her heavy eyelids and shook her head. "There is nothing to forgive. You tried to do the right thing. If everyone did that, we'd be living in a better world. I was very worried, but now that you are here, I'm fine. So, what about Gaziantep?"

"Yes, I'll go there. I still have a room there. But I want to leave Turkey. Can I use your computer? I want to find the closest German Consulate."

Nazaryan brought her to her office and started her laptop. They were surprised to find that there was an honorary consul for Germany in Gaziantep. Ahmadi noted the address and phone number.

They lugged Ahmadi's bag to the car out front and put it in the trunk. Nazaryan drove faster than she needed to, but it was all right with Ahmadi. She was done with Kilis. Nothing but memories of loss. Starting over would happen elsewhere. She pulled the piece of paper with the phone number of Vermeulen's daughter. Düsseldorf. *Why not there?*

FORTY-FIVE

THE SHUTTLE BUS dropped Vermeulen and Yaser near the provincial court building at the center of Kilis. They took a taxi to the spot where Yaser had left her BMW. He transferred his luggage to her car and they took off for her town house.

Vermeulen had argued that it wasn't safe. "It'd be the first place they look."

Yaser countered that it was better to be in a place where she knew the security features than some shabby hotel. "Trust me, I know how to handle my uncle. I'm his favorite niece."

"Does he have any others?"

"No, but that's not the point."

Vermeulen didn't press any further. No matter where they went, it'd be dangerous. Ceylen would be on their tail.

Yaser's town house lay just south of the university. The drive took twenty minutes. Vermeulen kept looking back, trying to spot any followers. He couldn't make out any black SUVs, but it was getting dark, so it was hard to tell.

"Are you sure we should drive straight to your place?" he said again when he sensed they were getting close. "I think we should check it out before we walk into an ambush."

"There won't be an ambush. My uncle wouldn't ambush me. So, please, relax. You are making me nervous."

In the dim light of the dashboard instruments, he could see her smile, but it wasn't a happy smile at all. *She detests her uncle.* Tessa had been right. Yaser was out for blood. This wasn't a transition of power, this was internecine war. Eventually, there'd be scorched earth, long after he'd become its first victim.

She drove into her driveway. Her house was dark. There were no parked cars on the street.

"Is it normal that nobody's parking on the street?" Vermeulen said.

"Yes, this is a newer development. All units have garages."

She pushed a remote button and the garage door opened.

"Let's not put the car inside," Vermeulen said. "We may have to get away fast."

"I don't think you understand the circumstances. There's no destination for a fast getaway, unless you plan on driving to Ankara."

"We may have to."

She said nothing. The dim light of the garage door opener showed a bare space with a door at the left rear leading into the house.

Yaser got out and walked to her front door. She unlocked the security gate, then the door behind it, hesitated a moment, and turned on the lights inside. He could see a room through the large window. She stood in the entrance, silhouetted against the light and turned as if to tell him to come. Vermeulen had already opened the door, ready to get out of the BMW. His gut told him she'd made a mistake. As usual, it was right. He heard two muffled bangs that sounded like an old man coughing. Yaser was gone. Inside already? No. She was lying across the threshold, most of her torso inside and her legs sticking out over the single step up.

He switched off the dome light of the BMW and rolled out of the car to the ground. His mouth was dry as sawdust. He strained to listen. There were no sounds, no steps coming closer, no cars racing away. He crawled to the rear of the car. The other side of the street featured town houses in a similar style. Some windows were lit. Some were dark. The shots must have come from one of them—a rifle with a suppressor. Anyone with a handgun would have stood on this side of the street. Vermeulen would've seen them.

With a soft click, the light in the garage went off. Vermeulen rose just enough to be level with the trunk of the BMW. The way Yaser had stood in the door, and the way she'd fallen forward meant that the shots could've come only from the two units right across the street. He raised his head a few more inches and looked at the town houses. No sign of an open window, nothing to see.

The thought of a shooter up there, his rifle trained on him, waiting for his next move made the hairs on the back of his neck stand up. He had to get away from the car. Vermeulen crawled to the front. The garage was tempting. If he could find the switch that lowered the door, he'd be a lot safer. *Not a good idea. The light would come on again.*

Still, it was the safest way into her house. He crawled inside. Opening the door to the interior of the house was less dangerous. The shooter in the window couldn't see him there. And if there were others waiting in the shadows, speed and surprise would be his only escape.

He felt the step and got into a crouch. The door felt cool, Yaser's air-conditioning was running. Halfway up, he touched the door handle. *What if it's locked?* People do lock the doors leading to their garages. He eased the door handle down. When it was all the way down, he gave it a slight bit of pressure. It didn't budge. Doors stick, especially those separating the outside from the inside. He increased the pressure and could feel the ligneous fibers holding the door to its frame let go.

He took a deep breath. His heart pounding, his adrenals pumping epinephrine into his body, he exploded upward from his crouch, pushed the door open and flew through it. He slammed it shut, found the key in its slot and turned it. There was no sound coming from the garage. The room he'd entered was dark except for the light from the front room shining through the door. There were no windows in this room.

The open front door was his next worry. The open layout of the house meant there were no doors. He reached an arched passage from what could have been a dining room to the front room. He crouched and peered around the corner. Yaser was staring at him. She mouthed something. He couldn't make out what it was.

"I'm hit, but not bad," she said a little louder.

He realized that she was playing dead.

"Turn off the light," she said.

He reached around the frame and felt for light switches. There were two.

"Which one?" he said.

"The one closest to you."

He flicked the switch, but that wasn't enough. The

street lights shone through the window. He crawled to the front door, grabbed Yaser's wrists, dragged her inside, and kicked the door shut. Not a moment too soon. Two bullets smacked into the door. Which told him that the shooter was still out there. And that he'd just made a terrible mistake. He was stuck in a house surrounded by men with guns.

"God damn it," Yaser yelled. "Did you have to toss me around like a rag doll? I've been shot."

"And you'd be dead now if I hadn't acted as fast as I did. You'll live. Where were you hit?"

She stepped past him into the dining room where she turned on a light. Her face was much paler than it had been earlier. The bottom of her T-shirt was stained with blood. She lifted it and Vermeulen saw a mean gash above her right hip bone. Blood was running down her pant leg.

"You're lucky, it's just a scratch. Any first aid things in the house?"

"Upstairs. There's a closet in the hallway. I have to lie down."

The stairs to the second floor were in the rear. The closet held towels and wash rags. A small first aid kit in a plastic box sat in the rear. He grabbed it, got a wash rag wet with warm water, grabbed a towel and ran downstairs again.

The garage door opener rumbled.

"I just closed it," she said.

"Okay. Let me see if I can bandage you."

She pulled up her T-shirt again. He dabbed the gash with the damp rag and mopped up the blood around it. She grimaced. Once clean, the wound didn't look as deep anymore.

"Here, press the towel against the wound," he said and opened the first-aid kit. He found a small bottle of disinfectant. "This is going to sting."

She lifted the towel and he dripped disinfectant on the wound. She pressed her mouth shut. He knew how much that stung. He made a three inch pad from a roll of gauze and taped it over the wound.

"There. That should hold 'till morning. Then you should check it and get some better bandages."

"Thanks," she said. "Now go lock the front door."

"Where's your gun? I might need it."

Yaser took it out of her pocket and handed it to him. It was a subcompact Glock. "If my brother is out there, shoot him. I bet he's the one who fired the rifle. That's the kind of scum he is."

"Who's your brother?"

"My uncle's driver."

"That's your brother?"

She frowned. "Yeah, I know. Doesn't seem possible, does it?"

"I don't think he did it. The shot came from a rifle across the street. Not an easy shot."

He gave Yaser his assessment of the situation. They were caught in her house, they were surrounded by armed men, in short, her town house was the worst place to be.

"You just like to be right, don't you?" she said.

"It has nothing to do with that, it's just an objective assessment of our situation."

"If it were, you wouldn't have that 'I told you so' tone. But I disagree. We are in a defensible space, we have weapons."

"What, a subcompact Glock with ten rounds?" He

racked the slide, a cartridge dropped to the floor. He put it back into the magazine. Okay, eleven rounds, better than ten.

"That's just my around-town gun, you know, when I don't expect an ambush."

She opened the door of a cupboard that displayed a set of expensive-looking dinnerware on its upper shelves. Fancy porcelain, a BMW, a town house. For all her rebelliousness, Yaser displayed rather petit-bourgeois tastes.

In the back of the cupboard was a safe. She opened it and pulled out two more Glocks, these of regular size, and an H&K MP5.

"Enough firepower for you?" she said.

"You got enough ammo?"

"Five hundred rounds, all 9mm parabellum."

That was a lot of ammo. Using even a fraction of it would mean one hellish firefight.

"Listen," she said. "Nothing's going to happen. Once the sun comes up, the men with the guns will leave. Even my uncle can't afford a fire fight in a quiet neighborhood. The police are already pissed off. He's not going to make it worse. This isn't as bad as you make it out."

As if to prove her wrong, a bullet shattered the window of the living room. A second one followed immediately. They busted plaster off the opposing wall. The room filled with thin white dust.

FORTY-SIX

THE BULLETS THROUGH the window could have been frustration shots. A guy with a gun not getting his target. Or it could have been a warning. But of what? His presence was no secret. Vermeulen checked his watch. Ten-thirty in the evening. Even if Yaser was right and the gunmen left once the sun rose, it was going to be a long night.

But she wasn't right. And they weren't going to spend a long night in her town house. Things were unraveling fast. It was time to press his advantage.

"I want you to transfer the two million dollars back to UNHCR," he said.

She looked at him with a mixture of bemusement and disbelief.

"Why would I do that? You haven't delivered on your promise yet."

"My promise is irrelevant. If you want to walk away from this and live, you need my help. And I'm only going to help you if you transfer the money. Now."

"You overestimate your importance."

"We have at best thirty minutes and the sooner you understand your circumstances, the better. They will attack your house and we will give up. What I say, once we are brought to your uncle, will determine if you see the end of tomorrow. I can play dumb and tell him that you didn't want the UN on your tail and that's why you decided to end the cash card scam. Or I can tell him all about the weapons delivery and your plan of pushing him out. His trust in you is already shaken and since I have no dog in this fight, he's more apt to listen to me than to you."

"Why thirty minutes?"

"That's how long it will take them to find tear gas. Unless they already have it and then we're out of time."

"I'd have to go to the bank."

"Nonsense, you have a computer. You can make the transfer from here, right now. Do it. Or deal with your uncle."

Yaser frowned. She paced, making sure to stay away from the living room.

"Why do you think they shot the window?" he said.

"To scare us?"

He shook his head. "Think. You said earlier that your uncle can't afford a firefight here. So how is he going get us out without it? Tear gas. They broke the window to have access to the house."

"Why not wait until they have the canisters in hand?"

"Maybe the shooter was a bit too eager. I don't know. But it hasn't happened yet. That tells me they're still getting it. That's your chance to save your life. Do it now. You wait, you lose."

"You wouldn't throw a good-looking girl like me to the wolves."

"Now you're overestimating how much I care about your looks. I need to get out of here and get the UN money back. I'll do what it takes to make that happen. If you turn out to be collateral damage, so be it."

She chewed her lip. Her face reflected the internal battle. Anger, disbelief, and rebelliousness were vying with each other. At last, she hurried upstairs. Vermeulen followed her. He wasn't going to take her word for it. In her office, she fired up a heavy-duty laptop. It had a fingerprint scanner she used to unlock the machine. He watched her navigate to the website of a bank, enter her credentials and pull up past transactions.

"This is going to take a moment," she said. "The money isn't in the original account anymore. I'll have to transfer it back and then make the transfer to the High Commissioner's account."

"Why not do it directly?"

"I don't want to give away my accounts."

"A little advice. By the end of the month all of these accounts will be frozen at the behest of Interpol which will have gotten the information from the UN. You have to understand that whatever your plans were, this is a radical caesura. Your plans won't work anymore afterwards. Do the right thing now, and I can keep your name out of it. I can always blame it on the fictional Oben Özbek. Just do it before it's too late."

She opened another browser tab, logged into another account at another bank and wrote down the account information. Back in the first tab, she initiated a wire transfer and entered the account number for the UNHCR. She was about to enter the fifth zero of the amount when a dull thud sounded from downstairs. It was followed by a muffled bang. A tear gas canister. The clock on her screen told him that only fifteen minutes had passed. Apparently, getting the tear gas wasn't as difficult as he'd anticipated.

Yaser stopped typing and stood up.

"We need to get out of here," she said.

"And go where? We're safer up here than down there. Tear gas is heavier than air. Finish the transaction."

"No, I'm going into the garage. The tear gas won't get in there."

"Remember our deal."

"Fuck the deal. My uncle is gassing me. That's it. I'm going to light up his ass. I got three full mags for the MP5. It'll blow away his guys with their pea shooters. Eight hundred rounds a minute. Watch me."

Her nostrils flared, she went to the stairs. "You coming?"

"Not until the transaction is complete."

He stepped to the laptop and started adding the remaining zeros. She yanked him away from the keyboard. He turned and was staring at the muzzle of her Glock. It didn't look very subcompact from that angle.

"Give me one reason why I shouldn't kill you right here?" she said, her eyes radiating death. "I'll blame everything on you and I'll walk away from this mess."

"You forget that you took the evidence of the arms deals."

"But he doesn't know that."

"But he will. I took pictures of the lists and emailed them to a friend."

Her hand wavered. The moment he'd waited for. His right hand shot forward and slapped the gun away. It tumbled to the floor. He grabbed her left arm, spun her around and twisted the arm behind her back.

"Fuck you," she screamed, more from anger than pain.

"Shut up and sit down," he said. "Or you'll regret it." He was done being nice.

"You wouldn't," she said.

"Don't try me."

She didn't make a move.

"Sit on the stairs and don't budge," he said.

She turned and he pushed her toward the stairs.

Back at the laptop, he entered the last two zeros and clicked the transmit button. The confirmation message appeared on the screen.

"At least the UN got its money back," he said. "Now comes the hard part."

He stuck the pistol in his pocket, grabbed the laptop with both hands, aimed the hinge between screen and computer at the edge of the desk and slammed down hard. The hinge broke off and the screen fell to the ground. Nobody was going to use this machine to reverse the transaction.

Her face was so full of livid fury, it made his skin tingle. He pulled the gun again. She'd be a worse enemy than her uncle.

Her phone rang. She stared at it as if it were a scorpion. "It's my uncle."

"Well, answer it."

"I don't think so."

"I don't think you've got much of a choice."

She shook her head. "I'm not going to talk to him."

"So far, he doesn't know what you did with the information about the arms deal. As far as he knows, you struck a side deal with me. He'd be angry, but I'm sure you can talk your way out of that."

She pressed her lips together and tapped her phone.

"*Merhaba,* uncle. How are you?"

She listened. Vermeulen could tell that she was getting a lecture because her face took on mask-like features. Strange that her uncle didn't know that lecturing her would only make her more determined. Vermeulen had figured that out in less than a day.

She put her phone down and said, "He found the weapons list in your briefcase out in the car. Why didn't you bring it inside?"

Damn, there went his bargaining chip.

"Forget it," she said. "I'm going to fight, no matter what. I'm done being bossed around."

"What does he want?"

"For us to throw our weapons out of the window and then walk out the front door."

"Does he know how many guns you have?"

"He doesn't know about the MP5 and the other Glocks."

"Good, we'll keep those. I'll disconnect the garage door from the opener and slide it up just enough so I can get outside. You talk to him through the window. Make some demands, distract them. Then throw your Glock out the window. I can sneak up behind them. With the MP5, I'll have enough fire power to keep them in check. When you see me behind them, use your gun."

She stared at him. "What makes you think we're on the same team?"

Vermeulen pointed the pistol at her and said, "If you thought I was ever on your side, you're more naive than I assumed. I'm not going to get caught between you and your uncle. Toss me your car keys and get into the bathroom."

She didn't move. He fired a bullet above her head. It smacked into the plaster wall. White dust wafted to her black hair. She stood frozen on the top step, her eyes wide, mouth open. Why did it always take a dramatic gesture before people took him seriously?

"The keys," he said.

She dug the fob out of her pocket and tossed it to his

feet. He pointed the pistol at the bathroom door. She hesitated, but stepped inside. He closed the door and jammed a chair under the handle. Not a very secure prison cell, but better than nothing.

He put the fob in his pocket, grabbed a towel from the cupboard and inched downstairs. Tear gas hovered like an evil fog. The air outside was quiet and it had settled in a dense layer above the floor. Walking through it would make it swirl up again. Damn. He should have gotten the towel wet. He covered most of his face and continued down the stairs. His eyes began to burn almost immediately. He clamped his eyes shut and hurried towards the door that led to the garage. Halfway there, he stumbled over the MP5. He grabbed it, just in case, felt along the wall for the door and slipped out.

The air in the garage was much better. He sat down and pressed his hands against his eyes. The burning was unbelievable. Snot ran from his nose. His throat itched as if he had swallowed a horde of ants. All this after encountering only a wisp of it. How much worse would a full-scale exposure be? All the images of protesters being tear-gassed became real.

After getting his breath back, he turned on the light and examined the garage door opener. It was a standard model and he found the cord that disengaged the door from the motorized drive. He pulled it and turned off the light again.

The town house was fairly new. There was a good chance that the garage door was still in good condition and wouldn't squeak or grind when moved. He found the handle and gave it a tentative pull. It moved easily. Okay. So far so good. He strained to listen for activity outside, but no sounds came through. He set the firing selector of the MP-5 to burst. Unlike in the movies, emptying an entire magazine in a few seconds was worse than useless. Continuous fire pushed the muzzle up. You ended up wasting ammo and giving away your position. Three bullet bursts were far more effective.

He pulled the door up a couple of feet. It moved smoothly and without sound. He lay down flat on the floor and peered out. The BMW was still parked in the driveway and the passenger door was still open. Pretty good cover from the street.

It was quiet. Then the faint sound of a phone ringing came from the house. A last ultimatum from Ceylen. Vermeulen heard the muffled sounds of shoe soles grinding grit on asphalt. Ceylen's men were moving into position. Definitely more than one, but he wasn't sure how many. It sounded like they were heading to the broken window.

He waited, willing his heart to quiet down so he could hear over the roar of the blood in his ears. There. A small tinkle, like cheap wine glasses. They were removing the glass shards from the window frame. Against the dim light of a distant street light, he saw a dark shadow in the void of the shattered window. Next, the door opened. Two more shadows walked inside. Then it was quiet again.

This was his moment. Take the car and drive away. He rose into a crouch. And stopped. What if there were more waiting outside? Or the shooter with the rifle, still in the house across the street. They'd take him out faster that he could shift from reverse to drive. The rag top of the Z4 offered no protection.

He left the car alone and crawled across to the neighboring town house. He tossed the MP-5 into a bush and kept crawling. Three houses later, he got up and walked. The sound of police sirens reached his ears. There were many of them and they were coming fast. He reached the cross street, and continued at a steady speed. Just a man out for a walk. Nothing to worry about.

FORTY-SEVEN

THE BUS LUMBERED through the night. It'd left Adana a couple of hours ago and still had another three hours to go before reaching Ankara. The Metro bus wasn't cheap, because the seats were wider and reclined more than on most planes. Even so, Vermeulen only dozed, because sleep was out of the question. It had taken the three-hour ride from Gaziantep to Adana just to get his pulse back to the normal range.

He'd gotten away. Not out of the woods yet, but close. Only after his plane had taken off from Ankara would he breathe easy again. He still had trouble comprehending everything that had happened in Kilis. He'd flagged down a taxi and cajoled the driver to take him to the center of Gaziantep. There, he'd taken another taxi to the bus depot, where he'd barely made the overnight bus to Ankara. He'd paid cash for all transactions. That should be enough to throw off anyone following him until he got on the plane.

All Vermeulen had on him was the cheap phone the skateboard kid had gotten for him, his wallet and his passport. His suitcase and his briefcase were still in Yaser's BMW. By now, Ceylen or his men had rifled through everything in there. The information on his laptop was encrypted. That should keep it from the eyes of Ceylen. He'd been told that the encryption was "military grade," whatever that meant. All he needed was enough time to write his report and submit it. After that, he didn't care what happened.

Suarez should be happy with the outcome. Vermeulen had returned the two million to the UNHCR. Even if Ceylen cancelled all the company registrations, he couldn't reverse that transaction. Vermeulen's report would highlight specific precautions for the future of UN operations. Always double check the legitimacy of a contractor, even if that means taking more time. Suarez would be happy with his report. And so would the Undersecretary for OIOS. With a smile on his face, he dozed off again.

The next time he woke up, the bus had exited the motorway and headed into Ankara. It wound its way through the early morning streets of Turkey's capital and arrived at the main bus station only ten minutes later than scheduled. He got off and took a taxi to the airport. There he went to the closest ticketing counter and booked the next flight to Düsseldorf. That turned out to be more difficult than he expected. In the end, he got a standby seat on two flights, one at eleven-thirty that morning, the other one at nine that evening. There was plenty of time, so he splurged on a nice big breakfast, which cost as much as a breakfast at the Waldorf-Astoria. He didn't care, this was one bill the UN owed him.

After eating, he still had two hours before the first flight. He walked to his gate and chose a seat behind a column. It wasn't so much a conscious choice, as an ingrained habit of finding a seat that allowed him to see without necessarily being seen. It was too early to call Tessa, so he called Gaby. She answered almost immediately.

"Dad. Where are you? How are you? Last I heard from Tessa, you were about to get in league with the daughter of the mob boss. That sounded like a really bad idea."

"I'm at the airport in Ankara. I'm standby on two flights to Düsseldorf. One takes off in two hours, the other one at nine tonight. With any luck, I should land around 2 o'clock your time. If not, it'll be late tonight. I'll let you know as soon as I find out."

"I'm so glad you got out of there in one piece. That's a real relief. I'll take the week off and you can tell me the whole story when you get here. I was on my way out for my morning run with my friend. Okay if I do that?"

"Sure, a male friend by any chance?"

"Oh Dad, quit asking about the men in my life. There aren't any because I have little time. Talk to you soon."

He settled back into the chair and waited.

An hour later, two women in colorful uniforms showed up and opened the counter next to his gate. One of them fired up the computer and the other disappeared through the door. A handful of travelers had assembled near the area already. Several of them approached the counter and spoke with the woman behind the computer. So Vermeulen didn't think it strange when two men did the same. They spoke, the woman shrugged, they spoke some more, the woman typed on her computers. The conversation lasted longer than any of the previous conversations. The men didn't hand over their tickets and they didn't get boarding passes. Which meant they weren't verifying their flight or their seats. Vermeulen checked the direction of the nearest restroom, got up and sauntered away, keeping his back to the counter. He stepped into a stall and waited behind the locked door.

There was no obvious indication that the two men had inquired about him. All he knew was that they weren't passengers. They were dressed casually, jeans, short sleeved shirts, sneakers. They could have been cops. They could have been mobsters. In either case they were bad news.

He left the restroom and lingered near the entrance, checking out the counter. The two men had left. He sauntered along the concourse and found a shop that sold travel accessories. He bought a baseball cap with the red and black emblem of Ankara's Gençlerbirliği soccer team. He added a pair of sunglasses. It wasn't much, but it'd throw off anyone looking for the likeness of his passport picture. The last thing he bought was a briefcase. No one was more conspicuous than a man traveling without any luggage. The sales clerk wanted to remove the paper stuffing from the bag, but Vermeulen told him he'd take care of it himself.

He settled in a chair at a more crowded gate. CNN Türk was playing on a monitor mounted to the ceiling. Most waiting passengers' eyes were glued to the screen. He took off his sunglasses and watched. He didn't understand the commentary, but the report had something to do with refugees crowding onto rubber dinghies, trying to get to Greece. More footage of groups walking along a street. Images of crowded railway platforms in Budapest. The anchor's face popped up again. His voice sounded breathless. All Vermeulen heard was "Kilis."

The image changed to a rather familiar street. The camera zoomed in on Yaser's town house. The broken window was clearly visible. Police tape sectioned off the house from the street. Stills of Yaser followed. One showing her in the BMW, hair flying in the wind. Another one taken outside a disco showed her in a rather risqué dress. Next came an interview with a police officer. Vermeulen recognized the Kilis station. He didn't understand what the cop was saying. Nor did he get what the medical person in the next interview said. Yaser was either dead or in the hospital. The final image was a still of Ceylen, his face angry and one hand raised against the camera. He turned to the man sitting a seat away from him.

"Excuse me, do you speak English?"

The man smiled an apologetic smile and shrugged. A professional-looking woman a couple of seats beyond must have heard the question and said, "Do you need help?"

Vermeulen got up and settled in the seat next to her.

"Could you tell me what that report was about?"

"There was a gangland shootout in Kilis," she said, shaking her hand. "I wish our president would do something about organized crime instead of smearing the opposition."

"Did they say anything about victims?"

"Yes, the woman was wounded. But not before she got the better of her uncle. They say he died on the way to the hospital. She claims it was self-defense. Too bad they didn't kill each other. Why do you want to know?"

The loudspeakers announced that his flight to Düsseldorf was boarding.

"Ah, that's my flight. Thank you very much for your translation. Have a nice day."

He walked back to his gate, wondering if the men were still waiting for him. Sure enough, he saw the two men standing near the counter. They were definitely waiting for him. There was a long line of passengers ready to board. His name was listed on a monitor. It was the last of four names. Two of the other names had a green check mark. He sat down behind the column and waited. The line of passengers got shorter and shorter. He decided to leave before he was the only one left in the gate area. He waited for the next group of people walking to their gates and joined in. Just another traveller getting to his gate.

The rest of the day was excruciating boredom. He had no place to go, but had to keep moving to keep out of the eyes of whoever was after him. Not for the first time did he wish he could enter one of those first class lounges. He ended up on the male side of one of the airport chapels, figuring it'd be the last place they would look for him. It was quiet and he found a bench in the corner that allowed him to doze. He didn't want to stretch out and annoy one of the visitors who came to pray. After lunch he found another chapel and did the same thing. He was too tired to think.

At seven he found the gate for his next flight. The routine was the same as that morning. The two men didn't show up. Maybe they'd given up, maybe they'd been called back. With Ceylen dead, and Yaser wounded, there'd be confusion as the various factions sorted out where they stood and who'd they fight for, or even if they'd try to take over the reign. He had no doubt that Yaser would fight hard for what she called her patrimony. Winning that fight was a different question.

Before the boarding started, he heard his name over the public address system. He approached the counter and was told that he indeed had a seat on this flight.

"Has someone inquired about me here?"

The attendant looked at him, eyebrows raised. "No," she said. "Why do you ask?"

He smiled and told her that it was nothing. She gave him his boarding pass.

He got in line. Others queued behind him. The woman checking the boarding passes opened the door behind her and started. The man before him passed his phone over the scanner, it beeped, the attendant smiled and he walked through the door. She turned her smile to Vermeulen who handed her his boarding pass. She scanned it, the scanner beeped, she said, "Have a good flight, Mr. Vermeulen." He nodded to her and kept walking, picking up his pace ever so slightly. The men hadn't returned for him. Which meant they hadn't been police. And that was a relief.

FORTY-EIGHT

VERMEULEN STRETCHED OUT on Gaby's pull-out sofa. It was a tad short for him, but better than any place on earth that morning. He smelled coffee brewing and checked his watch. Quarter after eleven. The longest he'd slept in a while. No wonder, after the weekend he'd survived. Gaby had picked him up after midnight and he crashed on her sofa almost immediately after arriving.

He used the bathroom and shuffled into her kitchen.

"Ah, the dead have risen," she said.

"I can't speak for all the dead, but the smell of coffee will do that for me. Sorry for sleeping so long."

"Nothing to be sorry about. I've already been to the office and explained that I would take some of my accumulated vacation days. My boss was happy. They hate paying it out in cash. I picked up croissants on the way back. You still like them, right?"

"You bet. Thanks."

He sat down and she brought him a cup. The first swallow restored some of his humanity.

"Tessa called while you were asleep. She said she found a ticket at one of those last minute deal places. She'll be here the day after tomorrow."

"That's a long way to come," he said, thinking they could have caught up at home once he got back to New York.

As usual, Gaby read his mind. "It's not always about

you, you know. Tessa and I haven't seen each other in a while and we thought it would be great to spend some time together. With or without you."

"Sorry. Of course you are right. It'll be fun. And I'll have a day to rewrite my report."

"Did you get it sorted out?"

"Mostly. I got the UN money back. That's the most important part. But that's about all I could do in the crossfire."

Gaby creased her forehead. "Why do you always get yourself into such situations? It's not in your job description to get shot at."

"I know. Believe me. I'm not looking for it. But I couldn't just ignore such blatant fraud. They were taking the money from people who'd lost everything. How could I just walk away from that?"

"Did the police at least arrest the gangsters?"

"I have no idea. In the end everything went south. The mob boss is dead. I saw that much on TV at the airport. I wonder if his niece has taken over. She was wounded and she's a nasty piece of work. She wanted me to help her bring down her uncle in exchange for letting me leave."

"From what Tessa told me, you agreed to help her, didn't you?"

"I thought it was the only way out. But I was wrong. We ended up getting caught in her house. There was a firefight, tear gas. In the end I escaped before it was over. I did send Tessa the pictures of the papers that proved the mob had made a big arms sale. I don't know if she did something with them. As far as I'm concerned, none of it made one whit of difference. Everybody is selling weapons in Syria, everybody's making money on the back of those refugees. It's enough to make your blood boil."

Gaby put her hand on his arm and looked at him. "I don't believe you. You would've stopped that arms delivery if you could've. I know you. But I'm going to say something very selfish. I'm glad you didn't. There've been enough victims already."

He grimaced. "Maybe you're right."

Gaby's phone rang. She answered, listened and looked very puzzled.

"Just a moment," she said, muted her phone and said, "It's a call from the German embassy in Ankara."

"What?" Vermeulen said.

"They're asking if I know a Rima Ahmadi."

It took Vermeulen a second to connect the dots.

"Oh, yes," he said. "Tell them you know her. She's a refugee from Aleppo and got caught up in this mob thing. I helped her escape. I gave her your phone number."

Gaby looked flustered, but said, "Yes, I know Rima."

She listened again, looked at Vermeulen and mouthed, "She's applying for a visa."

That startled Vermeulen. A visa? Why not asylum? Then it dawned on him. Applying for asylum would mean waiting in Turkey until the application was approved. Asking for a ninety-day tourist visa was much faster. And Gaby's phone number let Ahmadi claim that she had a contact in Germany.

Gaby muted the phone again and said, "What's going on?"

"I think Rima wants to come to Germany. She hasn't got anyone. Her whole family was killed. I gave her your phone number since I didn't have my phone anymore."

Gaby hesitated a moment before unmuting her phone and saying, "Yes, I've invited Rima for a visit. Is everything okay with her visa application?"

She listened some more and said, "Of course, here's my address." After reciting that, she asked if there was anything else. Apparently there wasn't.

She ended the call and put her phone down. She looked at him and said, "You're right, we can't end this terrible war on our own. We can't even do much for its victims. But I can do something for one of them."

THE NEWS OF the weapons delivery intended for ISIS hit the front page of *The Modern Republic* newspaper in Ankara on Tuesday morning. Tessa knew one of the editors and had forwarded the documents Vermeulen had sent to him. It was the only thing she could think of that would generate fast action. NATO or the UN would have taken weeks to do anything.

The Modern Republic reporter had arrived in time to see the trucks pulling into the Gaziantep warehouse on Sunday. He took photos of the convoy and individual trucks. Some of the tarps were loose and a peek under them revealed the military hardware. He tried to talk to the drivers. They refused to answer any questions. He contacted the Defense Ministry for comment. No responses were forthcoming, so the paper ran the photographs of the trucks and several pages of the ISIS order. Together, they told a damning story. The editor crafted the accompanying text carefully. Not having secured any confirmation beyond the photographed documents, he posed questions rather than state facts.

In the same paper, albeit far from the front page, appeared a small item that the body of Bilek Balbay, coordinator of the UNHCR sub office, had been found in the vicinity of the warehouse. Police were treating the death as suspicious. The two stories appeared to be unconnected.

The reaction to the front page news was at first muted. The only visible change was the Turkish military cordoning off the warehouse. The editor at *The Modern Republic* was surprised. He'd figured it would attract more attention.

That changed on Wednesday, when police arrived at the office of *Modern Republic* and arrested the editor and the reporter on charges of treason and espionage. They went along, knowing that resistance would only give the police an excuse to deny bail. As it turned out, they were denied bail anyway since national security was at stake. The lawyer for *Modern Republic* protested strenuously and cited both Turkish and European Human Rights law, but the judge remanded the journalists to custody.

It would be another year before the two were sentenced to five years in prison.

The war in Syria continued unabated, as did the flow of weapons and the stream of refugees.

* * * * *

ABOUT THE AUTHOR

MICHAEL NIEMANN grew up in a small town in Germany, ten kilometers from the Dutch border. Crossing that border often at a young age sparked in him a curiosity about the larger world. He studied political science at the Rheinische Friedrich-Wilhelms Universität in Bonn and international studies at the University of Denver. During his academic career he focused his work on southern Africa and frequently spent time in the region. After taking a fiction writing course from his friend, the late Fred Pfeil, he embarked on a different way to write about the world. For more information, go to: www.michael-niemann.com.